HER UNFLINCHING WARRIOR

OMEGA SKY, BOOK TWO

CAITLYN O'LEARY

D1603623

This book is dedicated to those who have, and continue to face, personal adversity with grace, with bravery, and with strength.

SYNOPSIS

She is the only woman he wants, but the one woman he knows he shouldn't have.

When Navy SEAL Gideon Smith gets a frantic call from Jada Harlow he drops everything to help her.

As a software designer, Jada often dug deeper into systems and issues than most people, but she never expected to find herself immersed in this much trouble.

Even though she had once loved and lost Gideon, she knew he was the only man who could save her. But would she be able to handle having him so close, with his heart so far away?

This is an action, adventure, romantic, stand-alone novel.

PROLOGUE

"WHAT DO YOU THINK YOU'RE DOING?" HIS FATHER GASPED from his wheelchair. This was not the man who'd raised him, through his dad's worn gray t-shirt, only shoulder bones stuck out where muscles used to bulge.

Gideon looked down at this shell of a man and swallowed hard. He couldn't show any emotion, not when the powerful Kendall Douglas was blackmailing him.

No weakness. I can't show any weakness.

Gideon turned away and started prowling around the small kitchen of the house he'd grown up in. His parents were sitting at the tiny kitchen table where their little family had eaten most of their meals, and he was doing everything in his power to avoid looking at them again.

Out of the corner of his eye, he could see his mother holding his father's hand. How often had he seen that unity?

Every day.

He'd seen his parents' solidarity almost every single day of his life, until his father's accident. Then Pops was plugged into too many machines, and there wasn't a way for Sela Smith to hold onto Henry Smith's hand. Now that his father was home, and not plugged into the machines, they could finally show their solidarity again. But Gideon knew it killed his father to not have the strength to squeeze the hand of the woman he loved.

"I'm packing," he quietly answered his father's question. "I've got a bus to catch."

"Well, stop," his mother said. "I'll report you as a runaway, and you'll be back by dinnertime." She was using her calm Sunday school teacher voice.

Gideon continued to roll up his phone charger he'd just unplugged from the wall and pushed it into his backpack. He pulled out a sheaf of papers and walked over to his parents. Two sets of brown eyes, so like his own, stared up at him. He set the papers on the table in front of them.

"What's this?" his father asked. He picked up the papers with a shaking hand. He tried to unfold them, but his wife had to help. They both started reading, and Gideon's mother finished first. It killed Gideon. Since his Pop's accident, even his mental acuity had gone downhill.

"This isn't legal," she burst out. "You're only fourteen, you can't be an emancipated minor. That's not possible."

"It's legal. Pops signed the paperwork, and it was notarized in front of him. Remember?" he asked as he turned to his dad.

He watched his father's typically mahogany skin tone turn to ash. "I was signing papers about my doctor bills and disability claims," his dad protested weakly. "It was when your mom was at work. You were helping me, Son."

Bile rose in his gorge and Gideon swallowed twice, forcing himself not to vomit on the kitchen floor.

"Is that true, Gideon? Did you trick your father into

signing papers to make you an emancipated minor?" His mom gasped out the question. She was holding the side of her face as if she'd been slapped.

Gideon couldn't verbally respond, knowing he might bawl. He nodded his head instead.

"Why? Why would you do this to us?" Gideon had never seen his father look so bewildered, not even when he'd first woken up in the hospital. "Why would you want to leave us? Your brother?" His father shook his head. It was like he was trying to get the idea of Gideon wanting to abandon his family to roll around in his brain until it would finally click into place.

"I gotta go. It's time." All of his planned speeches had disappeared under the weight of his dad's pain.

"Son, you know things are tough right now, but these are the times when families need to cleave together the most." His father gripped the arm of his wheelchair. "Gideon, we raised you better than this, in my heart I know this. Talk to me. Explain this to me, because I know this isn't you." His father was right. That was exactly how Gideon felt.

"You're wrong. It is me." Gideon kept his answer short, he needed them to believe him. He had to sell this story because lives depended on it, namely theirs. He couldn't let them guess how he really felt—if they got suspicious, it would be the end.

He knew his Ma and Pops, they'd keep at him until they found out the truth, and they'd try to take on Mr. Douglas themselves. They'd try to fight for Gideon, but it'd be no use. Gideon would end up in jail and his family would end up homeless.

His mother released her husband's hands and stood up. She had the bearing of the choir director that she was.

She lifted one hand and pointed at him. "I will go to court and make this right. You're only fourteen, this can't be legal, there is no way that any judge would allow this to stand. You deceived a sick man, and I will make sure the notary who did this will lose their license."

Yeah, like that's going to happen. Mr. Douglas' lawyers at Streetgamezzz were too slick for that. His mother would never find that notary.

"Ma, it's legal. What's more, you missed the court date. It's done."

She sucked down a deep breath until her ample bosom threatened to burst through the buttons of her housecoat. "What do you mean, it's done? What court date?" she demanded to know.

"There was a registered letter. It was sent to the house with the date and time of the hearing to protest my emancipation. You guys didn't show, so it went through. It's finished."

She wilted before his eyes. "The boy I raised would never scheme like that. He would not sign for a registered letter to his parents and keep it from us."

His father struggled to sit straighter in his chair, but it was no use. He ended up slumped forward against the strap around his chest. "Gideon, Son, tell me you didn't do this." Henry Smith lifted his head so his rheumy gaze could catch Gideon's.

Once again, Gideon thought he might lose it.

"Well, both of you thought wrong." He bit out the words and glared at his parents.

He turned around and picked up his backpack.

"Don't you dare turn your back on your mother," his father wheezed.

"I'll fight this," she whispered.

Gideon slowly turned around. He was tired. It was so hopeless. He'd looked for some kind of different answer, a way out, but there wasn't any. This was the only way, he was stuck.

"How will you fight it, Ma? With what money? Pretty soon, we're going to be living in Sister Ella's back bedroom, with Pops on the couch and you on a blow-up mattress. Maybe there'll be enough space for Mikey and me on the floor." He tried to keep the bitterness out of his voice.

"And you leaving is the answer?" his mother asked. She sounded like she was going to cry.

"Yeah. Yeah, it is."

"I don't understand, why would we live at Ella's?" his dad asked.

Ahh shit, Ma hasn't told him.

His mother looked heartsick. She looked over at her husband, her mouth opened, then closed. She took a deep breath. Gideon decided to rip off the bandage. He hated this for his mother, she'd worked so hard trying to keep things together. He needed to help her. It was his job while his dad was sick, he was the man of the family. He needed to rip the bandage off and make it easier for Ma.

"We're going to lose the house, Pops. There wasn't enough money to pay the taxes, even though Reverend Knowles took up a collection. And we're months late on the mortgage."

"What about Al Fortney?" His Pops asked, referring to his old boss at the body shop. "I know the accident was my fault, but you told me he was helping out," he said, staring at his wife.

"He did, Honey." His mother answered. "The money he gave us for three months helped augment my salary from the church and covered the mortgage before we got the donation from the church."

"How did I not know all this?" His dad sounded lost.

"Doctor Turner said your memory would be good as new in no time, Honey. As soon as we get you to a good rehab facility, things will be fine."

Yeah, with what money? I have to go work with Streetgamezzz, like yesterday.

"And our savings? Is it gone too?" his dad asked. "Everything we had to move out of North Highland to get Mikey away from the Crips, is it all down the toilet?"

His mother nodded.

For long moments his dad stared at her until finally, a tear rolled down his father's face. "Are those fuckers still trying to recruit Mikey?"

"Henry, language," his mother scolded.

"Sorry, Sela. But our boy is only twelve. We both were taking double shifts to get out of Highland so Mikey would be safe, and I screwed it all up by being careless. I still can't believe that you've forgiven me for fucking up so badly."

Gideon watched as his mother brushed a kiss on his father's cheek. "There's nothing to forgive. You're the best man I know, Henry Smith. You've done everything possible for this family. I love you so much."

Gideon turned away, not able to stand watching his father cry or the beauty of his parents' love when he had to be so cruel. He took a deep breath to force back his own tears.

"Ma, I gotta go, or I'll miss my bus."

His mother grabbed the edge of the tablecloth and wiped tears from her eyes. "Don't do this, Gideon. How can you break up our family? Now, more than ever we need to stick together."

"I need to leave." He zipped up his backpack, knowing that Mr. Douglas expected him by four o'clock.

"Where will you go?" His mother's voice was uneven, as she stuttered out the question. "When will I see you? Will you call?"

"I can't, Ma."

"Boy, if you do this. If you hurt your mother like this, I'll never forgive you." His father's voice was the strongest it had been in months. Maybe the rehabilitation center Gideon would be able to pay for *could* help him.

"I've got to go," Gideon said as he hefted his backpack over his shoulder.

"Please don't," his mother whispered. "Please don't go, Baby."

Gideon staggered, he thought his knees would give out. "I've got to go."

His mother jumped up and ran to him. She threw her arms around him and pulled him into the strongest hug he could ever remember. "You be safe. If anything ever happened to you, I would die."

He dropped his backpack and crushed her to him. "I love you, Ma. So much." He shuddered, forcing back a sob, but a tear escaped. He laid his head against her braided bun, breathing in her honey scent.

"Go hug your father," she whispered.

Gideon looked over her shoulder. His father was watching them both. She released Gideon and pushed him toward her husband. "Go."

"Pops?"

"Get out." His father slowly raised his arm and pointed

to the door. "If you're so determined to leave, get the hell out."

Gideon stood frozen.

"Henry. You don't mean that," his mother said, aghast.

"I mean it." He moved his arm, then pointed his finger at Gideon and jabbed his finger at him. "You want to leave, you want to hurt your mother? Then, you get the hell out of my house. You're dead to me, Boy." He started to cough, and Sela Smith rushed to his side.

"Henry—"

"What are you waiting for?" Henry asked when he got his breath back. "I don't ever want to see you again. Anyone who would turn his back on his mother at a time like this is a boy I don't want to know. Get the fuck outta my house."

His father meant every word. Gideon saw it in his eyes. This man he'd revered all of his life hated him. His knees wobbled. He thought he'd fall to the floor and howl with pain and grief, but he didn't.

Gideon picked up his backpack and walked out the kitchen door. Walked to a new future with a man who was blackmailing him. But it was worth it if it could help his family.

He made it down two of the last three steps, stopping on the third where he and Mikey had carved their names. Wet hit his eyes. How could he do this? How?

He turned back to the front door, desperately wanting to go back inside.

Ma.

Pops.

He looked up into the sky. *Please God, keep them safe. I'm begging you. Keep them safe.*

Gideon turned around and walked away.

1

NAVY SEAL GIDEON SMITH DOUBLED DOWN ON HIS SPEED as he entered his neighborhood. Sweat dripped down his forehead and back as he ran flat out up the long private drive to his house on James Lake in Virginia Beach.

He hit the brick of his house with both hands as he came to a stop, his grin huge. Then he began his cool down by jogging, then walking around his circular drive. He could hear Lucy at the mudroom door, wanting a chance to come and play. Gideon pulled out the smart lock that he'd modified and clicked it. The mudroom door opened and Lucy bounded out.

"Miss me, Girl?"

The Chornyi Terrier almost knocked him down in her enthusiasm at his return.

"It's only been two hours," he laughed as he wrestled with the big dog. Lucy was one hundred and thirty pounds of muscle who loved playing with her human. Whenever Gideon went on a mission, he had to have the Ellis family next door watch her. When he'd made the decision to adopt Lucy four years ago, he'd not-so-innocently suggested to Felix Ellis that he might want to meet the breeder too, since Chornyi were known for their intelligence, playfulness, protectiveness, and how kid-friendly they were.

Gideon knew that both of Felix's pre-teen girls ran track and played soccer, so there would be no problem with them giving the pup enough exercise. Plus, she would be great with their toddler, if she were socialized with the child early enough. He also knew that Pam Ellis was still having problems with her fucknut ex-husband, even though he hadn't been in the picture since before she'd met, married, and had kids with Felix. So having a guard dog along with the security system would be a nice addition to the family. The fact that the sibling puppies would be growing up next door to one another, and Gideon would have access to dog watchers while he was on missions, didn't play into it at all.

Sure it didn't. Gideon grinned to himself.

"Get the rope, Luce," Gideon pointed to the mudroom door. She gave him a big shaggy doggy-grin, ran back to the house, and came out with a thick-knotted rope.

"Good girl."

Lucy dropped it in front of Gideon, then looked up at him and gave a low growl.

"Oh, you think you can win today, do you?" Gideon picked up one end of the rope, and Lucy latched onto the other with her sharp teeth and strong jaw. She gave a mighty yank backward and Gideon laughed as she forced him to take a step forward. "You're full of fight today, aren't you?"

For five minutes they circled around one another, both refusing to give up their hold on the rope, until finally Lucy let go, and Gideon damn near landed on his ass.

Lucy panted; even with her black fringe of hair flopping over her eyes, Gideon could swear she was laughing at him.

"Good going, girl. Let's see what kind of treats I have inside for you."

He scrubbed his hand through the long black curly hair of her coat as they walked into the mudroom. "I'm going to have to groom you, real soon. You're a mess."

Lucy barked. "Uh-huh, Princess likes her primping time, doesn't she?"

Gideon winced when he heard what he'd just said. God, was he really calling his dog Princess and talking about primping?

"Fuck me," he said to the empty living room as he and Lucy walked through it on the way to the kitchen. She barked. Apparently, she agreed with his sentiment.

He went to the cookie jar of dog treats and pulled out one of the pieces of meat jerky. Lucy's tail was wagging so hard, her whole back end was shaking.

"Here you go." Gideon fed her the nutritious treat.

"Now it's time for my shower."

Lucy cocked her head consideringly, then meandered over to her huge doggie bed in the corner near the accordion doors that looked over his backyard and settled in for a nap. She knew that a shower was no fun.

Gideon pulled off his tee on the way to his bedroom suite and was soon luxuriating in a hot shower that eased all his sore muscles. Sure as hell beat the showers at the nearby Little Creek Naval Base. As he worked out the kinks it allowed him to think through all that needed to get done next week. His lieutenant, Kostya Barona, was out of action until the following Monday, which gave him time to whip the team into shape. It would be fun to really screw with his team.

The entire time he showered and toweled off he considered his plan. When he swiped the steam off his mirror he saw the big grin on his face as he deliberated exactly how he could screw with his team—and get them to up their game. It had been a long while since they'd done some Urban Training.

"A mindfuck," he purred.

When he dressed and got back to his kitchen he grabbed his phone and checked out the availability of the Zussman Urban Combat Training Center at Fort Knox in Kentucky. It turned out that a bunch of Marines just had to cancel, so it was open.

It was meant to be.

I'm going to have so much fun.

Lucy looked up from her doggy bed. Gideon wasn't all that surprised from when she was a pup she could read his mind. She knew that her human was excited.

"Sorry Luce, this is man play, you're not invited."

Woof!

Definitely disgruntled.

"Hey, you get to go play with your sister Aggie and the girls."

Woof! Woof!

"Oh, so now I'm chopped liver, I see how it is." He opened his freezer and fridge and started pulling out ice cubes, berries, yogurt, peaches, and coconut water. With all of that, he added protein powder and threw it all into the blender and he soon had a tall glass of ambrosia. He downed one quick, then poured himself another glass and headed down the hall into his den.

When he fired up his two laptops and his desktop, he

grinned. The last time some of the guys were over, they had laughed when they'd seen his tower of power. Dumbasses didn't understand that a man needed more than a phone and a laptop. Shit, Jase didn't even have a frickin' laptop, he just had a phone. He was pretty sure the man had calluses on his thumbs. How in the hell he managed to text with his meaty paws was beyond him.

Then there'd been Nolan and Ryker. They continued to give him a hard time when his four monitors flared to life. He'd just rolled his eyes at their laughter. Both of them *might* be able to tell the difference between VGA and USB cables, but they'd be hard-pressed to come up with their names.

Neophytes.

By the time that had happened, Jase was already out the door, stripped down, and in his pool. Thank fuck he'd left his skivvies on since he didn't have a privacy fence and the Ellis' girls really didn't need that much of an anatomy lesson at their age.

He shook his head at the memory.

Jase Drakos is nuts, but damn, I sure love having him watching my six.

Gideon finished his protein drink before sitting down at his computer station, because no food or drink was allowed at the tower of power, then he reserved the Urban Training center. He snagged his phone and placed a call.

Commander Clark picked up on the first ring.

"Gideon? Are you quitting already?"

Gideon laughed. It was good to hear Kostya's boss sound like his old self.

"No, Sir, I plan to take every advantage possible of being in charge while my boss is out of town."

"Ahhhh, now this sounds interesting. Tell me more."

"I was thinking of messing with their minds."

"That's always a good thing, keeps them on their toes. What's the plan?"

"I reserved MOUT at Fort Knox in hopes that I could get your approval to give them a little urban combat training."

"And how do you plan to screw with them?" Commander Simon Clark asked.

"I'm thinking it would be fun for their GPS to show downtown Cincinnati, then their radio frequency to be on five different wavelengths. If it were just two, they'd get that shit figured out in no time, but five should take them more than a minute to untangle."

"I like it," Simon chuckled. "Anything else?"

"I don't want any of them in on it, that would be cheating. But besides the electronics, I think that having some of their machinery failing would be appropriate as well. I want things to happen that are all fixable in the field."

"Like what?"

"Lithium batteries on the night vision goggles will die."

"Highly unlikely."

"So's everything else. They'll know I'm fucking with them, but figuring out how to deal with the unexpected is their job."

Clark grunted in agreement. "What else?"

"I'm going to send them out with 223 Remington cartridges for their M4s."

"Isn't that dangerous?"

"Nah, just irritating. If one of my guys clamps in a Rem cartridge instead of five-five-six, then I'll owe you a beer. They'll just be pissed as hell, and once more they'll be gunning for me. It'll be funnier than hell." Gideon clamped his jaw shut. Was that a giggle that was close to coming out? What the fuck?!

Giggling? Am I a girl? First, there was primping, now giggling?!

"I like it, Smith. When are you going to head out to Kentucky?" Clark asked.

"There'll be eleven of us. Landon Kelly is on leave caring for his grandmother in Alabama, Sebastian is—"

"On baby watch. Yeah, got it. Is his wife okay?"

"She's on bedrest for the rest of her pregnancy, so he's out for the duration," Gideon answered.

"They have another infant, right?"

"Yeah." Gideon pictured his namesake. "He's seven months old. Sebastian has his hands full. Neither of them has relatives that can help out."

"Got it. So that's twelve, who else is gone?"

"Ryker McQueen is off for a week. He's available if we need him, but I don't want to pull him in for just a training exercise."

"Got it. This sounds like fun. I think I'll come with you."

Gideon sat up straight. He couldn't remember the last time Commander Clark had been out in the field, let alone on a training exercise.

"That's great, Commander. I'll let you know when I have the flight lined up. I expect we'll be wheels up tomorrow."

"I'm looking forward to it."

The man hung up.

Lucy wandered into Gideon's office and woofed.

"I know, Girl. Pretty weird shit, isn't it?"

"THIS IS A TOTAL BUST," Ryker said over the phone.

Gideon held back a laugh. "So Amy isn't giving you the time of day?" he surmised.

"It's worse than that. As soon as I showed up at the restaurant, she stopped working the front of the restaurant and hid out in the kitchen."

"I told you that you needed to give her a heads up that you were coming to D.C. for a visit."

"I wanted to surprise her. Dammit, Gideon, we had a great time together, our chemistry was off the charts, she should have expected it," Ryker defended himself.

"You met Amy Linden when?" Gideon prompted carefully.

"Uhhm, three months ago?" Ryker answered. In his mind's eye, Gideon could see Ryker squeezing his bicep where he had his tattoo.

"And in those three months, how many times have you talked to Amy?"

"Maybe four times?"

"Maybe?"

"Okay, three times," Ryker admitted. "But they were long conversations," he argued. "Over a half hour each."

Gideon laughed. "Jesus, man, you are such a guy. Women like talking on the phone, so you spent what, five hours with the woman, flirting with her three months ago, and talked on the phone with her for a total of an hour and a half, then suddenly showed up at her place of business. Is that what you're telling me? What was your awesome opening line?"

Ryker took a long time to answer, so Gideon knew it was going to be bad.

"I might have said something along the lines of, 'Hey, Beautiful, did you miss me?'"

Gideon groaned. "It's amazing she didn't throw food at you. Seriously, you get laid with lines like that?"

"Well yeah," Ryker said. "But not with women like Amy. She's a whole different level. She reminds me of Kostya's woman, Lark. There's something about her that really got to me."

"So you decided to treat her like all the others," Gideon scoffed.

"That's bullshit." Ryker's voice sounded heated. "I've been calling...a lot. It's not my fault she only picked up the phone three times. Why in the hell do you think I finally hauled my ass up to D.C.? I don't need a bunch of shit from you, Smith. I need some fucking advice!"

Gideon forced himself not to laugh. But this was some funny shit.

"You there? Or are you just trying not to laugh?"

Gideon cleared his throat. "Have you talked to Kostya? Maybe he'd put Lark on the line, Amy *is* her best friend, after all."

"Come on, he's proposing this weekend, there's not a chance in hell I'm interrupting. Anyway," Ryker's voice trailed off.

"I know. You don't want to have to admit to Lark that you need help. You know, it's not the end of the world to ask for help. We do that all the time, that's what being part of a team is all about."

"Yeah, but Lark isn't part of Omega Sky, now is she?"

Gideon sighed. "I get your point. Okay, here's what I'd suggest."

His phone clicked.

He looked down and recognized Jada Harlow's

number and he frowned. He watched as the number continued to show on the screen. He waited to see if it would go to voicemail, but it didn't.

"Don't leave me in suspense, what's your suggestion?"

Another click. Jada's number popped up again.

"Ryker. I gotta go."

"Man, that's so not cool."

Gideon swiped his thumb, hanging up on his friend. "Hello?"

"Gideon, it's me, Jada." Her voice didn't sound right.

"I know." He really hadn't ever expected to hear from her again. Not after the way they'd left things. Well, how *he'd* left things.

"Gideon, I'm in trouble." She paused, he could almost see her licking her bottom lip. She did that when she was upset or nervous. "Big trouble. I stumbled across something when I was..."

Dammit!

"When you were what?" he asked harshly. "Hacking into some system you had no business being anywhere near?"

"Gideon, please listen." It almost sounded like she was begging. That couldn't be right.

His shoulders got tight. "I'm listening, Jada."

"There was something that looked wrong. Really wrong, so I dug a little deeper, and I noticed some anomalies." She paused. Gideon heard her take a deep breath. "Not just an anomaly. It was something bigger than that, it was purposeful. Gideon, I didn't know who else to turn to, and—"

He waited for just a second. It was sounding bad.

"And what, Jada?"

Nothing.

"Jada?"

Still nothing.

"Jada, talk to me."

He looked down at his phone.

Fuck!

Their connection had been lost.

He pressed her number to reconnect the call and it went straight to voicemail.

"Call me!"

He texted her.

CALL ME.

He punched in her number again. Voicemail.

Shit!

2

GIDEON PULLED UP THE PRINCESS QUEST PROGRAM ON HIS desktop computer. When he got the program running, he didn't click on O'Keefe or Nightingale, because Sebastian and Kostya knew where their women were at. But Jada? It sounded like she was in trouble.

Sounded like.

He'd stick with that.

Sounded like.

He breathed deep through his nose and squinted at his monitor. Jada was always knee-deep in crap she shouldn't be, it was her nature. This could just be another one of these types of situations.

Right?

"Bullshit!"

He slammed his fingers on his keyboard, knowing it wasn't going to do him any good, but it made him feel better. Maybe he could get his information just a quarter of a second faster. Almost from day one, Gideon had put her phone under the Princess Quest monitoring system. There was just something about that woman, despite the fact that he knew in his heart there wasn't a chance in hell that they could have a future, he just couldn't let her totally out of his sight. For some reason, he felt like he needed to watch out for her. So she was in the system and her avatar was Jolie.

Dammit! Why is it taking so long to find her?

Gideon drummed his fingers on his desk as he let the program run. Princess Quest was on the down-low; Kane McNamara, his counterpart on the Night Storm Navy SEAL team, had developed it. He initially used it to keep track of just his team's women, and others who they were concerned about, but he spread it out to the Omega Sky, Black Dawn, and Midnight Delta teams.

PQ was used to ensure that their women were safe. And after some of the crazy shit that had happened to some of those ladies, Gideon understood why he'd created the app. It was the 360 phone tracker app on steroids. The way Kane had built it, if the men could get ahold of the women's phones, they could install the app. After it was installed, the app could track the women even if the phone was turned off or if the battery died.

But Gideon wanted just a little bit more out of Princess Quest, and after working with it for a month he'd found it. He figured out a way to tweak it so that it could be implanted in their phones wirelessly. So, the first time he and Jada had been together, which was at Sebastian and Gianna's wedding, he had implanted the software. So far Jada hadn't discovered it, which had surprised the hell out of him. Jada was a tech genius. Though, she didn't have the years and years of experience to build up to his level of security paranoia.

His computer pinged—Jada's location had loaded.

Fucking finally!

Her Unflinching Warrior | 23

Gideon leaned forward, his nose almost touching the monitor as he glared at his screen. What in the hell was Jada doing in Oregon? And not Portland, Oregon. Hell, no. She was in some city called Tillamook. What's more, her phone had been powered down—no wonder it had taken the system more than a minute to find her. But seriously, Tillamook, Oregon?

He needed Gianna Durand. Maybe she would have some idea what was going on with her best friend, but he was going to have to go in soft. Sebastian was guarding his wife like a rabid dog.

Gideon picked up his phone and punched in the number for his friend.

"What do you want?" Sebastian spit out his greeting.

Yep, not in a good mood at all.

"Hey, Bastian," Gideon said with a smile in his voice. "What's going on?"

"Neil is teething and has the croup. Gianna's throwing up so often that I'm thinking about taking her to the emergency room."

"Have you called Nolan?" Gideon asked, referring to their team medic.

"Of course, I have," Sebastian said irritably. "He and Raiden Sato *and* Tanner are all at Fort Bragg for their refresher course. I always forget that Tanner is a medic too, I always think of him as a sniper."

"They'll be back tonight."

"Not soon enough," Sebastian bit out. "Nolan told me to get her doctor to come to the house. Like that's going to happen."

"Take her to the emergency room. Why haven't you called someone else to come help you with little Neil so you could get Gianna to the emergency room?"

"Because she's supposed to be on bedrest, I didn't want her standing up. It wasn't 'til I got the okay from Nolan that I felt comfortable taking her. Now that I did, I was just about to call you. This is crap timing. Jada was here for two weeks and she was a Godsend, but she left a week ago, said she had something urgent she had to get back to."

How did I miss that Jada was in town?

"Bastian—" Gideon started.

"What?" Immediately Sebastian was alert, all panic was gone. There it was, that was what made Sebastian Durand a damn fine Navy SEAL, he understood when something was really wrong and he immediately changed gears.

"I won't get into it, but I've got something."

"Is the team heading out?"

"No. As a matter of fact, I'm going to need some PTO."

"Damn, you're in charge, this has to be big."

"Right now we're focusing on you. I'm calling Jase and Mateo. They'll be over before you get Gianna in the car."

"Isn't that overkill? I mean, Jase?"

Gideon snorted. "I'm thinking overkill is appropriate at this point. Plus he has his bike, he'll make it in minutes. Get my Godson and your wife loaded up, and they'll be there to drive."

He heard Sebastian heave out a sigh of relief.

"Thanks."

"Go," Gideon commanded.

Sebastian hung up, and Gideon immediately started making calls.

AFTER HE WAS DONE GETTING everything arranged for Sebastian, he looked to see if he could hack into Jada's computer, but he wasn't holding out much hope. He gave himself twenty minutes, then wrote a down-and-dirty script and let it start to run so he could concentrate on the next steps.

They weren't great steps.

He swiped his thumb over his number one contact and hit send. Even though Kostya was in Northern California getting loved up with his now-fiancée Lark Sorensen, Gideon knew he would answer.

"Talk to me."

"I've got a problem."

"Figured." Kostya's tone was mild.

Yep, loved up.

"It's Jada Harlow. I think she's in real trouble. An hour ago I just briefed Commander Clark on a MOUT training op with a lot of bells and whistles at Fort Knox. He approved us moving out tomorrow."

"Will Nolan and Tanner be back in time?"

"Yep."

"Sounds like a good plan. Nolan or Jase could lead if you need to bail."

"No need. Commander Clark said he wanted to go."

"Simon?" Kostya's voice held surprise.

"Yep. I laid out my plan and he said it sounded like fun."

"Let me guess, you were going to screw with their heads." Gideon could almost see Kostya's grin on the other end of the phone.

"Maybe," Gideon drawled.

"No wonder Simon wanted in. Okay, does it have to be

you to rig up everything, or can someone else on the team do the twists and turns?"

"When it comes to the electronics, I should be able to do that remotely. I had some plans for the equipment that I laid out for the Commander. He liked it."

"I'm sure he did. He can be a devious bastard. Let Simon take care of it along with Jase or Nolan. Probably Jase, since Nolan's coming in late. I'm approving your PTO. How bad is the situation? Do you need back-up?"

"Nah, I've got this," Gideon assured his friend.

"Gideon?" Kostya stretched out his name, knowing that Gideon might try to handle a personal issue on his own, instead of asking for help.

"I appreciate the concern, but I just can't imagine Jada into something that requires anything more than some strong words. It'll be fine."

"Call Simon. I want you to report in to me within forty-eight hours, got it?"

"Aye-aye."

GIDEON DROPPED his head and shook it.

Fucking Kostya.

"Hey, Gideon," Ryker called out from across the concourse.

Really? Really? Am I two years old? Do I need a babysitter?

Ryker jogged over to him with a shit-eating grin on his face.

"Kostya wanted me to tell you that paybacks are a bitch."

"How'd he know my flight?" Gideon held up his hand. "Never mind, it was McNamara."

Ryker nodded. "You're not the only whiz kid in town."

"I thought you were busy pursuing Amy. Are you really such a putz that you'd give up that easy?"

"She took a powder. Took time off from the restaurant. Couldn't find her at her apartment. I finally called Lark in desperation. She told me that I needed to go in softer, that she had some heavy stuff going down in her life at the moment." Ryker hefted his duffel up on his shoulder, then pulled his phone out of his cargo pants. Gideon watched as he pulled up his boarding pass.

"Did Lark tell you what kind of stuff?"

Ryker gave him a frustrated look. "Much as I love and worry about you, man, do you think I'd be here if I knew what was going down with this woman? I haven't been able to get her outta my head for three months."

"Maybe I could help track her down," Gideon suggested.

"Lark was pretty adamant that I leave it alone for now, so I'm taking her at her word. I've got sisters, and girl cousins, aunts and a mother. When a woman tells you to back off the way Lark told me to back off, the shit's serious. I don't have the *in* with Amy yet to press it." Ryker gritted his teeth.

"What?" Gideon asked.

"I just don't like the idea of her hanging out there in the wind, is all. Lark told me she has it covered." Ryker jerked his head and Gideon saw that people were lining up over at their gate.

"Lark is the type of woman who would make sure her best friend is covered, it's okay."

"I know," Ryker sighed as they walked over and stood in line. "Right now we'll focus on Jada. Kane's checking things out. He said to tell you he can't breach her system, and he's impressed."

"Normally that would be a good thing," Gideon muttered as he placed his phone on the boarding pass reader and smiled at the gate attendant.

"Anyway, he also said to tell you that he's going to be working on things while we're in the air, and he's helping Commander Clark with all the evil you'd planned for the team."

Gideon frowned at Ryker. "What do you mean?"

Ryker held up his hands and grinned. "McNamara thought that would be your reaction. Apparently, it was decided above yours and Kane's paygrade. He said to blame it on the lieutenants."

"Fucking Max and Kostya," Gideon muttered.

"Excuse me? I don't appreciate that kind of language, Sir."

Gideon looked up to see the pretty little dark-haired flight attendant who was about to greet them as they were stepping onto the plane scowling at him. He heard Ryker laughing behind him.

"I'm sorry, ma'am."

She sniffed, only slightly mollified.

Ryker elbowed Gideon as they settled into their seats. "You sure screwed the pooch on that one. And here you were giving me shit on how I was approaching Amy."

"Just sit down and shut up, will you? I need to use this time before we take off to see if any of the scripts I was running found anything out."

He checked his phone.

Aw, hell no!

Gideon damn near ground his back molars to dust

and looked up to see that passengers were still boarding the plane. Good, he still had time. He placed a call.

"Kane," he started talking before Kane McNamara even had a chance to say hello. "I see what you're doing, and your code is all wrong. Just stay the hell away from Jada's system. I know her inside and out; let me try to break in, you focus on little Night Storm shit. Do you hear me?"

"Well, it's good talking to you too, Buddy." Kane drawled.

"I'm serious, McNamara. I don't have time for any of your bullshit. Jada said she was in trouble. The sooner I can find out what the hell is going on, the better. Me tripping over your lame-assed attempts at infiltration is not helping."

There was a pause. "Okay, Gideon, then tell me how I can help."

Gideon felt the tight bands around his chest ease just a slight bit. "Find out what she's been doing for the last five months. I haven't seen her since Neil's christening, and I haven't been keeping track. See if anything she's been working with, or anyone she's been talking to, is connected to Tillamook, Oregon."

"Got it."

"Also, about the plans for the training in Fort Knox," Gideon started.

"I've got that covered. Already talked to Commander Clark. I'm kind of pissed that I never considered doing it with Night Storm. It's evilly brilliant, it will totally fuck them up, I love it. You don't mind if I add a couple of things to it, do you?"

"You have my blessings, but if you—"

"You have my word, the thing with Jada is my top

priority. I've also tapped Dex and Clint. We've got your back."

The flight attendant came down the aisle and glared at him. He must have missed the announcement to put his phone on airplane mode.

"Sorry, ma'am.

"Gotta go," he said to Kane. Then he powered down his phone.

"You seem to be breathing easier," Ryker said as he leaned in to talk to him.

"I am. Kane called in the computer experts from Midnight Delta and Black Dawn. I don't know if they're all available, but Kane'll let me know when we land."

Dammit, Jada, what in the hell have you gotten yourself into?

3

"So, tell me about Jada," Ryker asked quietly.

Gideon turned his head and glanced at his teammate who was stuck in the crowded middle seat. It was the only small bit of happiness Gideon had been able to find in this hellish situation. He was still kind of pissed that Kostya had set Ryker on him, but after what Gideon had pulled a few months ago on Kostya he guessed he deserved it.

"Jada is all kinds of trouble," Gideon answered Ryker. "She's brilliant. The woman is on Kane McNamara's level of brilliance when it comes to tech. If she had his discipline she could rule the world."

Ryker nodded solemnly. "So she's as brilliant as you. Got it."

"What part of McNamara, did you not understand?" Gideon asked irritably.

"I thought you tech wizards were supposed to be all egotistical. I heard from Jase, who heard from Nolan, who heard from Sebastian that you were one of those uber-young-genius-freaks in Silicon Valley, so don't bullshit a bullshitter. If Jada's brilliant, that means she might possibly be in your stratosphere."

"Did you just say Jase to Nolan to Sebastian, like some kind of little girl game of telephone?"

Ryker grinned. "I so did. You being second-in-command with all your tech gear means you're outta the loop. We survive on gossip."

Gideon looked around and made sure nobody was listening, but he still whispered almost silently. "You're in special ops, all of you; nobody should be gossiping."

"And we don't, not about work. But about people's personal lives, hell yeah. Of course, you don't have much of a personal life. After all, babysitting your brother's kids isn't really exciting, so that's why we were forced to dig around in your past. Of course, this Jada connection, this is sounding juicy." Ryker waggled his eyebrows.

"God save me from children in men's bodies," Gideon groaned.

"Tell me more about Jada, is she a brilliant crazy chick? You know, stripper crazy? According to Sebastian, you two hooked up; isn't that more Landon's cup of tea? I didn't see you as into crazy chicks."

Gideon jerked upright. "Shut the fuck up. She is not crazy. She's impetuous. She's nothing like the 'throwing all your shit out a plate glass window crazy' that Landon hooks up with. Jada is the type who'll think she can go and save the world with a laptop, pair of high heels, and a can of mace. She scares the shit out of me."

Ryker laughed...loudly.

"Will you keep it down?" the guy in the window seat grumbled.

Ryker rolled his eyes.

"She sounds like a hoot."

Gideon sobered. "She's more than that. Much more." His voice trailed off.

"So why didn't you two last? According to the rumor mill, you're the one who broke things off. If you thought she was all that, why did you?"

Gideon felt his shoulders tensing again. "She's twenty-five, man."

"So?"

"I'm thirty-eight. I'm thirteen years older than her."

Ryker snorted. "Yeah, I did that math. So what? Landon's dating a woman eighteen years older than him."

Gideon gave his friend the side-eye.

Ryker shouted with laughter.

"I told you to keep it down." This time the guy was louder. Gideon leaned over to see a small man in a business suit glaring at Ryker who had eighty pounds of muscle on him. He had to give him props for not being intimidated. Ryker turned to look at the man. "I'm sorry, Sir. It won't happen again."

Ryker looked over at Gideon and grimaced. Neither of them ever wanted to be disrespectful, it just wasn't in their nature, nor was it how they were trained.

"Quit being funny," Ryker whispered.

"I wasn't. You were the one who gave credence to Landon's latest love interest. Come on, that's going to crash and burn big time. Hopefully, since he's home taking care of his grandmother she'll knock some sense into him."

"I'm not against the age difference. I'm against the fact he met and fell in love with her in less than two weeks. That kid is too impetuous."

Just hearing that description, Gideon thought of Jada.

Is that what happened to her? Had she done something impetuous and ended up in real trouble?

Ryker yawned.

"When was the last time you slept?" Gideon asked.

"I caught a couple of hours yesterday."

"We've got four hours before we land in Minneapolis, take a nap. Hopefully, by then we'll know more and we can talk through a game plan on the flight to Oregon."

"Sounds good."

Ryker leaned his seat back and closed his eyes.

After he heard Ryker's deep breathing that indicated sleep, Gideon decided to get some rest as well. He looked behind him and saw a man who was as big as he was. He didn't push back his seat, knowing that it would disrupt the guy's comfort. Instead, he got as comfortable as he could and closed his eyes to see if he could find some solace in sleep as well. But he highly doubted he could. Too many thoughts of Jada were swirling around in his head.

THINKING BACK to a year and a half ago, Gideon remembered the first time he'd even read the name Jada Harlow. It had taken less than fifteen minutes to have most of her life parsed out in front of him. She was the youngest child in a big boisterous family, so different from his own.

There were six kids, and she was clearly an *oops* baby because there were seven years between her and the last brother. Her mother, Camila Diaz, immigrated with her family from San Juan, Puerto Rico to New York. There she met and married Edward Harlow. He was a private in the

Marines, but by the time he'd put in his papers after twenty-five years, he was a Master Sergeant. Pretty damned impressive.

Jada was a go-getter from day one, and being raised by Camila and Ed, and following five successful brothers, she didn't think anything could stop her, and nothing rarely did. Which was why, when he first encountered her, she was embroiled in a mess of epic proportions, positive she could handle it and keep Sebastian's woman out of danger. Boy, had she screwed the pooch on that one.

Gianna Prentiss was Jada's college roommate and best friend and she had been kidnapped by the time Gideon was face-to-face with Jada, via a computer screen. It had been Jada and Gianna's screwball plan to get information to take down Sebastian's uncle and grandfather by having Gianna go undercover working at a bar.

It had all gone to shit by the time Jada had called in the calvary. She'd kept it tight, pushed and prodded Sebastian and Gideon to listen to her, and Gideon had to admit, he'd been blown away by her stubbornness, loyalty, and genius. Of course, he was pissed as hell at her recklessness. The only redeeming fact was that she seemed to realize it and was doing everything in her power to rectify her mistake.

Gideon was stuck in the middle—he ached for his brother Sebastian as he suffered over Gianna's capture, but he also felt deeply for this woman he'd just met as she agonized over her friend's plight. Yet, somehow Jada kept her shit together, and with her help, he and Sebastian were able to do what they needed to do to find and rescue Gianna. In spite of the fact that Jada threw buckets of attitude Gideon's way during the entire process, Jada was positive she knew best how to help during the rescue efforts, and what surprised the fuck out of Gideon—sometimes she was right!

The airplane hit turbulence and he opened his eyes and looked over at Ryker. His friend was softly snoring. Gideon gritted his teeth and tried to ignore his sense of dread. He knew Jada Harlow; the woman was hell on wheels. There was no way she could be in real danger.

Was there?

Yeah, like there was no way Gianna could have ended up kidnapped.

Gideon rubbed the top of his head, then smoothed his hand down until he was kneading the tense muscles in his neck. What the hell was she doing in Tillamook? Did she need cheese for fuck's sake?

You better be okay, because if you're not I'm going to paddle your ass!

Thinking about how Gianna ended up beaten and in a coma, Gideon found himself staring at the seat in front of him, imagining every awful scenario known to mankind.

Scad.

Scared and mad. That sounded plain stupid. Kind of like Bennifer. *Need to come up with something better.*

Mafraid.

Harlow, that's pathetic.

Frifurious.

"I like it," she whispered into the dank darkness.

I'm frightened and I'm furious, and some kind of fried food would not go unappreciated. Maybe crab wontons?

How many hours ago had it been since the two women and one man had snatched her from the crappy little motel room? She really thought she'd been safe, staying in a dive close to the river and cheese factory, far away from Oceanside, but not so much.

Seriously, how could she have been so naïve?

I wasn't thinking! Dad would be so pissed if he could see me now.

Jada squeezed her eyes shut, thinking about the flimsy locks and the fact that she hadn't packed a gun. He'd be so pissed.

The master sergeant would have my ass if he were still alive.

The unholy screams from the other side of the wall had stopped a while back. That was when she started coming up with different ways to define fear. She should really come up with ways to define being an idiot!

Stupid.

Stupid.

Stupid.

Jada bit her bottom lip. She wanted to hit something, but she couldn't. When she'd woken up she'd found herself locked up in this smelly, dark, damp room with her arms jacked up behind her back with a zip tie wound around her elbows and wrists. She was taking care not to roll around too much because dislocating a shoulder was not going to help her escape.

I should have called Gideon from the get-go.

She pictured him in her mind's eye. All six foot three inches of Navy-defined muscle. God, the military kept their men in tip-top condition. But it had been his eyes that had snagged her, to begin with. They were molten brown, swirled with a bit of gold. Nothing like her dad's green eyes. But Gideon did have the warm dark skin that was definitely reminiscent of her father, and the fact that he carried himself with that military bearing? She'd been a goner.

They'd fought and wrangled on how to handle things that went down when Gianna had been kidnapped, but he'd listened to her, despite the fact that he was crazy smart and had done legendary things in Silicon Valley that people were still whispering about, and probably secret stuff for the Navy that if she found out about it, she'd be killed.

Killed.

Killed.

Killed.

"Hey, you. Can you hear me?"

Jada had been thrown close to the wall where the screaming was coming from. The wall where the awful interrogation had been taking place.

She wriggled around, ignoring the searing pain in her arms so that she could get up on her ass, and when she did she pounded her boot-covered feet against the wall.

"Can you hear me?"

She heard the slightest bit of noise from the other side. It wasn't a groan or a sigh, it was more like a body shifting or rolling.

"Are you okay over there?"

Something scraped against the other side of the wall.

"I hear you. I hear you. Don't worry. We're going to get out of here. I promise. You're going to be all right. Just hang on a little longer okay?"

Another scrape.

Jada lost her balance and fell over. Her bound elbows crashed onto the concrete.

"Owwww."

Wet hit her eyes, and she had to force back tears. She

gritted her teeth against the pain, then grinned. She knew what her dad would say.

Improvise. Adapt. Overcome.

Damn right she would. Her partner in crime over there on the other side of the wall was alive. She could overcome this situation.

The door to her cell, room, whatever she wanted to call it, opened. She couldn't see who was in the doorway, they were backlit.

"What's all the ruckus about?"

It was the man who'd copped a feel. Scratch that, he'd copped more than one feel. Both of her breasts were going to end up bruised.

Jada didn't respond.

The wiry guy walked further into the room and started crooning to her.

"Did you miss me? Is that why you started making noise?" he asked in a low, sing-songy type of voice.

Jada kept silent.

"Girly, I asked you a nice, pleasant question. I want a nice, respectful answer," he said as he crouched down beside her.

The bastard wanted a response. Wanted some sort of sign of weakness, but he'd have to beat her bloody to get it out of her. No way was she giving in to this piece of shit.

As he smoothed his hand over her curly hair she kept perfectly still.

"How do you feel about foreplay?" he whispered at her temple.

She gave him nothing.

Hot, moist breath hit her as his tongue wormed its way into her ear.

"Akk. Akk." Jada tried to stop gagging, but she couldn't.

"Awww, is your tum-tum upset?"

His hand snaked around her body and she felt his oily touch reach up under her t-shirt and mash against the flesh of her stomach.

Bile rose.

Jada slammed her lips together and her eyes watered. His fingers twisted and pressed into her stomach. She gasped. Before she heaved she turned her head so she was facing the monster, then vomit spewed.

"Bitch!" he roared.

Jada's head hit the cement floor hard as he let her go. She heard him scampering backward, muttering obscenities.

Fucking asshole deserved it.

Blinding, unimaginable fire burst up her thigh.

"Fucking bitch!" he screamed as he kicked her again in the same place on her thigh, so hard that the burning pain blasted red fire that ran up her body and into her brain as she screamed.

"What's going on in here?" a woman yelled as Jada's world went from explosions of red and orange to almost daylight where she saw her tormentor swinging his foot toward her face before she rolled.

The blow to the back of her shoulders was fierce, but it could have been so much worse.

"Butch, what the hell are you thinking? If you kill her, the director won't be able to question her. If one of us fucks up, we'll all die."

"She puked all over me," Butch whined.

"Butch, have you damaged the merchandise?" another woman asked softly.

"N-n-no," Butch stuttered.

"I don't believe you, Butch. Come with me." Her sweet, kind voice scared the hell out of Jada. These people were all whacked. She didn't even want to think about how bad this director person could be.

"Naomi, check on Ms. Harlow. Make sure she doesn't die."

Out of the corner of her eye, Jada saw the wiry man leave with the much smaller woman. Then she watched Naomi crouch in front of her.

"Let's get these restraints off of you. You're locked up and in pain, the least I can do is take these off."

She pulled out a knife and cut through the zip-ties. Jada hated the fact that she had no feeling in her hands or arms and couldn't take the knife from her. And add that to the fact that the kick to the back of her shoulders and her thigh had pretty much incapacitated her for the next little bit. So much for 'overcoming'. Dad would not be impressed.

Naomi stood up and left the room, leaving the light on. Jada listened but didn't hear the door being locked—maybe she'd have a shot at escaping in a little while, after she could move again.

The door opened again, and Naomi came back inside. She was holding some kind of blue tarp.

"I know it's not much, but it's something." She laid it over Jada like someone would a blanket. "It's going to get cold here tonight, can't have you freezing to death. Sweet dreams."

This time when she left, she turned off the lights and locked the door.

"I am not frifurious," she said as she spit out the rest of the uck that remained in her mouth.

No, I'm getting seriously fucking frightened.
Think, Jada, think.

Try as she might, she couldn't. She winced in pain at the thought of trying to move, every part of her body now hurt.

Was it possible that Gideon might be looking for her? He'd sounded so cavalier when she'd called, but he'd come, wouldn't he? He was a hero, that's what heroes did.

The dark room started getting hazier, but she didn't want to go to sleep. Butch might break his leash and come back, so she needed to stay alert. If only Gideon were around, then she'd be safe.

Safe, and held in his arms.

Her bottom lip began to tremble.

Stop that!

Think of something good. Something happy. Think of Gideon. That first time in Kentucky, not the last time. Their very, very first time.

She closed her eyes. She just needed to rest her eyes for a moment. Just a moment.

4

"THIS IS GLORIOUS," SHE SMILED UP AT GIDEON.

"What?" he asked as he pulled her in, just a little closer.

"Wearing heels with a man, and still having to look up. I don't get to do that very often."

Gideon's hand tightened at her waist as he easily guided her around the dancefloor. That was another thing, she'd never been in the arms of a better dancer. Never. Not even when she'd gone to the military dances at Camp Pendleton as a young girl with her father. Nobody had it going on like Gideon Smith. When she told him that he laughed.

"They're Marines, Angel, what did you expect?"

"Hey, watch your tongue, my Dad was a Marine."

"Your father was the one exception." His thumb trailed a circle around the curve of her lower back, causing her to shiver.

"I like the maid-of-honor dress that Gianna chose for you to wear. It suits you."

"She designed it. She's crazy talented." Gianna had designed her own wedding dress too, which was amazing. With her design, there was no way she looked five months pregnant.

Gideon stroked her dress. "I can only imagine one thing softer than this material," he murmured.

A shudder ran through her body. A great dancer, so handsome, and a smooth talker. Maybe she'd been wrong about Gideon Smith. The first time she'd dealt with him over the phone and SKYPE, she was sure he needed to be committed to the fiery depths of hell for being an arrogant prick. The arrogance was still there, but the prick part seemed to have disappeared.

"It's angora. Only Gianna would want a winter wedding in Kentucky. She knew it was going to be cold and snowing, so I made her promise that I'd be warm. I don't like cold."

Gideon's laugh swirled around her like steam from a sauna. It promised to heat her from the inside out until all of her bones were melted into warm molten gold.

"You with me?"

"Huh?"

"I was just saying that you and Kostya have a lot in common, he hates the cold too. I wouldn't be surprised if he faked the whole meeting in California so he could avoid the snow."

"Smart man," Jada muttered.

"I'm not complaining. He would have definitely been trying to cut in on this dance."

Jada highly doubted it. "He knows about me, right?"

"Sure. You're the woman who helped save the bride."

"Yeah, and the one who was a pain in your ass while doing it," Jada muttered.

"As far as Kostya and the rest of the Omega Sky team are concerned, that's a plus. Apparently, they think that taking me down a peg or two is a good thing."

Jada moved her head from where it had been resting on his shoulder to look up at him. "They do? A plus?"

The song ended, and Gideon took her hand and guided her to a table in the corner, instead of the dais where they had been previously sitting. He pulled out a chair for her and she sat down, then he pulled up a chair close to hers. Instead of feeling penned in, she felt safe.

How odd. Must be because he's so big.

"Jada, let's get something straight, yeah, you can be a tad bit annoying when you think you're right about everything."

She couldn't help the giggle that popped out of her mouth.

"I didn't know that 'a tad' and 'a lot' meant the same thing."

Gideon laughed. "Okay, maybe *a tad* is an understatement."

"It is, because you're *a lot* annoying when you think you know every damn thing. Because you don't."

"Regardless," he replied with a grin. "I kind of like annoying. And, according to my performance evaluations, it would not hurt me to learn a little humility."

Jada frowned. "Your lieutenant would never put that in writing," she protested. "That would be on your permanent record. I thought you liked this guy."

"Relax. You're right, he wouldn't. Why do you know what would or wouldn't go into my performance eval?" Then his hand shot out and he grabbed hers. "Oh right, your dad was a Marine. I'm sorry for your loss."

"It was a long time ago."

"It still hurts."

His brown eyes were so kind, Jada let down a little of her guard. "You're right, it does. I was a Daddy's Girl. I love my Mama, don't get me wrong, but I was unexpected. Ronnie was their seventh, and they thought, last child. I came six years later. Daddy retired a year after I was born and moved his Platoon from Forster Hills, California to New York. Mama's family owns a construction company out there, one of my brothers was already working for Uncle Ricky, so Daddy bought in. He died of a stroke on a construction site when I was thirteen."

"He sounds like a good man."

"The best. I have five older brothers, all good men as well. And the number of uncles and cousins are too many to name or mention."

Gideon's lips tipped up.

"How many in the military?"

"Two of my brothers are Marines. One is still serving."

"Sounds about right," Gideon grinned.

"You got it. Once a Marine—" Jada started.

"Always a Marine." Gideon finished. "So where are all of your five brothers now?"

"Nowhere close by, so we don't have to worry about that tonight."

He raised his eyebrow.

"Well, now that I know that you're not *a lot* annoyed with me, I'm thinking I'd like to explore any chemistry that might be lurking about. But I'd kind of like to do it without an audience."

Gideon stared at her for longer than a moment, and she'd worried she'd blown it. Maybe propositioning somebody like him wasn't the way to go. The last guy she'd done this with was when they were both seniors in college. But hell, she'd definitely felt his level of interest when he was pressed up against her on the dance floor.

Shit, maybe he liked the shy and retiring types. Someone more like Gianna.

Jada bit her lip and tried to pull her hand away from Gideon's grasp.

"Look, I wasn't saying we should go to your or my hotel room. I'm not a sure thing, at least not yet."

Great. Now I sound like a slut.

"What I mean is, I'd just like to be alone with you, maybe talk to you, and very definitely like to kiss you. Is that so wrong?"

She finally yanked her hand away from his and pressed the heel of her sparkly amber heel into the wooden floor, intent on getting purchase so she could push up and away before she made an even bigger fool of herself than she already had.

"Jada," his voice was lower than before, darker and deeper. "Jada," he said as he brushed her curls away from her face and traced the line of Jada's jaw. "Are you listening to me, Angel?"

His voice was a low rumble that seemed to vibrate right into the center of her chest. She nodded. "I'm listening."

"I'm going to stand up, hold out my hand, and you're going to take it. Then you're going to stand up and we're going to walk hand in hand up to the happy couple and wish them good-night."

"But—"

"No buts. Sebastian and Gianna are dying to leave, us going will just spur them on."

She looked over her shoulder at where Sebastian and Gianna were sitting in front of everyone. Judging from the couple's stiff smiles, Gideon was not wrong.

She smiled up at him. "I like your plan."

He stood up and held out his hand. She took it and soon she was hugging Gianna goodbye. Her friend was so excited about being Mrs. Sebastian Durand that it didn't even enter her consciousness that Jada was leaving with Gideon.

As soon as they got outside she pointed to a dark spot in the corner of the reception hall lot. "My rental car's there."

"Jesus, Jada. You should know better than to park way the hell over there. Please tell me you're armed."

Jada spread her arms wide, holding her clutch purse and bouquet in one hand and her shawl in the other. "My bag's a little small for a pistol, don't you think?"

"Well, then I think you should have parked a little closer to the entrance, don't you?"

"Look here, Mr. Smooth-Talker, I was planning on having someone walk me to my car because I knew it was going to be dark out when I left. Okay? Happy now that you are back into my *a lot* annoying category?"

But he was hot when he was all alpha protective male, and he wasn't saying anything that any of her big brothers wouldn't be saying.

But.

But.

She didn't want to be kissing one of her big brothers.

Gideon caught her eye. "*A lot* annoying, huh?"

"Yes." She tugged his hand and started dragging him toward her rental car.

"Hold up there, Jada. Once you get into your rental, where are you planning on going?"

"To Boone's." She tugged at his hand again, but he wasn't moving, therefore, neither was she.

"Boone's Tavern, the bed and breakfast that Sebastian rented out for the entire wedding party?" Gideon clarified.

"Everyone, except for you," Jada reminded him.

"That's right. The idea of all that togetherness, when it wasn't with my teammates, gave me the heebie-jeebies."

"It's nice," she protested. "Are you walking me to my car or what?"

"I know the hotel is nice, but if you're serious about us taking a little bit of time to talk and explore our chemistry without ending up in either of one another's rooms, I've got a better idea." He pulled her closer and stroked his hand up her arm, up her shoulder, until he was holding her around the back of her neck and tilting her head up so they were looking each other in the eye.

"What's your idea?" she whispered.

"Let's swing by Boone's, you pick up just enough to tide you over for a night, and I call over to my hotel and book you your own room. Then we go have dessert in their restaurant and close down their bar as we get to take our time getting to know one another."

Heat swirled its way down from his hand to the center of her chest, then settled between her legs, leaving her aching.

All that from a few words and him touching my neck. I'm screwed.

When she didn't answer, he smiled. "I'm thinking you like that idea."

Jada nodded.

Once again, he grasped her hand, this time sliding his fingers through hers, and guided her to his silver Range Rover.

It had been a long time since Jada had woken up with such a sense of regret. Looking around the beautifully appointed hotel room, she pushed herself up against the headboard and banged her head against it.

Stupid.

Stupid.

Stupid.

How in the hell could she have let Gideon just kiss her goodnight at the door and not dragged his delicious ass into her room?

She dropped her head into her hands and blew out a big breath. Dammit. She had missed her shot, and he lived in Virginia and she lived in Manhattan; there wasn't a chance in hell they'd have another night like last night. Not with Gideon. And he was freakin' special! She'd never lit up with a man like she had with Gideon, and she'd missed out on a taste.

What had she been thinking?

And it was more than just sex, but that would have been awesome, she was sure of it. He was a *man*. Not one of those college boys and computer geeks she'd dated in the past. Granted, some of them had been built along the lines of Gideon because she didn't date small men, but she'd never been so turned on. And definitely never on so many levels. He rang *all* of her bells, physically, mentally, and emotionally.

Jada jerked up in bed.

"Whoa there! Are you kidding me?"

She threw back the covers and jumped out of the bed, making a beeline for the bathroom. *What in the hell am I thinking?* She barely knew the man, and she was getting this tangled up?

She yanked open the shower door and turned on the faucets to hot, then jerked off her nightie and walked her naked booty into the shower. She needed to clear her head and fast. She was supposed to have brunch with Gideon today, and she sure as hell didn't need to be mooning over the man and thinking about china patterns. Not that she ever intended to have china, what twenty-four-year-old woman wanted china patterns? Those were for her mother's generation!

"Harlow, get a fucking grip!" she yelled up into the shower spray. She slathered vanilla-scented body wash all over herself then used her honey-scented shampoo that helped to tame her curls.

When she was done, she bounced out of the shower. She wanted extra time to get ready. She'd brought a warm red sweater, black skinny jeans, and brown suede boots that zipped past her knees to wear for the next morning when she planned to spend time with Gianna's granny and great aunt.

"Shit!"

She needed to call them and let them know that she wouldn't be there at the brunch. Not that they'd notice, they had friends come in from far and wide. Those two had been in their element yesterday.

Jada slathered her hair with product, then used her own blow-dryer with its handy-dandy diffuser and styled her hair. When she was done, she unplugged it and put it back into her small carryall along with all of the product she'd used thus far. She went back into the bedroom and grabbed her cell phone to call the Boone Bed, Breakfast and Tavern so she could talk to Granny. It took a minute to be connected to her room.

"Jada? Are you about ready to head on downstairs?" Granny asked.

"I'm not at the Boone. I'm actually in Lexington at the moment."

"Now why aren't you here? Hold on a minute."

Jada heard the hotel phone clatter onto the nightstand. "I just took a peak outta the curtains. Why is your car here, if you're not?"

Busted.

"I decided to get a room here in Lexington. My own room," she stressed. "I wanted a chance to get to know Gideon a bit better."

"Hmmm."

Jada waited to see what kind of wisdom Gianna's Granny would have to impart. The old lady had taken Jada under her wing ever since she and Gianna had started rooming together their freshman year at NYU. Gianna had insisted that Jada come to Berea, Kentucky for the Fall Festival, whatever in the hell that was, to drink pumpkin cider and look at arts and crafts.

Then Jada had returned the favor and had Gianna come to Queens and celebrate Three Kings Day with Jada's family on January sixth. Of course, Gianna had to come two days early, and Jada's Mama had tried to teach Gianna how to make tamales and roasted pork, but Gianna was a bust in the kitchen. However, on the day of the celebration, Gianna shined. Uncle Ricky had her on the dancefloor doing the salsa like she was born to it. Her Mama was all disappointed that all of her sons were married, after taking note of Gianna's birthing hips.

"Gideon is one mighty handsome man," Granny said carefully. "I've seen pictures of your Daddy, he has the same strong look as him."

"Yes," Jada said carefully in return. She knew that Granny had a lot more to say, and she braced.

"He's a might bit older than you."

"Yes," Jada agreed. "I kind of like that about him. He keeps up."

Granny cackled. "You're smart as a whip, always have been. No grass grows under your feet, Girly. You'd need a sharp 'un to match you. Gianna's told me you dated some college boys who was book smart, but not smart-smart, I reckon you get my meaning. But, Girly, is it wise for you to be bedding some man twice your age just because he's all that?"

"I told you, we didn't share a room," Jada reminded the older woman. "And he's not twice my age."

"I saw you two on the dance floor, don't be tryin' to pull one over on me. You might not have shared a room, but there was some sparkin' going on. Now I don't want details. Are you spending the night in Lexington again?"

Jada didn't know how to answer, because she didn't know if she was.

"My point is made. You have a care, Girly. My new grand-son-in-law holds Gideon in high esteem. I'm not going to think anything but the best of both of you, no matter what you get on up to. I just don't want to see my girl hurt. You hear me?"

Jada's heart melted. "I hear you, Granny."

"Now, you tell this young man, I will *not* be happy if I

don't see the two of you before you both leave the state of Kentucky. I want my goodbye kisses. So does your Auntie and Grandpap. You hear me?"

"I do," Jada smiled.

"Get on with you."

5

"I thought we were going to be having brunch at the hotel."

"Are you disappointed?" Gideon asked.

"Uhm, not with a flight of bourbon for brunch. This beats the hell out of mimosas any day of the week," Jada giggled. "Thank God you're sharing it with me."

Gideon raised his eyebrow.

"Okay, maybe you're not. But this is good. Did you taste this one?" Jada pointed to the empty glass.

Again, Gideon raised his eyebrow.

"You should have." She pointed to the name. "It has hints of maple syrup, vanilla, and candied nuts."

"I like the name," Gideon said. "Angel's Envy."

"What are you drinking?" Jada asked.

"Gianna's grandpappy suggested that I try some Blanton's, so that's what I'm doing." He took another sip, then nodded to her empty four glasses. "I don't think I can keep up with you, Angel."

"They were just tiny little drippy drops of bourbon,"

she assured him. Then blushed as she covered her mouth as she hiccupped.

"Was that me?" she giggled. "It must have been the eggs benedict."

"Must have been," he agreed solemnly.

Jada stifled a giggle. She looked over Gideon; there he sat in a white t-shirt that molded across a chest that made her drool, and he sat there with an air of command that had not been lost on the hostess when he'd given her his name for their reservations. Jada would have been fine if all she had to do was throw a little shade at the little blonde teenager, but oh, no, things had to get *real.*

"I can seat you right now," the hostess said as she gave Gideon a blinding smile. She started to pull out their menus and a middle-aged man who could've passed as the hostess's father—except for the fact he didn't know how to smile—nudged her a little bit to the side. He looked Gideon up and down then stared down at the hostess stand.

"Which reservation is his?" he asked the hostess. Clearly, he was the boss.

The young girl pointed to the marked-up book that had many names, times, and lines drawn through them. She then looked back up at the self-important little fellow. "Smith, for eleven a.m.," she said. Jada could clearly see Gideon's reservation in the book.

He brushed the girl aside and then swept his glance between Gideon and Jada. "When did you make your reservation? Usually, we have a two-week waiting list for brunch, and I don't remember a Smith on our list."

Is he kidding?

Jada did a quick sweep of the restaurant. They weren't the only people of color, nor was Gideon the most dressed-down person, but he was the only black man in jeans. Jada looked over at the hostess who looked both resigned and mortified. Apparently, this wasn't her first rodeo with this clown.

"A friend put me on the list this morning," Gideon said with an easy smile.

"That wouldn't happen, because that's against policy here at Slade's." The manager pulled the menus from the flustered hostess and looked down at the reservation list on the stand. He then called out for the Parkers.

A clearly uncomfortable couple came up to the stand. "Weren't they here before us?" the man asked.

"There was a mistake. I'm rectifying it," the asshole said as he picked up a pencil and crossed out both Parker and Smith, as if he were seating both parties.

Fucker.

Gideon sighed, pulled out his cell phone, and sent a text. The snooty manager walked away with the Parkers following him.

"I'm so sorry," the young hostess said. "He's my boss." Shit, Jada thought that she might start to cry.

"Don't worry about it, Miss," Gideon smiled.

Jada looked at Gideon curiously. He was taking this pretty damn well. Too damn well, if you asked her. But it was clear he wasn't leaving.

Then she saw it. There was a small smile playing around Gideon's lips. Damn....The man definitely had an ace up his sleeve.

Jada relaxed and started looking around at the décor. From where she was standing she could see the bar covered almost the entire back wall. She'd never seen such a huge selection of bottles, and she'd been to a lot of clubs in Manhattan. What's more, the bartenders sure seemed to know what they were doing.

"Gideon!"

Jada looked up to see a huge red-headed mountain man all dressed in white making his way toward them. He had a huge grin on his face as he moved around the hostess stand. Gideon stretched out his hand but the lumberjack ignored it and crushed Gideon in a big hug.

"You made it! How long has it been?"

"Years," Gideon smiled.

"At least five," the man boomed.

"Slade, I want you to meet someone," Gideon said as he pulled Jada close. "Jada Harlow, this is Slade Edwards, he's the owner of this shack."

"Hey, my last restaurant was a shack, we call this one a joint."

The hostess giggled.

"Hey, Julie, when can we get my friends seated?" Slade asked.

"Uhm, Murray didn't think their reservation was legitimate, so he uhm, wouldn't let me seat them."

"Excuse me?" Slade's voice lowered two octaves. He gently pulled Julie away from the stand and lowered his voice. "Julie, what do you mean not legitimate? I put people on the goddamn list all the time, Murray knows that. Hell, he does it too. Tell me he wasn't refusing service."

Julie's face blazed red then she looked down at the floor.

Slade's gaze switched from Julie to Gideon. "Gideon, am I reading this right? He refused you and your woman service?" he asked quietly.

Gideon sighed. "Sorry, Slade, that's what happened,"

Gideon answered just as quietly, aware that there were customers all around them.

"Goddamned racist prick," came Slade's harsh whisper.

Murray had the misfortune to walk up at that point. Slade pulled two menus from the hostess stand and handed them to Julie. "Sweetheart, can you seat my two good friends? Their brunch is on the house."

Murray's eyes got wide.

Julie looked up with relief and grinned. "Why don't you follow me."

Gideon had his hand on the small of Jada's back as he guided her past the hostess station. Jada was able to hear Slade talking before they were too far off.

"Murray, I need to see you in my office, right now." He sounded pissed as hell.

Jada smiled.

Class, her man was all class.

"IT'S BEAUTIFUL HERE," Jada commented, counting her blessings that she hadn't packed her spiked-heeled boots for the walk through the park, otherwise she'd be a mess. Her feet would be killing her, and she'd be wobbly.

"Yes, it is," Gideon said as he looked down at her.

Jada swallowed. She got the distinct impression he wasn't talking about the stark landscape and the pretty bridge over the river.

He took her hand. "So have you walked off your meal?"

"My meal, the bourbon, or my mad?"

"Any of the above," he grinned.

"My meal, yes. The bourbon, almost. My mad? My mad was gone as soon as I heard Slade growling at that racist buffoon." She smiled up at him. "But can I ask you something?"

"Almost anything." His eyes twinkled.

Honest to God twinkled! Whose eyes did that?

"Jada, are you with me? What question did you want to ask me?"

"Oh yeah," she shook her head. She really needed to focus on the topics at hand, instead of mooning over what a handsome man Gideon was. She cleared her throat. "You seemed really cool dealing with the racist bullshit that Murray pulled at brunch. How did you manage to stay so calm?"

She watched as he tipped his neck to the side as if he were relieving sore muscles. Who could blame him?

"Over the years—and I mean years—unless somebody is getting hurt, I'll normally just ask to talk to management and explain and let them know what's going on. These days I'd say eighty to ninety percent of the time, management will do something about the problem, unless it's the owner who's the problem. In that case, I just walk away."

"I suppose that's a more mature way of handling things," Jada admitted.

Gideon grinned. "What's your immature way of handling things?"

"I bury them with negative online reviews with, or..."

"Or?" Gideon asked.

"Well, there was this one time, it was a little clothing store on the upper east side. They actually accused one of my friends of shoplifting. She was picking something up to take it into the dressing room. Sheila was the type to wither and die, but she was with Raylene that day, who threw down. Thank God!"

"To tell you the truth, I still think it's messed with Sheila. She's careful where she shops. Raylene told me all about it. The owner of the boutique came out and told both of them to leave or she'd call the cops."

"So what'd you do?" Gideon asked.

Jada grinned at the memory. "Somehow their inventory, bookkeeping, and social media software all got wiped. I thought about making it look like they were cheating their suppliers, but I drew the line at making it look like they were stealing."

Gideon laughed.

"See, I showed restraint." Jada buffed her nails on her sweater. "But I still don't understand how you can just walk away without doing anything to that other ten or twenty percent. Doesn't it kill you?" she asked.

"No," Gideon answered. "As it is, my job requires me to literally hold people's lives in the palm of my hand. When I'm confronted with something like our friend Murray here in the states, it's not a life or death situation. Is it bullshit? Yeah. But I believe that Karma will eventually balance the scales. Jada, I have to believe that, otherwise I couldn't handle the raw pain and suffering I see in the world."

His words cut like a knife through warm butter. She stood there staring up at him like she was seeing him for the first time.

"How do you do what you do?" she finally asked.

"Because I can. Because it needs to be done."

Jada reached up and cupped his jaw, brushing her thumbs over his lips. "Take me back to the hotel, Gideon Smith."

Slowly, he pulled her close, sifting his fingers through her curls. His intense brown eyes flared with passion...for her.

"Are you sure?"

She could only nod.

His eyelids slid down as he focused on her suddenly dry lips. She swiped her tongue across her bottom lip to moisten it.

"You're killing me, Angel," was all he said before he swept down and took her mouth. The beauty of it burst across her mind, before the power of it had her wrapping her arms around his neck and pulling him down as she did her best to burrow into his body.

Gideon seemed to be on the same page. His fingers went from sifting to clenching, and his other hand swept under her sweater and spanned the base of her back. He kneaded her flesh as he made a low rumbling sound that made her clit throb. Jada squeezed her thighs together, tight.

Senses swirling, it took long moments for her to realize that the mewing sounds she was hearing were coming from her.

"Easy," Gideon whispered in her ear. "I've got you."

Jada's eyelids fluttered open and tiny bits of fluff were beginning to lazily drift down around them. She'd insisted she didn't need to wear her coat for the walk so Gideon had been holding it for her, but he now held it out, then helped her thread her arms through the sleeves.

"You're a nut for not wearing this earlier."

"I'm a New Yorker," she said proudly.

"Well let's get your New York ass back to our hotel."

"And to your hotel room?" she said hopefully.

"I do have quite the view," he allowed.

"I'm sure it's magnificent, I can't wait to see it," she grinned. "Now get a move on."

———

JADA NEVER NOTICED the view from his room. But what she was seeing right now was still magnificent. Incredible, unbelievable, out of this world. A naked Gideon Smith was a work of art, and having him kneeling above her, a look of passionate intensity on his face, made her toes curl.

"Angel, you with me?"

All she could do was nod.

His grin flashed white. "You're with me." He eased down beside her and then he did that man move where he curled his arm around her head as he cupped one of her breasts, his thumb and forefinger playing with her nipple.

"Gideon, no teasing. We're past teasing," she protested.

"More kissing."

"We've already kissed," she whined.

"Not naked kisses," he whispered.

His leg pressed its way past her smooth thighs, rubbing against her core. She jerked up and as she cried out, he captured her mouth.

His kiss was hot, deep, wet, and mind-blowing. Their tongues tangled and rubbed against each other. His fingers continued to toy with her nipple, but then he lifted his head, licked his fingers, and plucked at her other nipple. She hissed at the erotic feel, then the bastard had the nerve to blow across her tightened nub.

"Gideon," she hissed.

He plucked harder, and she loved it, but two could play this game. She untangled her arms from around his back and raked her nails through his chest hair until she was scraping over his perfect male nipples.

"Again," he ordered.

Jada complied, loving the way his light brown eyes turned dark with passion and his thigh pushed higher against her core. She opened her legs even wider, rubbing her clit against the rough hair on his leg. Sparks lit her up, and she started to tremble.

"Nuh-uh," Gideon smirked as he rolled them over. Jada found herself flat on her back, Gideon kneeling over her like some kind of perfectly formed God. She reached out to grasp his cock, but he grabbed her greedy hands in one of his.

"Nope. You tried to get away with something without asking permission."

Jada scowled. "What the hell is that supposed to mean?"

"We're in this together, or not at all, is what that means. We pleasure one another equally, no little side hustles."

"A side hustle? That means I was working for something." Jada tried to free her hands so she could touch his glistening chest.

"Weren't you working for it? I work for your pleasure, you work for mine, and then we find pleasure together."

He had a point.

"Trust me, Angel. My way is going to be so much better." With that, he took his free hand and cupped one of her generous breasts and lifted it to his mouth. Jada cried out. It was like she was plugged into an electric circuit.

"I wanna touch," she gasped.

He didn't stop what he was doing, he just started doing

it better. How that was possible, she didn't know. He moved to her other nipple, and soon her head was moving side to side, her curls tossing across the pillows. When he finally stopped and looked up, he gave her a soft kiss.

"I wanna touch," she whispered.

Gideon let go of her hands. With both sets of their hands loose, touching, holding, and caressing began all over again, only this time in earnest.

Jada sighed when Gideon brushed the inside of her thigh and gently pressed it outward. He groaned as she ran her fingertip along the vein under the bottom of his cock, until she began to tease the engorged head.

"Open," he commanded as he pushed her legs even farther apart. Jada gladly complied.

"Beautiful," he murmured. "God, you're gorgeous."

Jada felt her cheeks heat at his outrageous compliment, but seriously, how could she blush when she thought his sex was superb? She licked her thumb and swirled it around the head of his swollen cock.

"Jesus, Angel, you're going to kill me."

"But what a way to go, huh?"

Gideon pulled out of her grasp and slid down the length of the big bed. Before she knew it, his big hands were spreading her legs even wider and his eyes were looking up at her from over her stomach.

Oh, God.

Oh, God.

Oh, God.

No guy she'd ever been with had been any good at this. As if he could read her mind, Gideon gave her a wicked grin, then she watched as his gaze turned downward and she felt his thumbs brush against her intimate flesh. She jolted when she felt him part her wet folds. When he lowered his head and licked, she dropped her head against the hotel pillow and let out a lusty breath.

Oh, God, indeed.

Again and again, he licked. His tongue curled, then his fingers began a tortuously slow slide inside her wet channel. Were those her gasps? Was she panting? Pleading?

When her pleas stopped, she heard his hums of pleasure, and her body started to tremble as she realized Gideon was getting pleasure from all of his giving. His fingers plunged deep and curled up as he sucked in her clit and raked it softly with his teeth.

An inferno of heat blasted its way up her body from her core. The fire burst through her, knocking all conscious thought from her mind as incandescent pleasure permeated her every cell. Wave after wave after wave of ecstasy continued to soar through her body. It wasn't until she felt Gideon's lips on hers as he pulled her leg up and over his hip that she drifted back to the here and now.

"Angel?"

"It's true. I am an Angel, 'cause I flew," she whispered. "You took me right up into the sky."

She felt the heat of his condom-covered cock nudge her slick core. "Wanna take another ride?" His voice was a deep rasp.

"Don't think it can get any better," she admitted.

"A dare. I like it."

He hiked her leg up higher, and she tilted her hips to give him access. "I triple dog dare you," she smiled slowly up at him.

He didn't say a word, but he took the dare with one

slow slide forward. His thick flesh filled her deep, like she'd never been filled before. She moaned.

"Again."

His eyes hooded, and one of his arms came up around her back while the other curved around the back of her head, cocooning her in a feeling of warmth and safety as he slid back out and slowly thrust back in. Jada wound both legs around Gideon's hips, drawing him even closer, glorying not just in the tidal wave of pleasure, but also in the sense of ease and comfort she was feeling in this man's arms. He continued with the slow rhythm that filled her deeper and deeper, until he was finally rooted inside her like they were one being. It was beautiful. They both stopped moving, savoring the moment.

Then Jada felt Gideon tremble and searched his expression. His face was harshly etched with passionate need, and she realized just how much he was holding back.

"More, Gideon. I need more," and she was not wrong. She needed all that this man had to give.

He studied her face and must have found her truth because he slowly slid back out to the tip, then he drove back like his life depended on connecting with her. In and out, Gideon powered through her slick folds, expertly moving her body so that his cock would light up the right spots and rock her world.

"Gideon," she screeched.

He paused, a trickle of sweat dripped down one of his pectoral muscles and Jada licked it up. "I'm wonderful. You're wonderful. Keep going."

He threw back his head and laughed, then gave her another Gideon kiss, as he continued to drive her insane with his powerful strokes. Every single time he hit her sweet spot, he would twist and the base of his penis would rub against her clit. Sublime.

Jada began to pant, big gasping breaths; this seemed like so much more than what had come before.

"Come on, Angel," Gideon coaxed. "Reach for it."

She didn't know if she could. It was massive, she wouldn't survive. Gideon's eyes looked almost black, his face a mask of ferocious passion. He drove in again, and it was so good. So good, but too much.

"It's all right, let go, Angel." He bent down and kissed her, then he took her bottom lip between his teeth and bit down. The little bit of pain sent her over the edge of the world. Jada clamped down on Gideon's cock as she screamed out his name.

Over and over again he pushed her past any limit she'd ever had as the eternal beauty of the stars shot by. Then the beauty burned brighter as she felt and heard Gideon join her as he found his release.

Oh yes, magnificent.

JADA ROLLED over and let out a sharp cry of pain.

What?

It was pitch black, she couldn't see anything, and it stunk. She tried to sit up, but it hurt too badly.

Why did I have to wake up? Why couldn't I have just kept dreaming? Remembering all the goodness?

"Gideon, please help me. Please say you're coming," she begged the darkness.

6

It was nine o'clock in the evening in Portland Oregon. They'd gained hours on the flight. Ryker was driving so that Gideon could do research, but Ryker had taken the first opportunity to pull their rented full-sized SUV over at a closed Costco parking lot. The lot was almost two acres and he parked them in the back corner where they could unpack their hard case suitcases and pull the ammo out of one suitcase, and the guns and rifles out of the other.

"Two rifles?" Ryker asked.

"You never know," Gideon shrugged. "Just be happy." Actually, he had wondered if he was going to need to tap Kostya from Northern California, and if he did, he wanted to make sure they each had weapons.

Ryker and Gideon made sure that each M4A1 Carbine was locked and loaded, then they were back on the road, which gave Gideon a chance to study things on his tablet.

"Whatcha got?" Ryker asked after they'd been on Hwy 26 for thirty minutes.

"I'm in Jada's cloud account."

"I thought those were locked tight?" Ryker said. He sounded amazed.

"Yeah," Gideon said, not looking up. "They're password protected; if you have a lead on the password, then they're not bulletproof."

"I thought you said she was good. Wouldn't she use one of those password generators?"

Gideon looked over at Ryker. "You're kidding me, right? Thousands of hackers are working to infiltrate those companies every single minute of every single day. Whoever figures out a zero-day for one of those companies, will be bigger than the MVP of the Super Bowl game."

Ryker looked away from the road and scowled at Gideon. "There you go again, talking all tech. What in the hell is a zero-day?"

"It's basically a system vulnerability that the company doesn't know they have. That vulnerability would allow someone to install malware, or download their data."

"Why call it a zero-day?"

"Because the company has zero days to stop this from happening. Now the hacker who finds this will be able to name their price on the black market."

"How will he or she know who to sell it to?"

"Trust me, they'll know. There is a big underground marketplace on the dark web. Hell for something like that, if the hacker is savvy enough he or she could do an auction....but."

"But what?"

"It's called zero-day for a reason. At any time, the company could plug that vulnerability, and then your zero-day isn't worth a dime, so sitting around trying to haggle over a price isn't always smart."

Ryker started tapping the steering wheel with his ring finger.

"What?" Gideon asked Ryker, the man was obviously thinking about something.

"Were you ever involved in hacking? It sounds like you know a lot about it."

"When I was a kid, yeah," Gideon answered uneasily. He didn't really like thinking about his time with Kendall Douglas. He did not like thinking about all of the things that he was forced to do with that fucking sword hanging over his head. Even though he'd eventually gotten out from under Kendall, that time had left a stain that he still hadn't totally scrubbed off his conscience.

Ryker caught onto how Gideon had answered the question because he went back to his original line of questioning. "So, how did you crack Jada's password?"

"She screwed up. She allowed four of her regular passwords on clothing store sites to be captured on her computer's memory. When I went in and found those, I figured out her password naming convention. It's complicated, and unless you were her, you wouldn't know it. Or unless you had four other passwords to figure out the pattern."

"So basically you could get into my computer if you wanted to?" Ryker asked.

"Who's to say I haven't already?" Gideon grinned over at his teammate.

"No wonder Kostya loves having you as his second-in-command. You're scary."

"And don't you forget it."

"So, have you figured out where Jada is?"

"I have her phone locked at a small motel in Tillamook. Since the call, she hasn't moved. I've had the motel manager do a welfare check, and all of her stuff is still there, her suitcase and purse. The woman at the motel wouldn't look in her purse, but she did confirm that Jada's car is still in the parking lot. I told her that was great, that my wife has diabetes, and since I hadn't heard from her, I was concerned. We both agreed she was probably out seeing the sights."

"Tillamook has sights?"

"Don't be an ass."

"For real, the manager didn't mention any sign of a struggle? What about her computer?"

"I asked about her iPad, and that wasn't there, but again, the manager and I agreed she could have taken it with her."

"But Gideon, no signs of struggle, that's good news."

Gideon nodded, then turned his concentration back to his computer tablet. Now that he was in Jada's Cloud, there was a shit-ton of information that he had to go through. Jada was one busy woman.

RYKER WENT into the motel and got the key to the room that Gideon had rented online. From where Gideon was sitting in their rental car, he would bet his last dollar that the woman manning the front desk was the same one he'd talked to ten hours ago to check out Jada's room. That was the reason he didn't want to go in with Ryker, he didn't want to draw any attention to himself and have her remember his voice.

Ryker slipped back into the driver's seat. "We're at the back of the motel, close to Jada's room."

"Good."

"Have you had any ah-ha moments yet?"

Gideon shook his head. No fucking ah-ha moments, and if he had any hair on his head, he'd be ready to pull it out. Jada was doing work for a new company, a legitimate company called Risk Guard, and its mission was to protect other companies from cyber-attacks. Jada was doing freelance work for them, and she was getting paid a huge chunk of change for once.

Gideon's lips twitched as he remembered all of the shoes she had packed for baby Neil's christening; the woman *needed* money to support her shoe habit.

Her job was to probe the clients that hired Risk Guard and see if she could get past their security and firewalls. She'd been assigned twenty-three companies, and she'd already breached five. It looked like she'd managed to break into their systems within twenty-four hours.

Twenty-four hours? She must be losing her touch.

She had various scripts running against the other eighteen companies. Offhand, Gideon recognized the basic components of half of the scripts. They were pretty slick and should get the job done. He didn't have time to break down the code for the other nine. He needed to pull in some of the other SEAL team tech gurus.

Once again, Ryker found a dark place to park and they grabbed their bags and headed to their room.

"Oh, I forgot to tell you, she said there was only one room left, and it had just a king-sized bed, even though you had booked us two doubles. I said that wouldn't be a problem. I call dibs on the bed," Ryker said as he slid the card key into the slot.

"Asshole."

Ryker pushed open the door and Gideon immediately saw the two double beds.

"So did she get it wrong, or did you feel a need to fuck with me?" Gideon asked Ryker as he threw his suitcases on the bed closest to the door.

"Fuck with you. Wanted to see you smile."

"After we find Jada," Gideon said as he pulled out his gun and rifle from his case, then threw on a shoulder holster. He took a second look to make sure his Sig Sauer was locked and loaded and watched as Ryker did the same thing.

"Ready?" Gideon asked.

Ryker grabbed his wallet, then pulled out what looked like a hotel key, only it had many holes in it. Gideon recognized it. "You think a hotel punch card will do it? That's pretty old tech."

"This is a pretty old motel," Ryker said. "But if you're thinking I'm relying just on this, you're wrong. Trust me, I've got you covered."

"I really don't want to use the boot to the door method," Gideon said wryly.

Ryker looked at him with surprise. "Breathe in some calm. Seriously, have I ever let you down?"

Gideon rubbed the back of his neck. "No, you haven't."

"And I won't now," Ryker assured him. "Anyway, I checked out our door lock, this works on it." Ryker grinned and winked as Gideon opened the door.

"You really are an asshole, you know that?" Gideon chuckled. So, Ryker had accomplished what he'd intended. He hadn't laughed since that spine-chilling call from Jada.

"I know, but you love me anyway." Ryker's whisper was barely audible as the two of them crept down three doors to Jada's room. The modified key card got them into her room in seconds. When Ryker flipped on the light, Gideon's heart sank. He saw her purse sitting on the desk. He hadn't known dick about purse brands, or shoe brands for that matter, but in the little time he'd spent with Jada, he'd learned. That was her pride and joy, it was a Prada purse. With the money she spent on it, he could have bought a used dirt bike. The woman was crazy.

Another thing he knew—she hadn't left of her own free will.

"Why are you staring at that ugly orange purse?" Ryker asked. He was gently pulling Jada's stuff out of her ratty suitcase.

"Because it proves that she was taken against her will. This thing was practically glued to her shoulder the last time I saw her." Gideon picked it up, smoothing his fingers over the exceedingly soft leather.

"When was that?"

"Sebastian's son's christening."

"Sorry, you're going to have to do better than that. I don't keep track of time in baby christening increments," he said with a smirk. "Is that purse expensive?"

"Oh yeah." Gideon carried over to the unmade bed to peruse the contents of the suitcase that Ryker had just pulled out.

"She wasn't dressing to impress. Check out these boots; these are some serious work boots. So are these gloves. It looks like she was planning on mending fences out on the cattle range with these, but then if you look at these," he said pointing at a pair of very fine, thin leather gloves, "these look like she was planning on some dirty deeds."

Gideon unlocked the decorative lock on her purse and rifled through it. He wasn't surprised when he didn't find her phone. She was talking to him when she got spooked. Was she at the desk? Sitting on the bed? At the chair?

He squatted down and looked under the bed. No phone. He went over to the desk and looked all around it and under it. No phone. Then he went over to the one sadly padded chair next to the window. Again, he squatted down. It wasn't under the chair, but when he pushed back the curtains, he found it. He knew down to his bones that she'd turned it off and dropped it on purpose. She'd hoped he'd find her.

He thought for a few moments. Her iPad was missing, so hopefully, if they wanted info, they'd be going over that first. That would give them time to find Jada before they started on other ways of extracting information straight from her.

Please, God, say I'm right.

———

"HAVE I told you how much I hate this part of a mission?" Ryker asked as he flipped the channel again. He was a TV surfer. Jesus, couldn't he do that with the volume off?

"What part of a mission, McQueen?" Gideon mumbled the question as he sent another text, this time to Dex Evans, the comm/comp guy on the Black Dawn team.

I'm going to fucking rip the remote out of his hands!

"The waiting-for-you part of the mission. Isn't there anything we can do? Even if it makes no sense, and it's just chasing my tail, please let me do it."

"Food."

His phone rang.

"Food?"

"Not fast food. Decent food. Go now." Gideon didn't give a shit that he practically roared the last few words—anything that got Ryker out of the room was a blessing. What's more, his friend knew it. Ryker knew he was useless at this stage of the game, and that's why he was so damned antsy.

"Aye, aye." Ryker grinned as he shut off the TV then bolted out the motel room door.

Gideon's phone rang and he pounced on it. "Yeah, Dex, thanks for calling. I've got a situation."

"I figured. What are you doing in Oregon?"

"Long story. A woman has been kidnapped. She called me and mentioned an anomaly in a system she was checking out. She's doing contract work for a company that provides full cyber defense; she's the one who looks for ways to break in. She said she was in trouble, big trouble. Then her phone went dead. I have her on the Princess Quest app, but her phone was left in her motel in Oregon."

"Got it. Was she working on a project that resulted in her going MIA?"

"Probably, but she's working on eighteen systems at the moment, so I don't know which one could be the culprit. Some have similar scripts running against their security, but some are unique. I pulled down information from the cloud, but without her actual laptop, comp, or iPad, I can't tell which one she was working on at the moment."

"Shit. So, somebody somewhere caught onto her hitting their company and got cranky."

"If she was playing on the up and up, all of these eighteen companies would be on her employer's list. Can you get with Clint at Midnight Delta and Kane with Night Storm and divvy out what I'm going to send you? I'll also send you everything I pulled down from her cloud about Risk Guard, so you should be able to see if any of the eighteen aren't on their list of clients."

"Consider it done. Anything else?" Dex asked quietly.

"If I think of something, you'll be the first to know."

"I'll update you in an hour via text, just to give you status."

"I appreciate it, Dex."

Dex hung up, and Gideon rolled up his sleeves. It was time to get to work. Now, he hadn't sent the other men on wild goose chases—every lead needed to be checked out —but Gideon had a hunch. It was a wild one, but then again, Jada was a wild card. It was the reason she appealed to him more than any other woman ever had.

There was no record on the cloud of her having hacked Risk Guard, Inc., but his girl was too smart to leave any kind of trail. It was possible—and fuck, likely—that a company like Risk Guard would try to monitor their employees. In that case, there would be no record of what she had found anywhere. His girl would have been doing this with totally different equipment, a different persona, and she'd be arranging for her log-in to be coming in from somewhere in Outer Mongolia. There's no way he could follow in her footsteps without some kind of in, and he didn't have it. Gideon would bet his left nut that she had nothing from this other account and persona touching her Jada Harlow identity.

I'm fucked.

On the bright side, it would take the kidnappers a

couple of days to realize it, if the kidnappers *were* a part of Risk Guard, which was what his gut was telling him.

Unless they decided to just beat it out of her.

"Okay, okay. Fuck this noise. It's Risk Guard that has her, I'm sure of it. Look for some connection with the company and Tillamook."

7

THREE HOURS, ONE COBB SALAD, VEGGIE BURGER, AND FIVE calls with the other technical team members later, and Gideon's brain was running faster than a coked-up hamster in a greased wheel.

"Any luck?" Gideon asked Ryker as he came back into the motel room.

"I didn't find anything in Jada's rental car; it was clean as a whistle."

Ryker sat down on his bed. "What have you got? You're looking a little too calm for once." Ryker came closer, then sighed. "Shit, it's an act."

Gideon took the last bite of his burger and nodded, then swallowed. "Fine, I'm not calm, but I'm better than I was."

"Why?"

"Because I know what we're doing next. Risk Guard has two subsidiaries, one of them does real estate investments."

"That sounds odd. Why would a company like Risk Guard have anything to do with real estate?" Ryker asked.

"So, they could have property wherever they wanted. This allows their execs to live the high life all over the world without having to have silly little things like mortgages. Tillamook might not be the end-all-be-all, but Oceanside Oregon is pretty damned nice and it's forty minutes away. And guess what? This real estate company has a multi-million dollar estate with ocean access. That makes it very convenient for the yacht."

"Yacht?" Ryker queried.

"Yep, it's good sized, and what's more, they keep it moored off the house's dock."

"Define good-sized." Ryker was starting to grin, and Gideon didn't blame him.

Gideon wadded up the bag that had contained his food and tossed it in the trash. "Forty-two feet. Mount up, cowboy. Let's go get her."

"Are you sure that's where Jada is?" Ryker asked.

"I've got a good feeling about this, and I want to get there yesterday."

"You got it pulled up on Google Earth?"

Gideon cocked his head, and Ryker held up his hands in supplication. "Sorry I asked."

Gideon handed him his tablet. "Look at this."

He watched as Ryker looked at the multi-million-dollar mansion that overlooked the ocean. There was a big-assed boat house at the dock, and the four-car garage was another building that was separate from the main house. There was a large decorative security fence surrounding the property, except on the side facing the ocean, so they'd need to approach from the beach.

Gideon looked down at his watch, it was now one in the morning. He yanked his military backpack out of the larger suitcase and started slamming ammo, knives, and his gun into the pack. Then he checked on all the other things to make sure he was covered. Anything he could spare, he threw Ryker's way. Ryker had his civilian backpack that he'd used for his flight from D.C., and he was now loading that up with his ammo, gun, knife, and whatever else seemed useful. They both changed and layered up with their swim trunks beneath their cargo pants.

Gideon hefted his backpack up onto his shoulder, grabbed his room key, unplugged his tablet, and turned to Ryker. "Ready?"

"Yep."

They left the room and headed for the SUV.

"HE SAYS IT'S HOT, so it needs to go." The woman sounded mad.

"What a waste," Jada heard a man's voice say. She hadn't heard him speak before.

"Quit thinking and just do your job," the woman ordered. Jada recognized her voice, she was the one who had given her the tarp. Naomi, her name was Naomi.

Wait a minute, it wasn't as dark anymore, but it wasn't exactly light either. Jada turned her head just a little bit so she could see past the tarp to find out what was going on. It was colder than earlier.

Jada saw that she was outside. She could see the moon reflected off the ocean, and now that she saw that she realized she could hear the sound of the crashing surf.

"I didn't know I would need enough C-4 to take down the house, boat house, and garage," the man said tentatively. "It's in Butch's car, and he had the keys. I think you killed him?" His voice went up as he asked the question; it was clear he was scared to death.

C-4? What's going on?

Jada tried to move her head a little bit more. She needed to get out of here. She couldn't trust that the director guy still wanted her alive. Maybe she was supposed to go up in the explosion. As she moved the tarp she saw a pylon with a life preserver hanging off it. A dock. She had to be on a dock.

The marina! I'm at the marina!

"Help!" she screamed. "Help!" she screamed louder. "Rape!" she screamed even louder.

"Shut her up," the woman said in a bored tone. "I don't want to have to listen to her screaming and whining."

Someone yanked the tarp off her and she blinked her eyes.

"Heeeeellp!" Jada continued to scream the word.

"Should I drug her?" the man asked.

"No, gag her. The director could be coming. I'm not sure. If he does come, he wants to be able to question her."

Someone kicked her head. Unimaginable pain exploded through her skull. Her mouth went slack.

One of them stuffed a rag in her mouth, then wound a rope around her head. Around and around, until she thought she was going to choke. Her eyes were watering and she blinked rapidly, trying to clear them.

I can't pass out. I'll choke to death if I pass out.

The redheaded woman crouched down beside her and grabbed her chin so she was forced to look at her. "That was very annoying, and a waste of time. We're nowhere near anyone else."

There was no way that what she'd found out about

Risk Guard was this bad. Sure, someone might be angry and questioning her. But this? Torturing a man to death? C-4?

What the fuck did I get myself into?

"Who?" Jada mumbled behind the gag.

The redhead laughed. "I can't understand you, Baby."

"Who?" Jada tried again.

"You're a regular comedian."

"Who?"

"She probably wants to know if we're going to kill her," the man said.

"Shut up, Luke. You concentrate on finding a way to make everything go boom," she said over her shoulder.

"Actually," another woman said. "She's just saying one word. I think our little genius is asking, 'who'."

This was the woman who'd referred to Jada as merchandise. The one who had scared away the pervert.

"Is that it, Baby? You want to know who?" Naomi asked.

Jada nodded and pain sliced through her temple where she'd been kicked.

"It's our director. You never want to fuck with him. He can get just a tad bit grumpy, and when he does," she giggled, "well, take a look at yourself and you can see. Bad things happen."

She turned around and stood up from her crouch. "Luke, you better have figured out a way to blow everything up, otherwise bad things will be happening to you," she growled.

"And it'll go slow," the other woman said in a sweet voice. "Actually, fuck it up, Luke, I would enjoy a project. I'd really been hoping to work on this little girl, but apparently, I'm not allowed. So please, Luke, I'm begging you, fuck it up."

"I'll make it work," the man grit out the words, obviously scared. "You keep your sick games pointed elsewhere." His booted feet stepped over Jada's head, and he started running up the dock.

"Jenny, you need to keep it in your pants," Naomi sighed. "You already tortured our Risk Guard leak, and then you got to cut up and kill Butch after you found him going at it with our little genius here. Really, Sis, two men in one day should be enough, even for you."

"It's this job," the woman grumbled.

"No, it's not, it's the director who has you stressed. He's been stringing you along for two years, you need to be shot of him."

"Naomi, don't tread there, never tell me to get rid of my man. You know your boundaries, don't stray over the line."

"I'm your sister, and I'm telling you that you're heading for a fall. He's using you, and therefore using me."

A cell phone rang.

"Fuck, that's his ringtone," Naomi said with disgust.

"You watch her, make sure she doesn't choke to death. My man needs me."

As soon as Ryker started the engine, Gideon started to make calls. Even though all signs pointed to his hunch being right, he still knew there was a chance he could be full of shit, and he was putting Jada's life on the line with a hunch.

"I gave you an update a half hour ago," Dex answered

the phone. "We've tracked down nine of the leads, so far everything looks clean."

"Get everyone on the line," Gideon demanded.

"You got it, I'll do it now." Dex hung up.

That's why he liked working with the best; these men knew when not to ask questions and just get shit done.

It took less than a minute. "We're on. You've got me, Clint, and Kane."

Gideon had his phone hooked to the car's speaker system so that Ryker could be in on it too and they could all hear the same thing at the same time.

"I had a hunch. I thought Jada might also be doing a search on Risk Guard."

"Something totally off the grid?" Clint asked.

"Yep. Using a different identity, different hardware, IP, the whole nine yards."

"And we would have no way to know what would make her that suspicious, right?" Kane asked.

"Nope," Gideon agreed again. "So, I had to go at this another way. I asked myself if there was anything here in this area that was connected to Risk Guard. The only thing that we found is a shell real estate company that they created under a couple of subsidiaries. That real estate company owns a huge house, isolated on the coast, located on the water with a dock. They have a forty-two-foot yacht that they own as well. That's where Ryker and I are heading now. I've already texted the address to Dex."

"I received it and forwarded it to the rest of you," Dex said.

"Heading to the house is your only play," Kane agreed.

"That's what we think, too," Ryker said. "Gideon came prepared. I don't know how he thought he could Rambo it with two automatic rifles, but I'm glad he did, because that means I got one to play with one too."

Everyone on the phone laughed.

"Do you have specs on the house?" Clint asked.

"No," Gideon answered.

"You will in under five minutes. Lydia grabbed the address, she'll have the architectural CAD in a PDF format to the house sent to you via e-mail soon. You do want it e-mailed, right?" Clint asked.

Gideon chuckled. "Yes, I want to see it on my tablet, not on my phone."

"Who the hell is Lydia?" Ryker asked.

"My wife," Clint answered. "She can run rings around every man on this call when it comes to finding out shit."

"Just remember that, Querida," a woman with a Hispanic accent laughed in the background. "Gideon, I've sent you the specs."

"Anything else?" Kane asked.

"Just continue a deep dive on Risk Guard. I have no idea what we're looking for, but try to find something that shows them paying for outside mercenary consultants. If someone was so stupid as to build a shell company to pay for this shit in Tillamook, they might be paying their goons through the company too."

"We're on it," Dex promised. "From now on, you call in to me. Got it?"

"Yes," Gideon promised.

They hung up.

"How much longer?" he asked Ryker.

"Five minutes."

8

BREATHE.

Breathe.

It took all of her concentration to breathe through her nose and not choke on her saliva, since the rag barely let any of it come out of her mouth. Now she felt her nose filling up with snot. Dammit, why had they zip-tied her hands again before taking her to the dock?

"I've got the charges set," Luke said as he stepped over Jada's head.

"Wonderful. You did your job." Was Naomi's sarcastic reply.

"Wonderful, you're going to fail at yours. Looks like you're going to end up killing the director's pet."

"What?"

Naomi crouched down next to Jada. "Ah shit. You can't breathe, can you, Baby?" She stroked Jada's hair and Jada jerked away. Now she started to cough or tried to. She was going to die for sure.

Luke laughed. "Yep, look who's fucking up now."

"Give me your knife, you asshole," Naomi hissed.

"What, you need a favor from me?"

Jada couldn't catch her breath. She felt black closing in around her. Her body heaved.

"You fucker, give me your knife!" Naomi shrilled.

Jada's body bucked again as she tried to get air in through her nose and couldn't. She felt pressure near her temple. Then she felt a sharp pain.

"Dammit."

"Oh, did you cut the director's toy?" Luke laughed again.

Another stinging cut, then relief—Jada could breathe!

"What in the fuck is going on around here?" the scarier sister asked as she stepped over Jada.

"Your girlfriend screwed up. She almost let your little guest choke to death, then when she tried to fix things, she cut her. I'm sure the director is going to be real happy with the work you two lesbo bitches have managed to do," Luke taunted.

A shot rang out and Jada flinched.

Luke screamed. "You shot me in the leg!"

"It's only a flesh wound. Now tell me you have all the charges set."

"You shot me!"

"Tell me about the charges, or I'll shoot you again," the crazy sister named Jenny said calmly.

"I'm bleeding."

Another shot rang out.

"You hit me again!" the man screamed. "You're a psychotic bitch!"

"Did. You. Get. The. Charges. Set?"

"Yes! Yes! Yes! I got all the C-4 from Butch's car, there was more than enough, everything will go up like the Fourth of July. The detonator's right here, in my hand."

Jada winced—weren't they close to the house?

"You dumbshit. We need it on a timer." Jenny sounded even angrier.

"I-I-I c-can do that."

"Well, get it done."

"How long?"

"Half an hour," she said. "No, wait. I need to get this one's comp and my bag from the house. Make it forty-five minutes."

"Jenny, I'll run up to the house," Naomi told her sister.

"No, you get her onto the ship. I need to wait for Miles, anyway."

Jada startled at the name. *I knew Miles Albright was involved!*

"He's coming?" Naomi sounded surprised.

"Of course, he's coming," Jenny said irritably. "He wants to find out what this bitch knows. What's more, we haven't seen each other for a while."

"What about Bonham? Are you just going to leave him to die?" Naomi asked.

"He betrayed us. Of course, he's got to die." There was a pause. "Luke, change the charge so it's an hour. I want to make sure we give Miles enough time to get here and on the yacht."

"W-Whatever y-y-you want," came his shaky reply.

"Damned right," she laughed. "Don't you forget that. Now pick yourself up and get going."

"I can't. I need to get to the hospital," he gasped.

"You know what I did to Bonham, you know what I did to Butch, do you want to be next?"

"No," was his weak reply.

"Then get your ass up and hobble the fuck away and

do your fucking job," Jenny sneered. "Also, remember to never use the term lesbo again. It's derogatory. Got it?"

"Y-y-yes."

Jenny laughed. "Get to hobbling."

Blood splashed on Jada as he stepped over her.

Jada somehow managed to hold still, even when she felt a drop of blood drip down her eyelid.

"Naomi, I expect you to take care of him when he gets back. I don't want anyone alive."

"Got it," Naomi replied. "And her?"

"Get her up and walking. Get her ass on the ship, then we'll call you on where to meet. In the meantime, head for Hayden Island. Got it? He's coming to the front gate, and I'm meeting him there."

Naomi must have nodded because another pair of boots straddled her.

Naomi crouched down and swiped at the blood on Jada's cheek, then her eyelid. "Now that my sister is gone, you can quit playing possum." She bent further, and before Jada knew what was happening, she kissed her softly on the lips and tried to further the kiss by pushing her tongue forcefully into Jada's mouth. Jada jerked her head away. The pain in her head was excruciating, but that was so much more acceptable than Naomi's assault.

The redhead laughed.

"Ah, Sweetheart, you're so pretty. It's going to be a shame to see Sis hurting you. I hope you just talk." She stroked her fingers down the side of Jada's jaw, then she violently forced her thumb past Jada's lips, then pulled it away and sucked on it. "Your flavor is exquisite, even with a hint of vomit."

"You're sick." Jada's voice was hoarse.

"Jenny and I both have our kink," Naomi laughed.

"Jenny says you were a brilliant college girl. Were you in a sorority? I bet you have a lot of fun girl-on-girl stories to tell me. But I gotta tell you, when it comes to sex and pretty girls, I like being in control. A lot. Not taking it to the point of pain like Sister Dearest, but having my little bunnies scared is yummy."

All the time Naomi was talking, she was using the muzzle of her gun to push up Jada's t-shirt until it was up above her bra.

"You have beautiful breasts, Jada. No wonder Butch wanted to play with you."

Jada looked into Naomi's eyes and saw the crazy. Feeling the cold steel against her breastbone scared the hell out of her.

"Now, do you think you can stand up and walk to the ship, or do you want to continue to lie here on the dock and let me play?"

If I can get on my feet, maybe I can get away.

Jada tried to push up from the wooden slats, but fell back down, hitting her shoulder, hard.

"Aww, you don't want any more bruises, look at what Butch did to you. Naomi pushed the gun against Jada's breastbone, right over her heart, then she bent over and licked Jada's nipple over her lacy bra. She crouched upward and looked Jada in the eye. "You taste like ambrosia. Here, let me help, my love."

Naomi put her arm under Jada's shoulders, and between the two of them, Jada was soon shuffling toward the end of a long dock. She saw the gleaming front of the ship and the name *Avatar* in sparkly gold letters.

"You're going to need to be careful," the redhead said as she helped her climb aboard.

Jada thought about jumping into the water, but there

was no way she could swim in the state she was in. She'd just drown. Would that be better?

No! I'll fight. No matter what. I'll fight this bitch.

As soon as they were aboard, Naomi grabbed her by her hair. "We're going to have so much fun before we get to the island."

"Over my dead body," Jada growled.

Naomi yanked Jada's head back by her dark curls so that she could pull them face to face. "Let's get one thing straight. I'm the one with the gun and I have a knife. I'm not afraid to use it. I'll just tell them you tried to escape, and my sister will believe me. So, get smart, and get smart fast. You need to treat me as your new best friend."

Jada thought of Gianna; now that was a best friend, not this twisted sister.

"Let's get you below deck," the redhead purred.

Not a chance in fucking hell am I going downstairs with this ginger-headed bitch.

Jada swung out, aiming for the woman's jaw. She clipped her good. Naomi brought up her gun, but Jada didn't care. There wasn't a chance in hell she was going to let herself be raped. She tried to balance on her right leg, and swung out with her left one, intent on kicking the shit out of the sick bitch. She lost her balance and fell backward, knowing she was going to hit her head on the brass railing.

Her last thought was, 'Not again,' just as her head hit. Everything went dark.

———

"Jesus," Gideon breathed.

"What are you seeing?" Ryker demanded to know.

Gideon was staring at the yacht through binoculars. Jada had just rushed the woman with the gun. What in the hell had she been thinking? Did she have a death wish?

"Jada's out. She just hit her head against the brass ship railing. Fuck, Ryker, she hit it hard. I can't see her now. There's a woman with a gun. I don't know how many more are on board."

"Got it."

They were about one hundred yards from the dock, behind some rocks. Between the rocks and the dock, there was nothing but sand. They were going to have to swim to get to the yacht if they didn't want to be seen.

"Let's hit it," Gideon said as he started toward the ocean. Ryker followed him. Gideon grinned; there wasn't anyone on the Omega Sky team who was better in the ocean than Ryker McQueen. Ryker was the stronger swimmer. Not only was he ten years younger than Gideon, but the little shit had also grown up surfing the beaches of Southern California.

"I'll wait for you," Ryker promised.

"Obliged," Gideon said before he dove into the surf.

It didn't take long before they were both at the hull. They each swam in the opposite direction so they could make better time. As Gideon swam, he listened and watched and peered into every window to see who was on board. Gideon's gut clenched when he looked into the third window and saw Jada. She was halfway off a bed and there was a blood stain around her head. It looked like she had been thrown there like yesterday's trash. Gideon continued to swim around the rest of the yacht, looking for any other signs of life. When he met up with Ryker, he reported in.

"I found Jada. She's in the aft portside cabin. I didn't see anyone else."

"Understood." Ryker acknowledged. "I found one woman looking over the bow like she was waiting for something. She had a gun in her hand."

"Must be the one who attacked Jada."

"That's my take," Ryker agreed.

"Let's board."

Ryker nodded. They swiftly swam to the hull and quietly climbed up the ladder. They pulled out their rifles. "You go below decks," Gideon ordered. He needed to make sure that they were safe so that he could concentrate on Jada's safety.

Ryker raised his eyebrows but nodded. They split up. Gideon meticulously checked every part of the upper deck. He was surprised to find even the cockpit empty. He could see the woman peering over the hull, looking past the boat house, up toward the house. Gideon slung his rifle around to his back and pulled out his pistol. He didn't make a sound as he moved up behind her. Before she knew what was coming he had the gun's muzzle shoved into her temple, and her pistol wrested out of her hand.

"What?" she shouted in confusion.

"Down on your knees."

"Who are you?"

"Down on your knees. Don't make me repeat myself."

She knelt. "Who are you?"

"Shut up and put your hands behind your back."

He had her hands and ankles zip tied in moments. He shoved her onto her stomach. "How many others?"

"Fuck you!"

Gideon pulled out his knife then grabbed a hank of her red hair and yanked her head up so he could look her in the eye, his knife at her throat. "Lady, I will fuck you up. Now, tell me what I want to know. How many more of you are there?"

"I don't know. Maybe three, maybe just my sister."

Gideon frowned. "Explain."

"I'm supposed to kill Luke."

"And the other?"

She spit at him. He pressed the knife until there were beads of blood oozing from her neck. "Tell me who else."

"The director. Miles Albright. They should be gone by now," she whimpered.

He let go of her hair, letting her face slam into the wood deck.

Gideon turned and ran to the stairs that would take him below deck. Ryker had found a first aid kit and was wrapping Jada's head with a bandage. She was fighting him.

"Get away from me." Her words were slurred.

"Move," Gideon shoved Ryker out of the way. "Call an ambulance."

"On it." Ryker pulled a baggie out of his drybag and unwrapped his cell phone. Vaguely Gideon heard him calling emergency as he turned his attention to Jada.

"Get your hands off me, you pervert." She took a weak swing at him. He grabbed her fist in his hand, and kissed her knuckles.

"Jada, it's me. Gideon. Let me help you, Angel."

"Liar."

"I need to stop the bleeding."

He pushed her hand down to her side. He took the steri-pad and gently placed it against the bleeding wound. "Fuck," he mumbled.

"Ow," she groaned.

"I know it hurts, Angel. Just let me do this, and soon it will be all better."

"Ambulance is on its way. We need to get her to the main house so they can get to her faster."

"No," Jada turned her head to peer at Ryker. "No house."

"Yes, Jada. We've got to get you to a hospital," Gideon insisted.

"Blow up."

"What?" Gideon didn't understand. He wrapped the bandage around her head. She groaned and he winced.

"No."

"Jada, I know it hurts, but I have to stop the bleeding."

"No house, blow up. Gotta save..." Her eyes closed.

Gideon looked up to Ryker. "Explosives?"

"Sounds like."

"But who is she talking about saving?"

Jada moaned. "Angel, Honey, I need you to wake up. Come on, I need to know who we need to save." Gideon gave her a gentle shake. He looked down at her; even with her dark coloring, her face was ashen. Just how much blood had she lost?

Slowly her eyes opened. "Gideon?"

"Yeah, Angel, it's me."

"Charges. Going to blow up..." Her eyes closed, then opened. "Save him. They hurt him."

"Who? Who did they hurt? Jada? Jada? Open your eyes, Angel."

Gideon gave Ryker a frustrated glance. "She's lost too much blood. We were lucky to get as much information as we did."

"I've got to go see about the explosives, see if I can stop the charges. If this place blows, we're going to have a fuckuva time getting her to an ambulance. Plus, I need to see about the guy she was talking about."

"Agreed, do what you can."

"I'll keep you informed."

Gideon nodded, all of his attention on Jada. He pressed his fingers to her carotid artery. Her pulse was weak from all the blood she'd lost. "I'll call emergency and tell them the situation. I'll make sure they don't come too close," he yelled after Ryker.

Ryker was already out of sight.

"Good," he yelled back from a distance.

Gideon ran his hands down her body to check for other injuries. Her ribs seemed okay, but when he skimmed her breasts she winced. He continued to probe. When he touched her thigh, she let out a low cry of pain. Carefully, he pulled up her oversized tee and pulled down her yoga pants.

"Goddammit."

Bootprint.

For the first time in his life, Gideon saw red. It colored everything he was looking at. He shook his head and looked down at Jada. She wasn't moving, and he was scared to death.

Gideon thought for more than a second, then hustled his ass to the galley and made an icepack. He got back to Jada in record time. "Are you with me, Angel?" he asked.

Still nothing.

He took a couple of pillows, one to elevate her head, then took all of the bullshit decorative pillows and shoved them up against the side of her head so they'd hold the icepack in place. He bent over and started to whisper in her ear.

"I fucked up, girl. I was such a dumbshit. I see that

now. Open your eyes and I'll lay it all out for you so you can gloat."

He traced his fingers from between her eyebrows, down her nose, then tapped the end like he'd done in Kentucky. "Wake up for me, Angel. I need you to open those gorgeous brown eyes. Don't you want to hear what I have to say?"

Gideon felt his throat begin to close up. *Don't let me be too late. Not like Pops.* He couldn't bear it.

What am I talking about, I won't be able to bear it if she leaves me? I need her. I need her in my life. Please, God, don't take her away from me.

"Jada, I am too old. I'm fucking ancient. What's more, I'm damaged goods. But if anyone is strong enough to handle me, it's you. You were right all along. I've needed someone exactly like you in my life for forever. You told me, but I just wouldn't listen."

Gideon looked down and grabbed her left hand because it wasn't swollen. He opened it up so that he could kiss her palm. "You have to be okay."

He looked down at her, his stomach roiling with anguish, then his brain clicked into gear.

"Fuck me! Angel. Hold on. Just hold on for a minute."

Why hadn't he thought of this before? He ran out of the cabin and rushed up to the cockpit. No keys. He should be able to hotwire the motherfucker. How stupid was he? He pulled out his phone.

"Ryker, get back here. We're taking the yacht to the marina."

"You have the keys?" Ryker asked.

"No, going to hotwire it. So come back."

"Can't. I found one of the charges. It's set to blow in fifteen minutes. Gideon, this place is fucking huge, I won't be able to find whoever Jada was talking about. What I can tell you is the C-4 is not enough to take out the whole house. There has to be another bomb somewhere. This was easy to find, so I'm sure I can find the other one."

"Goddammit!" Gideon knew there was no way that Ryker was going to leave an innocent behind, not if he could help it. It just wasn't in his nature.

"Get the fuck out of there in five minutes," Gideon ordered.

"I'll evaluate things in five minutes, now let me work," Ryker answered. Then he disconnected the call.

"Fuck!"

Gideon needed to concentrate on his task and work fast. He looked at the console. He'd never seen anything like it before. *Think man, electronics are electronics.* He ran back down to the cabin where Jada was and saw that there was no change. He started praying as he grabbed his pack and headed back up the stairs to the cockpit.

He analyzed the control panel. The first thing he spotted was that the yacht had an electronic kill switch, which was good news for him. That meant that somewhere on the yacht was the equipment he was going to need to hotwire this ship, and if he had to guess, it would be really close to the starter switch and battery. Gideon hauled ass to the stern so he could access the engine. He skidded on his knees and when he got there, he started clawing through his pack for tools.

He looked at his watch. Two minutes had passed.

He used his flathead screwdriver to take off the panel covering the engine, while his eyes scanned for anything that looked like it might be an emergency kit. Red caught his eye and he lunged. He pulled it to him and yanked it open.

"Yes!"

He pulled out the battery-operated screwdriver, then made quick work of removing the panel. He peeked in the goody bag again—yep, it had everything. He saw the wires and a three-wire ignition. He was in business! He connected the right wire from the on terminal to the negative terminal on the battery.

He glanced at his watch, four and a half minutes had passed.

His phone rang. Ryker. "Charge is disarmed. I don't know how many others. I'm going to search for the guy. Ambulance is waiting at the gate."

"No need, hot-wired the yacht. Get here ASAP, we'll head to the marina."

"Got it."

"You only have five and half minutes if there are more charges," Gideon pointed out.

The line went dead. Ryker had hung up again. Gideon was wet from his time in the water, but he began to sweat anyway. He bent back down and worked to finish the job so the engine would start.

He connected the third wire from the off terminal to the positive terminal on the battery. Gideon switched on the gas tank and turned on the three-wire switch. He was almost a hundred percent sure he did it right, so he hustled up to the cockpit, and pressed the button to start the engine.

It roared to life. They were in business.

He looked at his watch. It had been seven minutes since Ryker told him that the charge was set for fifteen minutes, and he still didn't know what was going on. He couldn't call him; he didn't want to do anything that might distract his friend.

The boat house! Of course, they would have set a charge to blow up the boat house. It was located where the dock met land, so even if Ryker found the guy and made it out of the house and headed to the yacht, he could still be killed when he got near the boat house.

Gideon was over the side of the ship, and running down the dock, in seconds. It was killing him not checking on Jada, but he had to concentrate on the mission. As soon as he opened the boat house door, he saw the C-4 and the detonator. It was the sloppiest job he'd seen in his life. Obviously, whoever set it didn't give a damn. When he got down on his knees to disarm it, he realized he was kneeling in a pool of blood.

"What the hell?"

Aw, who cares?

His phone rang, it was Ryker. "Found another charge and a dead guy who bled out beside it. It's got enough C-4 to blow the whole front of the house. This has to be the last of it."

"There's still the garage," Gideon warned.

"Shit, you're right," Ryker agreed. "We're down to four minutes."

"Skip it. The garage is far away enough that the explosion shouldn't impact you. Try to find that guy that Jada was talking about and get him to the yacht. But, wait until the four minutes are up."

"Why?"

Gideon hung up and concentrated on disarming the bomb in front of him.

His smile was grim.

Three minutes.

Thank God it was electrically primed. He pulled out his knife and unfolded it. He carefully pulled up one of the wires that was set to channel the current to the blasting cap, and he cut it.

"One down." He cut the next one.

"Hot damn!" He looked at his watch; hell he had ninety seconds left—easy, breezy.

He closed his knife, got up, and shoved open the boat house door. He sprinted down the dock.

Gideon didn't even remember how he got down to Jada, but he was beside her, touching the pulse in her neck. It was beating steadily.

"That's it, Angel. You've got this."

He felt the engine fire up.

"Ryker," he yelled at the top of his lungs.

"I've got this," his teammate yelled back, echoing his words. Gideon slumped in relief knowing that Ryker was at the helm and they'd soon be at the marina and could get Jada the help she needed.

Gideon looked down at Jada. "Hold on, Angel. I love you. Hold on."

9

"OH FOR GOD'S SAKE, WHO STAYS IN THE HOSPITAL MORE than a day anymore? Get my doctor in here right now, I want out," Jada demanded.

"She's a feisty one."

"And who the fuck are all of these studs? Did you call up Abercrombie and Fitch and say you needed some models to cheer me up?" Jada glared at Gideon.

One of the models laughed.

"You." She pointed at Laughing Boy. "Name, please."

"Do you want my rank too?" he asked.

"Jesus, would you start with a name, and tell me why in the hell you think it is okay to be in my hospital room when I'm basically wearing tissue paper?" She pulled her blanket higher over her boobs.

"My name is Lincoln Hart, Petty Officer First Class, United States Navy."

Jada squinted at him. Lincoln was wearing a white tee. With muscles covering muscles, he looked like daddy Hemsworth had another kid that ended up a SEAL. She turned her head and regretted it.

Fuck, I hurt.

"I saw that wince. You have a serious concussion. They want to keep you for at least three days," Gideon said patiently.

Jada ignored him and pointed at another man, who scowled at her. "Name and rank."

"I'm here under protest." He crossed his powerful arms over his navy blue t-shirt. "The name's Nolan."

"I asked you—"

Another unknown hottie came and stood next to Gideon. "Am I hot too? I gotta tell you, after the shellacking I've been taking from my woman, I could really use a boost to my ego." His green eyes twinkled down at her.

"You're not hot, you're SexySuavey, will that do?" Jada's voice trailed off. That was about all she had in her. She knew she was on some kind of intravenous painkiller that was making her tired, but even with that, she still hurt.

"Okay, everyone out," Gideon ordered. "We'll ask our questions tomorrow."

"Gideon." She turned her head to look at him, not caring if it hurt. "Why'd you bring all these men?"

"I wanted to introduce you, Angel. One of them is going to be with me while I watch over you at all times until we capture whoever kidnapped you."

"Director, named Miles Albright," she slurred. "He's stringing Psycho sis..."

Her eyes closed.

"Sleep, Angel. I'm here. You're safe."

She felt Gideon place a gentle kiss against her forehead. It was nice.

GIDEON STRODE out of the room. Everyone but Linc followed him. He was taking first watch. Ryker beat him to the elevator button by half a step and hit it.

"Did you get anything from the sheriff?" Ryker asked Gideon softly.

Gideon gave a small shake of his head. "Let's wait til we get to the cafeteria."

When the door opened there was an older couple who took two steps back when the three of them entered the elevator.

"Hiya," Ryker smiled. "We're visiting a friend. This seems like a really nice hospital."

The couple bowed their heads and looked at the floor. Ryker was not making them feel more comfortable.

As soon as the elevator door opened, Gideon and his teammates stepped back so the couple could exit before them, then they left and headed in the opposite direction toward the cafeteria.

"I'll get the food," Ryker volunteered as he saw the line. "You two grab a table and talk. Gideon, you need to bring Nolan up to speed anyway."

Gideon nodded and walked to a back corner and sat down.

"Thanks for dropping everything and coming. I can't tell you how much I appreciate it," Gideon said as soon as they sat.

Nolan frowned. "You do realize you're being both patronizing and insulting, don't you, Chief?" When Nolan was pissed his Southern drawl became more pronounced. By the sounds of it, Nolan was well and truly pissed.

Gideon rubbed the top of his head. O'Rourke was right. "You're right."

"Good. Glad you realize it."

"This thing with Jada has me twisted up."

One side of Nolan's mouth tipped up. "You don't say."

"You know, you should be a little bit more obvious when you bust somebody's balls, I'm sure your subtlety goes over Landon's head."

Nolan smiled bigger. "Maybe his new lady love will educate him about a few things."

Gideon snorted.

"I like your girl, even if I don't know what in the hell Abercrombie and Fitch is."

"It's a clothing store that's known for its all-American good-looking models," Ryker said as he put down two loaded trays of food.

"Jada's funny, fiery, and fantastic to look at. You scored, Chief," Ryker said as he sat down and started pulling food off the trays and putting it in front of all of them.

"It's the feistiness that has me worried," Gideon said as he grabbed a plate with scrambled eggs and bacon. "There isn't a chance in hell she'll let us handle things. She'll want to be on the front lines."

"Say no," Nolan said right before he put a forkful of eggs into his mouth.

"She's going to get me to promise to let her help before giving me any information."

Nolan washed down his eggs with water. "So lie."

Ryker laughed and pointed his fork at Nolan. "Do what he said."

Gideon realized that it wasn't a bad idea, he just wasn't going to do it. He respected her too much.

"Ah hell, he's not going to do it," Ryker groaned.

"You can read him?" Nolan frowned.

"About Jada, yeah. I saw him bust ass to get here. He sees her as an equal."

"She *is* an equal," Gideon snarled.

Nolan put up his hand. "Don't get your panties in a twist. You know goddamn good and well what we're talking about," he drawled. "I will tell you I'm fucking amazed that you consider someone, man or woman, on par with your comp and tech skills. But there's no way she's an equal to our other skills, and you know it."

Gideon blew out a long breath. "You're right."

"So, she's not on the front line. She can do research, she can be giving us all the blow-by-blow support we need as we do our op, but that's it." Nolan's gray eyes were the color of steel.

"That's the second time you're right today. That means it's the second time I'm wrong today, so I'm going to cut that shit out." Gideon shook his head ruefully.

"Would be obliged, Chief," Nolan smiled.

"He screwed up while I was getting food?" Ryker said.

"Drop it," Gideon ordered as he looked around the sparsely filled cafeteria. There was nobody close to them, but he still intended to speak softly.

"Okay, where are we?" Ryker asked.

"We'll get more when Jada wakes up, but right now I sent Nolan and Linc a summary of what we knew up to the point when you got on the plane, so here's the latest."

Nolan and Ryker leaned forward.

"I found out there's another woman who's her sister, a man named Luke, and a guy called Miles Albright. I didn't share that info with the authorities. She's being held based on my testimony that I saw her assault my girlfriend, and that she had a weapon and that's why I put her in restraints."

"What's Jada's prognosis? I mean she seems with it, but you could tell she was in a lot of pain," Ryker stated.

"That's because she's refusing pain meds until she absolutely needs them. She was pissed when she found out they were giving some via IV. She thinks she should be able to handle the pain without having to rely on narcotics. She's stubborn as hell. I mean she's the definition of stubborn. Her father was a Marine and two of her older brothers are Marines. She shares their attitudes."

"Lovely. So, she really is a wildcard," Nolan grimaced.

Gideon nodded and grabbed a cinnamon roll.

"What else you got?"

"Of course, we weren't allowed anywhere near the questioning of Naomi Sims, they didn't get the info I did. Of course, they didn't put a knife to her neck."

"You researched him?" Nolan asked.

"Yep, I did a deep dive on him. He got his start at MIT, then started with the Department of Defense when he got out of college with his Ph.D. There isn't a lot of information on his time with the DoD; he spent twenty-five years there though. It must have been some top secret shit he had clearance for, because I still haven't been able to crack through the walls of what exactly he'd been working on. Four years ago he just up and left, and became Chief Technology Officer for Reynolds, Inc. Man kept a very low profile until he joined Risk Guard's Board of Directors, then things changed."

"How?" Nolan asked.

"He started digging deep into Risk Guard's business. It was clear that the CEO of Risk Guard was pushing back. I still don't know what anomaly Jada found, but it had to have been something directly involving Miles, otherwise, why would he have her kidnapped?"

"Do we question him?" Nolan asked softly, his tone deadly.

Gideon knew what he meant. This definitely could be done off the books. Nobody would know who had touched him, and they *would* get their answers.

"No, that's not the play I want to make right now. Miles waving a flag is too big of a risk, he has too high of a profile. I know he's guilty, but blowing up that mansion, kidnapping Jada, and hell, just putting something like this in play, means he has an ego. He'd report our questioning."

"Putting what into play? Did I miss something?" Ryker turned to Nolan who shrugged.

"If you missed it, so did I," Nolan agreed.

"Sorry, you're right, I wasn't clear. I've been talking more to Clint, Dex, and Kane. Here's the deal. We think the companies that hire Risk Guard to evaluate their systems, are in essence, clean. However, we've been thinking someone at Risk Guard doesn't want to inform them of their findings. They instead want a big fat client who will think they do in fact need to hire Risk Guard. Therefore, they insert malware into their client's software, or better yet, into their firmware, and voila. They now have a huge contract that will last indefinitely."

For the first time, Nolan actually grinned. "Sounds like you've figured it all out. So, why not just make this Miles guy confess?"

"Because that's not even close to being enough. There were three bodies found in the house, so that's three unsolved murders alone, right there. Right now the police haven't been able to identify them, but Jada told me some names. She said one was named Luke, who set the explosives. One's name was Butch, he's the motherfucker who'd dared to put bruises on her body. There was also another guy they'd been torturing. She didn't get his name, but they'd referred to him as a leak at Risk Guard. What I don't know, and what Jada isn't sharing, is what made her suspect Risk Guard to begin with, and how that brought her to Tillamook."

"Ah, she's holding out until you promise you'll let her in on the op, right? Nolan asked.

Gideon nodded. "So until Jada gives me the info, or we figure it out on our own, we're in a holding pattern."

"Are you telling me, you brought these two in and we're just going to sit here with our thumbs up our asses in the cheese capital of the world?" Ryker asked impatiently.

"No, I'm not telling you that. Our girl Naomi said Miles and her sister were due to arrive back at the ship, so they were, and maybe still are, around here. I want to track them down and watch them. First off though, I want eyes on Jada at all times. I'll figure out where we're going to set up home base for a while."

He looked over at Nolan. "How'd you and Linc get away? What'd you tell Commander Clark?"

"Funny thing that. We both said the same thing—we had a friend in need, and asked if we could be released from training. He was cool with it. We have five days until Kostya is due back, then we're to talk to him and reassess."

Gideon nodded. That was another thing he put on his mental *to-do* list, he needed to inform Kostya what was going on. He took the last sip of his coffee. "I'm going to find places for us to stay, and not at that shitty motel Jada was staying at."

"Shitty's fine, I'm not particular," Nolan drawled.

"When did you become so hoity-toity?" Ryker asked. "I

believe we have slept for five days in our same stanky uniforms on dirt and rocks with our packs as pillows, so what in the hell's wrong with Jada's motel?"

"It's exactly because of those days in the desert, jungle, and mud that I like my amenities when I can get them," Gideon smiled slowly.

"You Princess," Ryker scoffed with a twinkle in his eye.

"Quit giving Gideon shit and let's go stretch our legs. The sooner he can get on his comp, the sooner we have rooms where we can get some sleep."

Gideon smiled at Nolan who got up, bussed the table, and handed one of the full trays with debris to Ryker. He took the other, and they both walked off. Gideon pulled out his tablet to make reservations, then to check in with the other team's computer experts.

10

"YAY ME, I GET TO LOOK AT AIRPORT VIDEO FOOTAGE," Ryker groused.

"You lost rock, paper scissors." Linc shrugged. "Maybe you should stop choosing *rock* all the time. With paper, you get to go to Seattle and check out a waterfront condo."

"Meanwhile I have to go to D.C. where all of the politicians live." Nolan O'Rourke looked like he was sucking on a lemon. Every other man grinned. Nolan wasn't really known for his ability to schmooze.

"I got you a nice place to stay," Gideon coaxed.

"I'll trade you, straight up. I'll throw in eight hours of working on your car," Ryker promised. Nolan gave him a confused look.

"Amy," Linc said. "If Gideon is twisted up about Jada, then we can say that Ryker is tied in a constrictor knot over Amy."

Everybody busted out laughing. "I don't know who the hell Amy is," Nolan said as he continued to chuckle, "but she obviously has him by the short hairs."

"She's Lark's best friend. She's given our boy Ryker the brush-off, and his little ego can't handle it," Linc laughed.

"Hold up," Ryker said in a serious tone. "You haven't met her. None of you have. Yeah, I might be tied up in knots, I'll cop to that. But she has herself put together, she is a great friend to Lark, she's making her way in life, she's nice, has a great sense of humor, and is someone I want to get to know better. If there's an opportunity to be in her city and spend some time with her, fuck yeah, I'm going to take it."

Gideon's eyebrows went up so high, he thought they might crawl off the top of his head. This was for real; Ryker was dead set serious on this woman and he'd been giving him shit.

"Man, I'm really sorry. I didn't realize just how deep this went. Apologies." Gideon said.

"Yeah, same," Linc said.

"I want to meet her," Nolan said with a slow grin. "She sounds amazing."

"She is," Ryker concurred, "but I saw her first."

"Well, in that case, hell yes we can trade," Nolan smiled.

"Since you know why, do I still have to work on your car?" Ryker asked.

"Hell yeah, you do," Nolan smiled wider.

Everyone but Ryker busted up laughing again.

"WHERE IS EVERYBODY? Without the Chippendales, my blood pressure might not be high enough to even register," Jada complained.

Gideon walked further into Jada's hospital room. "You'll just have to cope with me."

She crossed her arms and *humphed.*

Gideon laughed, but even though she gave him this much lip, he knew they had an elephant in the room, and he didn't know how to broach it, how to mention the way he had left things the morning after baby Neil's christening.

"What?" she asked belligerently. "You look pensive. What's going on?"

"We need to talk about everything you know about Risk Guard."

Way to avoid the topic. God, I'm a chickenshit.

"Fine, let's talk. What do you want to know?"

Gideon pulled up the chair beside the bed even closer so that he could see her pretty eyes and not miss one word that she said.

"Tell me what you were working on that had you coming to Oregon."

She slowly turned away and bit her bottom lip. Gideon couldn't tell if she was in pain, didn't want to tell him, or was just thinking.

"What, Angel?" he prompted.

Her head whipped around and her eyes spit fire. "Don't call me that. Don't ever call me that again."

Gideon could see the pain on her face. It gutted him. He suspected she hurt from both turning so fast, and because he had been such an utter dick the last time they'd been together in Kentucky.

"Alright, Jada, I'm sorry, I won't call you Angel. But please be mindful of your injury. There's a reason the doctor is keeping you here for two more days."

"Which is utter bullshit," Jada gritted out. Then she

clenched her teeth and it became clear that her pain was indeed physical.

"You need to take the pain meds the nurses bring to you. Did you sleep last night?"

"Sure, I passed out on you and the underwear models, remember."

Stubborn, the woman redefined the word stubborn.

"Are you saying I'm not an underwear model?" he teased.

She twisted her lips.

"Tell me why you're here," he asked again.

Again she remained silent.

He sighed. "I need to know why you came to Oregon. Did it have anything to do with the eighteen companies you were on contract to penetrate for Risk Guard?"

Jada closed her eyes, then opened them up and looked at the ceiling, but a smile was playing on her lips. "You got into my cloud account. How?"

"Not telling, but yes I did."

She turned her head to look at him, this time a hell of a lot more slowly. "You want info, well so do I. I'm not saying a word until you tell me how you were able to hack my cloud account and promise to let me in on your little soldier games."

Gideon rubbed the top of his head. "I figured out your password."

She sat up straight in bed. "Bullshit."

"Nope, it happened."

"I never use the same password for anything. Everything is at least, *at least* sixteen characters, with numbers, upper and lower case letters, and three symbols. Bullshit you figured out my password."

"I did."

Her eyes got even wider. He watched as she thought through how he could have possibly come up with her password.

"Okay, you figured out how I sequence my passwords. No two are the same, but there are pieces of them that stay the same, but how could you even know that?" She wasn't asking him, she was talking to herself. He continued to watch her process. It was fascinating to see how her mind worked. He loved it.

"Fuck! Fuckity, fuck! It was Jimmy Choo and Louboutin! I totally fucked up! My password was captured on my computer when I shopped, and I didn't ensure it was scrubbed after I was done shopping. You found out how I sequence my passwords! Dammit!!!"

Gideon fought hard not to grin, but she saw it.

"Do not laugh at me," she pointed a finger at his face.

"I'm not laughing."

"Bullshit! You're laughing that my shoe habit is what screwed me over."

He saw the twinkle in her eye. And this was one of the many reasons he adored her—she could laugh at herself.

"Those shoes will look good on you, An—" he stopped himself before he called her Angel.

"Damn right they will. I hope nobody steals them off my doorstep before I get home."

Gideon winced. He'd never liked the apartment she lived in. There was no doorman, it was just a walk-up in what he considered not the nicest part of Manhattan.

"I see that look on your face, Gideon Smith, but we're not going to get into your Neanderthal worries. Now you're going to tell me what my scripts have found."

"That was not the deal. The deal was that if I told you

how I got your cloud password, you would tell me why you came to Tillamook, Oregon."

She huffed again. "Fine. But after that, will you tell me what my scripts have found? Please?" she wheedled.

"I promise."

She gave a small nod. "The anomaly I found wasn't on any of the existing eighteen clients I was working on."

"How long have you been a contractor with Risk Guard?"

"I got the contract three weeks after Neil's christening, so about five months, almost six."

"What's your position there?"

"My job is to play black hat. Companies that call Risk Guard ask them to do a threat analysis against their firewalls and security systems to see how protected they are. That's where I come in. It's been pretty easy. I've been able to break into almost everyone they've sent my way."

Gideon grinned. Of course, she had.

"And the eighteen you're working on now?"

"I'm using the same standard scripts that I've used to break into the others. I should have cracked about five by now, so that's why I want to know where I stand."

"We'll get to that. I still want to know what brought you to Oregon."

She gave him a cagey look.

"You promised," he reminded her.

"I know I did, and you promised I would be part of your operation to take down Risk Guard, especially Miles Albright. How do I know you won't go back on your word?"

"I don't do that." Gideon was offended.

"Yeah, yeah you do. You inferred that we had something. You led me to believe that we weren't just some kind of fling, that we were building something more, and then you kicked me to the curb. If that's not going back on your word, I don't know what is."

It felt like that time he'd taken a bullet dead center in his Kevlar vest. It knocked him down, he lost his breath, and it hurt like hell.

"You're absolutely right. I did that. You don't know how sorry I am. I want to talk about that. I need to talk about that, I was wrong in so many—"

"Stop. Just stop, Gideon. I can't listen to this right now. I'm in pain, and you rehashing the worst moment of my life will gut me. Let's just focus on the now. Are you telling me when it comes to your work I can trust you?"

Gideon nodded. He couldn't say anything else.

"Okay, you asked why I'm here in Tillamook, right?"

Gideon nodded again.

"It's just going to sound a little crazy."

"Jada, you were kidnapped and three people were killed. We're past the realm of crazy and are at the point of deadly."

"Well okay then. I need to start at the beginning. Risk Guard found me by word of mouth and I signed the dotted line in two business days. The money was crazy good, so I didn't do my normal deep dive on the company."

"So, you dove in after you went to work for them," Gideon surmised.

"Yep. It always makes me itchy, working for somebody I don't know inside and out, but they said I could only consider the offer for forty-eight hours, and then it was off the table."

"Didn't that send up a red flag?"

"Gideon, it's a well-respected, publicly traded

company. Plus, I had the opportunity to quit at any time. The only thing that I was dealing with was a non-compete and an NDA. I figure the NDA goes out the window if I can prove Risk Guard employees tried to kill me."

"You can bet on that," Gideon growled. "So you started to dig deep on them after you were employed. What did you find?"

"I looked at all of their financials, those that they reported to their stockholders, and then the ones in their enterprise management systems. I was surprised to see those actually matched, kind of stunning in this day and age. But one of the things that bugged me is how they went from a no-name company to almost top of the field in two and a half years. That really got me into digging."

"Understandable."

"They had to have changed their tech, marketing, sales, something, but I couldn't find any evidence of any of those things happening. The only thing I could find was that they landed six huge clients and Miles Albright joined the Board of Directors."

"Let me guess," Gideon said wryly. "You dug deeper."

Jada gave him a blinding smile. The kind he'd gotten when they'd *first* met in person. The kind he'd killed right before they parted five months ago in Kentucky. The *last* time they were in Kentucky together.

"I did dig deeper, and I found some gold." She actually rubbed her hands together with excitement. "Gideon, it was awesome. Yep. Each one of those six big clients? Somehow, mysteriously, within months of one another had huge flaws in their company's security. Flaws that would take a year to fix. Boo-hoo for them, yay for team Risk Guard."

"Are you telling me nobody questioned this before you?" Gideon asked in surprise.

"No, because they were so different. This wasn't a piece of malware or anything as easy as that. Each one of these companies had a different kind of vulnerability, the kind I'm tasked to find, a zero-day. Not all in the same place, not the same type, but definitely a vulnerability that could be tapped. It seemed kind of suspicious to me that within two months' time, these six heavy hitter companies had system vulnerabilities that could be exploited, don't you think?"

Gideon cocked his head. "I have to agree, even if they all looked different, the odds are against it. So, what did you find?"

"It definitely took a hell of a lot longer than a minute," Jada grinned wide. "But, when I went back into their systems, I finally found four identical signatures where they'd been hacked, all going back two and a half years ago. You just can't convince me that was a coincidence."

"Nope. No way it was that. Could you trace it back to anyone?"

"Just an I.P. address in the Philippines, so no."

Gideon nodded. "Probably defunct now anyway."

"That was my thought. I've been looking at all of the software developers here at Risk Guard who were employed during that time, to see if any of them have that same kind of signature when they write code, but so far nothing. I'm only halfway done. The thing that's been really hurting my investigation, is that I haven't been able to track down the contractors they had on staff during that time. This is definitely something they could have sourced out."

Gideon nodded. "You've thought this out."

"Are you thinking I wouldn't have?" she asked tartly.

"Nope, this is exactly what I would have expected. But now tell me how this brought you to Oregon."

"Well, like I said, the other thing that was different two and a half years ago, was Miles Albright came on board as one of the Board of Directors. So, I've been doing a little digging on him. They love him over at Reynolds, his current company. He's a star. There is no conflict of interest with him sitting on the board of Risk Guard, but the fact that he does makes Albright shinier when Reynolds puts out their yearly bios of their company officers."

"What a load of horseshit." Gideon hated all the maneuvering in corporate America.

"Wait a minute, let me tell you about Reynolds."

"You don't have to. I've already looked into Albright, I know all about Reynolds," Gideon told her.

She frowned. "Why would you have done that? I hadn't told you about him."

"The woman who was with you on the yacht, she—"

Jada bit her lip and her breath hitched.

Gideon was so in tune with Jada that he immediately noticed her distress. "What's wrong?" he asked gently.

She shook her head and he knew that had to hurt. When her curls covered part of her face she didn't brush them away. Instead, she hid behind them. Gideon reached out and carefully brushed back her hair to put it behind her ear. She flinched.

"Baby, what's wrong?" He had to know. Something had set her off, and it was bad.

She turned her face to the wall. "Nothing's wrong."

"Can I hold your hand?" Gideon asked.

Jada continued to look at the wall, but she turned her

hand over and he placed his palm on top of hers, then tangled their fingers together. She gripped him tight.

"Jada, what is it?"

She continued to avoid looking at him. Gideon watched as she shook her head and mumbled. "Nothing. It's nothing. Tell me how you knew about Miles," she asked softly.

She was scaring him.

"Jada, look at me."

She looked at him out of the corner of her eye, then looked back down at the flimsy blue and white blanket covering her legs. She was examining it like it held all the answers to life's mysteries.

Gideon replayed what he'd said. She'd reacted when he'd mentioned the woman on the yacht. The woman who had been holding a gun on Jada. Was Jada reliving that moment when she might have died?

"I know it can be frightening the first time you're faced with your own mortality," Gideon started.

Jada snorted. "Yeah sure, that was it."

Well, that sounded like his girl; there was a little more spark, but she still wasn't meeting his eyes.

"Angel, can you talk to me? Tell me what's wrong?"

Her hand trembled underneath his.

"I told you, nothing."

Bullshit.

Gideon's antenna was up and it was pinging like a motherfucker. Since this was the first one-on-one conversation with Jada that he'd had since she'd woken up in the hospital, this was the first time he was really seeing things that her over-the-top bravado had masked on previous visits. His girl was hurting.

"You know you can talk to me about anything, right?"

"Sure." She dragged out the word for a while, making sure he knew she was being sarcastic.

"Should I maybe call your mom and have her fly out? I'd call Gianna to come, but she's on bedrest right now."

This time she did meet his eyes, and she was pissed. "Gideon Jason Smith, I don't need my mom or my best friend flying across the country to hold my damned hand. I am perfectly fine. I am not some kind of simpering miss who faints at the sight of blood, or at the first little hit of adversity, or the second, or even the third. I'm a survivor. Let's all bow down to Gloria Gaynor, and sing a chorus of 'I Will Survive'."

She yanked her hand away from him so that she could cross her arms over her heaving bosom. It would have been a great speech if her eyes weren't glistening tears.

11

"I HAVE NEVER DOUBTED YOU WERE A SURVIVOR. JADA, YOU are one of the strongest women I've ever met. Hell, I think you're the strongest," he said wryly.

"Damn right," she muttered sarcastically.

"But even the strongest among us need to lean on others from time to time. Sometimes life gets pretty damn ugly, and we need someone."

"I was only under their tender mercies for a day and a half. Two days? It was no big deal. Just a couple of bumps and bruises. Gianna ended up in a coma for God's sake, this was nothing."

"One person's nothing is another person's something," Gideon pressed.

"Shut it, Sailor Boy. For fuck's sake, you have to know they did a rape kit, there was nothing, ergo, I'm fine."

"You had bruises on your breasts. You might not have been raped, but some man sexually assaulted you." She needed to admit it, talk about it.

"It was nothing," she protested. "Somebody felt me up. Nothing," she spat out. Her eyes filled with tears. She was killing him. He brought their linked hands up to his lips so he could brush a soft kiss against her knuckles.

"What are you doing?" Her voice was fierce.

He kissed her knuckles again.

"Gideon, what are you doing?" This time her voice was tremulous.

"I'm kissing the hand of a survivor."

She dropped her head backward and looked up at the ceiling. A tear clung precariously to her lower lash. "Don't do this to me. Don't be nice to me like this. You don't even like me, remember? Let's focus on that, not this be-nice-to-Jada moment. I can't take it, Gideon, I can't."

"I more than like you, Jada." He rasped out the words, regretting every moment where he made her feel unwanted and unloved.

"Don't, Gideon."

"Tell me what happened. Don't let this fester, Angel. You're safe with me."

She turned her head. Tears spilled down her cheeks. "Am I?"

"Absolutely. From now on, your heart will always be safe with me."

For what seemed like an eternity she just stared at him, assessing. She must have decided she could trust him. "I was scared, Gideon. I could handle it if they were going to beat me. Gianna was so brave, how could I be any less?"

He waited for her to say more, but when she didn't he answered. "You're just as brave as your friend. Braver, even."

"But I'm not, I stumbled at the first hurdle." Her voice quavered.

"Tell me," he coaxed.

"I think I remember you seeing the boot print on my thigh, right?"

Gideon nodded. He didn't think he could even say yes without wanting to yell.

"He was fine. Butch, I could handle. I mean, he was your garden variety sicko that you find down in the subway every day in Queens. Nothing new."

Gideon kept his hold on her hand gentle and soft while he ground the toe of his boot so hard into the linoleum it was a wonder it didn't pop off. "What do you mean, garden variety, Jada? I grew up in the Bay area, I'm not familiar with your New York sickos," he attempted to tease.

She looked at him out of the corner of her eye. "You're just bound and determined to make me talk about this, aren't you?"

"Yep."

"Do you feel guilty about it, seeing as how I don't want to?"

"I can get someone from Victim Support Services." He let his voice trail off. He knew enough from his brother Mike, who was a police detective, that victims of violent crimes often needed help from those kinds of services.

"Are you trying to piss me off?"

Gideon let his thumb trail circles around the top of her hand. Her eyes fluttered and she seemed to relax, so he continued.

"Jada, I'm not trying to piss you off, I'm trying to help. Talk to me, Angel."

"I let a woman get the best of me," she whispered. "How did that happen?" Her eyes looked anguished.

It took three heartbeats for the words to sink in with

Gideon. This wasn't about the garden variety subway sicko, it was the woman they had in lock-up.

"How'd she hurt you, Angel?"

She turned wet eyes to him. "That's the thing, Gideon, she didn't hurt me. Butch did. He pawed at me, and hurt me, but Naomi didn't. She just kissed me against my will. She put her hands on me. She threatened things. She scared me. But I knew it was going to get worse, and I was scared. That's why I fought so hard. Underneath all my rage, I was as scared as a snot-nosed kid."

Gideon brought her hand up to his face, slowly opening it up so that he could give her palm a reverent kiss. Then he looked up at her. "Being raped is one of the worst things that can happen to a woman, of course, you were scared," Gideon said softly.

"But she was a girl. It wasn't the same thing as when Butch was after me," she protested weakly.

He continued to hold her hand against his mouth as if he were breathing life into her through their connection. His other hand grasped the side of her neck, his thumb brushing against her wildly beating pulse. "Can you look at me, Angel?"

"I asked you not to call me that," she said tremulously.

"I'm sorry. Please look at me, Jada. Move your eyes and look at me."

"I'm looking, now what?"

He traced her pulse again, it beat even faster. He kissed her palm, then placed it against his jaw, holding his hand over hers.

"Imagine if Gianna was telling you this story, would you feel compassion for her? Would you know, all the way down to your soul, that Gianna had almost been raped and she should be afforded the same care, the same empathy as if a man had assaulted her?"

Jada's throat worked as she swallowed, then she slowly nodded her head.

"What?" Gideon queried. "I didn't hear you."

"Of course, I would hug and hold her, and let her rant and rave. It wouldn't matter if it was a man or woman who did that to her. She was still sexually abused. I would take care of her."

"Then let me take care of you. I'm begging you, please let me take care of you. Will you? Will you do this for me?"

Her hand moved, stroking down his cheek. "All right."

HER HEAD HURT like a son of a bitch, but she'd be damned if she would admit it. She put a smile on her face and waited at baggage claim, holding Gideon's hand.

Gideon squeezed her hand. "Just hang tight. Sebastian will be here any moment, and we'll get you outside, out of this noise."

"I'm fine, really," Jada assured him.

The doctor had strongly advised against her flying so soon after leaving the hospital with a severe concussion, but she wanted to get back to the East Coast, even if she was staying at Gideon's house for a couple of days, before switching over to Gianna and Sebastian's place.

God, I hurt.

"Jonas is driving my SUV and picking us up."

"Not another model," Jada complained. And she was serious. Just how many of these ripped and chiseled-jaw men was she supposed to have to deal with? Was this part of the SEAL recruiting process?

"Nah, he's more like me. You'll see, he's one of us everyday kind of guys."

"You do own a mirror, right?" Jada asked from the side of her mouth.

Gideon squeezed her hand again and she looked up at him. "Don't be giving all my men big heads, they already have oversized egos," he teased.

"If they're anything like you and Sebastian, then of course they do."

"There's your bag," Gideon said pointing to her suitcase. "Wait here."

She watched as he made it past the hoard of people to grab not just her suitcase, but his luggage as well. As soon as he made it back to her, he was pulling his cell phone out of his back pocket.

"Smith here."

"About time you showed," he said irritably. "Are you parked?"

"We're at baggage claim three," Gideon said.

He disconnected the call and looked around. "Jonas will be here in just a moment, Angel."

Jada scowled at Gideon. She no longer had a shit-fit when he called her that, but she also let him know she wasn't happy when he *did* use the endearment.

Out of nowhere a big blond man came up beside them and took the suitcase out of Gideon's hand.

"Is there a reason you live somewhere that requires me to take four different freeways to get from my house to your house?"

"I did it to piss you off," Gideon said. "Jonas Wulff, this is Jada Harlow. Like I told you on the phone, she's been injured, so keep the growling to a minimum."

Jada shook her head and then regretted it. When

would the pain go away? "Well, Jonas, it's nice to meet one of Gideon's friends who isn't wearing a tight t-shirt, even though you are named after a predator."

A burst of laughter shot out of the big blond man.

"You, I like. My boss, not so much. I'm pretty sure he has a tracking device in his Range Rover that tells him if I go over the speed limit."

"I do. You didn't. I appreciate it. Now let's get my girl to the house, where she can lie down."

Jada let that pass, even though the wolfman gave Gideon a significant look. She wasn't up to her normal weight class for a fight.

"Huh?" She looked up startled when Gideon's arm was suddenly around her waist. "What are you doing?"

"I'm holding you up before you pass out. You're ready to drop. It's either this, or I carry you to the car, your choice." By the look on his face, he was not kidding. Jada wrapped her arm around his waist and held on.

"Smart move," he muttered.

They were now in a parking garage, and she heard the distinctive sound of a car being unlocked.

"Do you want to drive?" Jonas asked Gideon.

"No, I'll sit in back with Jada."

Jonas gave a low whistle. "Well okay, then."

Apparently, there was something significant about that, but Jada just didn't have the energy or brain power to figure it out. What's more, she was more than fine having Gideon help her into the backseat. Grateful, even.

"Aren't you hot in that jacket?" he asked before she buckled her seatbelt.

Jada thought about it for a second, "I guess I am. It's hotter here than in Oregon or New York."

"Humid, too," Jonas said from the front seat.

She struggled to try to get out of her vintage designer jacket; the big, square buttons that connected along the diagonal were too much for her.

"Let me help." Gideon brushed her hands away and swiftly unbuttoned her jacket and helped slip it off her arms and shoulders. When he had the jacket in his hands, he scowled. "This doesn't have a real lining, what kind of jacket is it?"

"Vintage," Jada said as she made a grab for it.

"That's code for second-hand, Gideon," Jonas piped up. "My girlfriend is always scouring second-hand shops for deals, and she makes good coin. Makes no sense to me. You going to get into the car, or what?"

Gideon shut Jada's door, then hot-footed it over to his side of the SUV, got in, and buckled up.

"Give me my jacket."

"When we get home. You already said you were too warm," Gideon said reasonably. "Jada, don't get worked up, just lean back and rest your eyes...and your mouth, and see if your head doesn't start feeling better."

"You're not the boss of me," she grumbled. Jada balled up her jacket and placed it against the window and used it as a pillow so she could sleep.

12

"HUH?" JADA STRETCHED LIKE A SLEEPY KITTEN—ALL SOFT, cute, and cuddly—but Gideon knew there were pinpoint claws that could tear the shit out of him.

"I told you we were here," Gideon said again.

Jada blinked a couple of times, then lifted her head off her jacket. "How long was I out for?"

"An hour. Traffic was bad."

"Where's Jonas?"

"He's already taken off in his tiny little car," Gideon scoffed.

"Huh? Tiny? But he's huge."

Gideon laughed. "That's what makes it so funny. German boy insisted on a German car built in the states. Go figure. Do you need help getting out of the car?"

Jada shook her head, then regretted it. Gideon winced. "Words, Angel. Don't nod or shake your head. Use your words until we get you some meds and rest."

He undid her seatbelt then bolted out of the car and was at her side before she could blink. He slowly opened her door, as if she would fall out of it or something.

"Let me help you out."

"I don't need help. If you need to be a Boy Scout, go find a little old lady to help cross a street or something."

Gideon shook his head. Yep, the kitten's claws were showing again. But Jada wouldn't be kittenish for long. He'd better enjoy it while he could.

"You live here?" Jada asked. She sounded incredulous. Then her head cocked. "Is that a dog barking?"

"Are you okay with dogs? I should have asked before bringing you here."

Smart move, Smith.

"Yeah, we grew up with a Great Dane when we lived in California. He died before we moved to New York. Mom got Tuesday when we moved to Queens, she's a Scottie dog."

"Good, so you're used to big dogs. But I think I'll put off having you meet Lucy until your head is feeling better. She can be exuberant when she meets new people."

Jada turned to him as they started up his walkway to the front door. "Please, can I meet her now? I think she'd be better than ibuprofen."

Gideon's lips twitched. "Okay, but don't say I didn't warn you." He pulled his key fob out of his pants pocket and clicked it. The mudroom door opened and they were met with three excited woofs, before the big black mound of hair bounded her way toward them. Gideon moved a couple of yards to the right, away from Jada so that Lucy would aim for him. She hit him full bore.

Her front paws hit his shoulders.

"I missed you too, you pretty monster," Gideon crooned. He heard Jada's giggle. It wasn't laughter, it was actually a giggle, and he loved it.

"Oh my God, what type of breed is she?"

"A Chornyi Terrier, also known as a Black Russian Terrier."

"She's huge!" said with a gleeful smile. "Come here, girl." She patted her thighs.

Lucy lunged off his chest toward Jada and he saw a problem of epic proportions about to occur. Jada was about to be knocked on her ass. Normally that would be just fine, but not when she was hurting like she was.

"Lucy, Stop." He said loud and firm. His big dog stopped in her tracks, then looked over her shoulder at him. Gideon knew he was getting a what-the-fuck look from underneath her long black bangs.

He walked over to her and ran his hands through her fluffy curls. One of the Ellis girls must have groomed her in his absence. "Lucy, soft." He knew that wasn't a normal command, but it worked when he wanted Lucy to do a soft approach with smaller animals, or children. Immediately his dog took shorter steps and led with her nose, making a snuffling sound. As she got to Jada, she looked up at her, pandering to be petted.

"Oh, you're just a big ole marshmallow, aren't you?" Jada chortled as she sank her fingers into Lucy's ruff and started scratching. Lucy was in heaven. Of course, she was —all that attention from Jada, who wouldn't be?

"Come on, ladies, let's get you inside. One of you needs to get a little food and then take a nap." Lucy's head whipped around, and Gideon stifled a groan. It sucked having a dog who knew so many words. As soon as he mentioned food, Lucy was all over it.

"I'm not very hungry," Jada protested.

"Maybe a little something to go with the meds, even if it's just some crackers. What do you say?"

"I say you're probably right."

"I'll get the bags as soon as you're seated and eating. Then I'll set you up in the guest room. Sound good?"

Lucy took that moment to butt her head against Jada's leg, wanting another scratch. Jada laughed. "Yeah, that sounds good."

As soon as they got into the great room, Jada stopped and stared. "Just how much space does one man need?"

"I bought it as an investment. But it's turned out pretty nice for my brother and his boys to come over on the weekends."

"I'll say, they must love it here."

"They do," Gideon admitted. He guided her to the couch. "Do you need the bathroom before I insist you sit down and I get you something to eat?"

Jada shook her head.

"Okay, why don't you have a seat here, and I'll bring you a little something to eat? What would you like to drink?"

"Do you have something with bubbles? Like club soda?"

"I think I can rustle something up."

Lucy plunked down at Jada's feet. "I think somebody has decided to watch over you."

Jada gave a wan grin, which told Gideon to move his ass and get her ibuprofen and food. When he looked in his fridge, he found some cheese, and a cantaloupe that still looked good. He quickly sliced them both up, added that and some crackers to a plate, along with some pills and a glass of club soda, and took it all out to Jada. He quickly noted that Lucy was now sitting on Jada's feet.

"Off," he commanded.

Lucy gave him a sorrowful look, but she hoisted

herself off Jada's feet and shuffled a step away before plopping down again.

"I think you've made a friend." Gideon smiled as he set the plate down on a side table next to the couch.

"I adore her. That's one of the things I regret about my apartment, no pets."

"Hold out your hand," Gideon said. He deposited the pills in her outstretched hand and watched as she swallowed them down with her drink. "You should be feeling better soon. Now, are you willing to tell me how bad your pain is?"

"No," she gave him a wry grin. "You'd just hover more."

She had him there.

"Is there anything else you need?"

"Yes, my iPad." Jada's tone was melancholy. "I feel like I'm missing a limb."

"You have your phone," he tried to placate.

She shot him a look of disgust. "Yeah, yeah, I know you're right, but it still stings not having it."

"I can get an iPad here for you by tomorrow. That way we can download everything from your iCloud account and you'll be back in business."

She sighed. "Not everything."

"Time to 'fess up. What else have you got on Risk Guard? You're checking them out on a whole different system and account, aren't you?"

"There's some work that I want to make sure is totally under the radar. And don't get high and mighty with me. If you say that you don't have the same kind of set-up somewhere I would call you a liar."

Gideon gave her a steady look. He wasn't going to confirm or deny a damn thing.

"Uh-huh," she said as she pulled the plate onto her lap and started to eat. "That's what I thought."

"So are we bickering, or are we fighting?" Gideon asked as he sat down on the couch beside her.

"Huh? What are you talking about?"

"I'm just trying to get a handle on things. I thought we'd made some headway in the hospital, that we were in a better place, but since you found out you have to stay with me for a couple of days we're back to mouthy you, and I can't tell if you're really mad and we're fighting, or if you're just mouthing off because that's your nature and we're kind of bickering."

Jada's mouth twitched as she popped in another piece of cantaloupe.

"I'm not up to a good fight. Head hurts. Body hurts. Plus, I like your dog. So, we're bickering."

"Do we have to? What would I have to do to bring it down a notch, maybe to a level of pleasant conversation?"

Jada rolled her eyes. "You and I would be bored within an hour with pleasant. Hell even stimulating conversation would make my eyes roll back in my head and I'm pretty sure drool would start forming in my mouth. Nope, bickering is the way it has to stay."

"And the hospital?" Gideon asked quietly.

"Don't be an ass, that was soul-bearing shit. I hated doing it. Didn't you hate listening to it?"

"Now who's an ass? I wanted to be there for you. Of course I didn't hate it."

Suddenly Gideon was holding a plate of food and Jada was halfway across the room.

"What, you only like it when I'm the simpering woman, is that what I'm hearing? Is that what turns your crank, Smith? Is that why I didn't make the cut and you had to kick me to the curb? Well, sorry for being me. Tell me where the hell I'm sleeping here in your mansion, and I'll make sure to stay the hell out of your way since you made it abundantly clear at Neil's christening that you didn't want to have anything to do with me."

Gideon tossed the plate on the sofa and stood up, hating it when Jada took a step backward. Lucy stood up and gave a low bark. "Settle," Gideon said pointing to her dog bed. He didn't wait to see if she followed her command. Instead, all of his concentration was on the beautiful, angry, and sad woman in front of him. He'd done that, he'd done that to her.

"Jada, we need to talk about that. I was totally wrong in Kentucky. I'd really like a chance to explain where my head was at, and what I'm thinking now."

Her laugh sounded like her throat was filled with crushed glass. "I don't think so. You did all the explaining in Kentucky too. I remember how that made me feel. I don't want another turn around that merry-go-round."

It hit him like a gut punch. He'd been trying to do the right thing. The good thing. Instead, he'd scorned and hurt a woman who had really been in love with him. A woman who had loved him as deeply as he had loved her.

Jesus.

How am I going to fix this?

Jada was holding her arms around her middle like she was trying to hold her guts in after having been eviscerated. More than anything, he wanted to go to her, grab her up in his arms and tell her that he would somehow make everything all right again. But he'd lost that right.

No, I threw that right away.

"Angel," he started.

"Don't call me that. I told you not to call me that." Jada's voice was shrill as she gripped her head, and Gideon thought he'd lose his mind.

"Jada, you're right," he said softly. Gently. He took a couple of steps closer while her eyes were closed. Then a couple more as she continued to hold her head. God, just how bad was she hurting? He needed to call Nolan and find out what to do.

"I'm sorry," he repeated. Her eyes slowly opened. He could see that she was having trouble focusing.

"Let me get you to your room. There's a connecting bathroom, and I'll bring in your case, okay?"

"Yeah." Her voice was weak.

"Do you need to lean on me?" he asked. "I promise not to let it turn my crank," he teased gently.

"Ha, ha. Very funny. Kick a woman while she's down."

An image of the boot print flashed in front of his eyes and Gideon gritted his teeth.

Keep your shit together!

Gideon put his arm around her waist and felt like he'd won the lottery when she relaxed into his side.

Please say I haven't totally fucked things up for eternity.

Gideon opened the door to a large guestroom that was painted a soft gray, with yellow curtains and bedding.

"This looks like a hotel room. A fancy hotel room, not the one I was staying in while I was in Tillamook," Jada clarified. "It's lovely."

"Glad you like it. Lie down or use the bathroom, and I'll be right back with your suitcase."

"Okay."

Gideon left her sitting on the side of the bed. She looked so small and beaten down, and he knew he was partly to blame. He felt like shit.

He jogged out to his Range Rover and pulled out the luggage and brought it in. The first thing he noticed after he closed and locked the front door, was that Lucy wasn't in her huge doggie bed.

He went to the kitchen and got Jada another glass of club soda and more cantaloupe since she'd eaten all the slices on the plate; it looked to be a hit with her. Then he juggled that and her suitcase to her room. Lucy looked up at him expectantly as soon as he entered. Jada was already under the duvet. Gideon could still see that she was wearing her blouse, and he would guess she was still wearing her jeans because all he saw lying on the floor were her ankle boots. He remembered that she used to like to sleep in just a sleep shirt or nothing at all.

Goddamn those assholes!

"Are you guarding our guest?" Gideon asked his dog.

Lucy gave a soft woof in the affirmative that didn't disturb Jada in the slightest.

"Good girl."

Gideon set the drink and plate of fruit on the nightstand, and the suitcase on the chair near the foot of the bed. Unable to help himself, he placed a light kiss on her forehead.

"Sleep well, Angel."

13

JADA WAS ALMOST FEELING HUMAN. THE FACT THAT GIDEON had gone out three days ago and bought her an iPad might have something to do with it, but she didn't care what it took, she was just glad she was feeling better. Thank God, horse hooves no longer clattered through her head. Another plus was that her brother Ricky had grabbed some things she'd needed from her apartment, which included her secret computer. He'd overnighted it all to her. Ricky was the most laid back of the Harlow brothers; he knew that eventually she'd tell him what the deal was, and he trusted that she could take care of herself, so he hadn't asked questions, he just did her a solid.

Then there was the fact that she and Gideon had come to some sort of detente. They didn't talk it through, but somehow they both knew not to discuss anything personal and keep everything focused on Risk Guard and figuring out where Miles and Psycho Sister were hiding.

Okay, so Gideon *had* tried to bring up personal shit a couple of times, but she'd shut him down, and he'd allowed it. The fact that he'd been at work for the last four days really helped.

Cuddling into the corner of the most comfortable couch in the world, Jada picked up her phone and made a facetime call to Gianna. She grinned when her friend answered it on the first ring, but frowned when she realized she'd only picked up the audio portion of the call.

"Thank God you called, I'm going bat guano crazy staying in bed. I swear, Sebastian has implanted some kind of tracking device inside me that tells him if I've moved two feet from the bed. He comes into the room like the hounds of hell are after him as soon as I make a move."

Jada snickered. "That sounds about right."

"It's not funny," Gianna wailed.

"Yes, it is."

"Sebastian is running himself ragged trying to be the perfect husband to me, and the perfect father to Neil. He isn't taking any downtime. He hasn't slept more than three hours at a time since they told us I needed to be on total bedrest."

"So, it's back to the good old days like when you first brought Neil Gideon back from the hospital," Jada laughed.

"No, it isn't. It's something else entirely."

Jada heard something in her friend's voice, and it wasn't just exasperation. She sounded sad.

"What's going on?" Jada probed.

"I'm not sure."

"But you've got an idea, don't you?"

"Yeah," Gianna admitted in a whisper.

"Tell me." Jada winced when she realized those were the same words that Gideon had used on her.

"Sebastian refuses to sleep with me. He's sleeping in the guest room."

"What?" Jada was appalled.

"He says it's because he has to get up in the middle of the night to check on Neil and doesn't want to wake me. But that's bullshit." Jada was surprised when her friend used a curse word. That was *her* bad habit, not Gianna's.

"Why is that bad? That seems considerate to me."

Kind of.

"It's ridiculous. We have the baby monitor, so if Neil cries we'd hear him. But he doesn't cry during the night anymore, he sleeps all the way through like a champ. Unless he has the croup or something..." The last few words faded away and Jada could swear she heard Gianna start to cry.

"Gianna—"

"Don't worry, Jada, I'm not expecting you to be able to make me feel better," Gianna said in a wobbly voice.

"Honey, you have to ask him what's going on," Jada said softly.

"I can't. I just can't. What happens if he tells me our marriage isn't working anymore?"

"You're out of your mind," Jada scoffed. "He thinks the sun rises and the moon sets according to your smiles. Remember, I was just at your house for two weeks a month ago. There is no way the devotion I saw suddenly went up in smoke."

"But ever since they put me on total bedrest, it's like he can't look me in the face. The three kisses we've had since then, I've had to initiate, and that's after I had to ask for the hug. How pathetic is that? I've had to ask for hugs from my own husband."

"As soon as Gideon comes back from work, I'm going

to take his Range Rover and come over to your house and sort this shit out. There is something smelly in Denmark, and I'm going to figure it out."

"No!" Gianna cried. "You are not interfering in my marriage."

"Well, someone's got to since you're not doing it. I swear to God, Gianna, he loves you. He worships you. There is nothing wrong."

"Yes, there is!" Gianna wailed. "My husband hates me!"

"Gianna, what's wrong?"

Jada heard Sebastian's worried voice over the phone.

"Nothing you'd care about," was Gianna's petulant reply.

"What are you talking about? I care about anything that has to do with you." Sebastian sounded distraught.

Good.

"No, you don't. You don't care about me. You hate me. Admit it."

As much as Jada wanted to know how this was going to play out, she didn't feel comfortable listening in to her friend's conversation, so she ended the call. She'd wait for Gianna to tell her what happened, and she prayed she'd have to wait until tomorrow because they'd take all night to make up.

Jada put her phone and iPad down on the coffee table then uncurled from the couch and got up to go to the kitchen. Lucy perked up from her doggie bed. "You want a treat?"

That got the big dog bounding off the bed and skidding along the wood floor to meet Jada in the kitchen.

"Thought so," Jada smirked. "Tell you what. We can both have treats, how about that?"

Jada got out the fixings for a bacon, lettuce, and tomato sandwich, and Lucy woofed as soon as she smelled the bacon. "I told you, we're going to eat together, like a family, so you just set your ass down near the couch, and I'll bring your treat when I bring my food. *Comprender*?"

Lucy wagged her tail so hard, most of her body shook and Jada laughed. She pointed to the couch and Lucy immediately trotted toward Jada's place in the corner. Jada finished making her sandwich and grabbed a small bottle of Sprite out of the fridge. She cut her sandwich, smothered it with potato chips, and threw three additional slices of bacon on top of the chips. Hopefully, Gideon wouldn't notice all the bacon she'd pilfered from his fridge.

Jada went and curled up on the sofa, balancing her plate on top of a paper towel on her crossed legs.

"Aren't you a good girl, waiting so patiently."

Lucy lifted her head and gave Jada her best pathetic look.

"Don't lie to me, you had plenty of food in your food bowl. I know because I saw how full it was this morning."

Woof, woof.

"Sure. That's what you say now. But what's your story going to be when Gideon gets home?" Jada loved having these nonsensical conversations with the big dog. She was such a love.

She held out a piece of bacon, and Lucy delicately nipped it away from her fingers, careful not to touch Jada with her massive teeth.

"You're such a good girl," Jada crooned. Jada started in on her potato chips, then wiped her fingers off on the paper towel before she picked up the older laptop that she'd used to infiltrate Risk Guard. She'd checked out Gideon's internet connection, and it was tight. Very few people would be able to track down his IP address. *Very few.* But that didn't mean it was perfect.

It took a whole sandwich and one and a half more pieces of bacon for Lucy until Jada was satisfied that she had rerouted everything.

"Who's my good girl? Here you go," Jada held out the last half-piece of bacon, but Lucy shot up off the floor and raced toward the mudroom instead. Jada gave a forlorn sigh. "I hear you, girl. I would pass up bacon for Gideon any day of the week."

Don't go there. That ship has sailed.

Jada set her computer on the coffee table, then headed to the kitchen with her plate so she could put it in the dishwasher. She hated leaving any kind of mess for the Chief. It was fun calling him that—she'd heard some of his teammates call him Chief and she knew it made him uncomfortable when she did, which only made it more fun. She had to do something to make the situation lighter, since she knew she was stuck in Virginia for a while. The game plan had been for her to eventually go and stay with Gianna and Sebastian, but after the call she was just on with Gianna, that didn't look too promising.

She sighed again.

Jada looked up from the kitchen counter when she heard Lucy's loud barking outside.

Gideon must be doing some serious playing with the dog. He must not have had to dress up like he did yesterday.

Jada opened the refrigerator and pulled out the fixings for the smoothie that Gideon liked to have when he got home.

"Hey, Jada. Did you have a good day?" Gideon asked as he walked into the great room.

"Yep," she smiled.

He leaned over the kitchen island. "Whatcha doing?"

She cocked her head. "Really? You really need to ask?"

Gideon chuckled. "Okay, a better question would be, why are you doing this?"

"How about the fact that you're letting me stay here to recuperate?" she responded mildly.

"Jada, we talked about that. It's not just because you need to recuperate. We haven't found hide nor hair of Miles Albright. He's gone to ground. Until he's found, you're a target."

"And I totally disagree. Right now, Risk Guard is being audited with a fine-tooth comb. Reynolds is doing their damndest to disassociate themselves with the man. I'm telling you, he's on a plane to some tropical island with Naomi's sister, never to be seen or heard from again."

"Until we track him down, you're not allowed anywhere he can find you."

She gave him a dirty look as she grabbed the raspberries out of the refrigerator.

"Look on the bright side; there are still strings we can pull and angles we can look at. We need to trace back what Bonham was working on, and who he might have been leaking to," Gideon reminded her. "The guys are working on that, and they're going to update us in two days."

Jada threw the raspberries into the blender and started to peel a banana, turning her face away from Gideon. She hated thinking about her time in the boathouse and Bonham's screams.

"Hey, look at me," Gideon prompted. She shook her

head.

"Are you still upset about Bonham?" he asked gently.

She whirled around. "Of course, I am," she practically shouted. "He's dead, and I couldn't save him."

"Ah, Jada, there was nothing you could have done to save him. You told Ryker and me about him as soon as you could. Hell, you were barely conscious, but you got us the information. Unfortunately, it was already too late. They'd killed him before you told us about him."

"I know, but it's just that we were in it together, you know? He was in the room right beside me in the boat house."

Gideon came around the island and pulled her close. "I am so sorry about that man. So sorry. I wish we could have saved him, I really do."

Jada turned and pressed her face into Gideon's chest. She took a deep breath of his woodsy smell. He'd taken a shower at the base—she could smell his soap and the other scent that was all Gideon.

His arms came up around her.

"Are you going to be all right? I thought you'd come to terms with Sid Bonham dying."

"I did. I do. I am." She looked up at him and fell into his gaze. "It's just I feel so bad that he was all alone in the world, you know? He didn't have anyone. He was all alone. He didn't have a wife, kids, or even living parents."

Gideon's arms tightened. "I know, Angel." His warm brown eyes were so sympathetic, so caring, and Jada suddenly realized that Gideon only really talked about his brother Mike. She knew that his father was dead, and his mother lived in San Jose, California. But why didn't he talk about her?

"Do you ever feel alone?" she asked.

"No, I've got my team," he answered at once. "Then there's Mike and the boys," he smiled. "With Felix and Kyle, it's like I have four nephews, not just two."

Jada bit her bottom lip and she saw Gideon's eyes flare. "What about your mom?" she asked tentatively.

"Ma?"

"Yeah. You never talk about her. You've heard about all of my brothers, my mother, and my uncles ad nauseam. I bet you could recite all of their names by now."

"I don't know their middle names," he teased.

"And your mother? How often does she come out to Virginia and visit you two?"

Gideon sighed. "It's complicated."

Jada frowned. "What does that mean? Family is family. Sure, it gets complicated—you fight and yell and throw down—but in the end, you always have each other's backs. Don't you go visit her?"

"Mike does."

Gideon tried to extricate himself from her hold, and Jada considered letting him go, but this was too important so she hung on.

"Gideon, you've been wanting to have an important conversation with me ever since I got here, haven't you?"

He stood still, his eyes turned molten, and he nodded. "Absolutely. I want to talk to you about what I said in Kentucky six months ago. Are you ready to listen?"

"If that conversation is going in the direction I think it is, then we need to be able to speak about a lot of things. Things like why you and your mom aren't speaking."

Gideon sighed. "I agree," he said as he pulled her closer. "But Jada, I'm only going to share that kind of information with someone who is sharing my life. Is that going to be you?"

Jada gasped and fell backward in his hold.

Sharing his life?

"Gideon," she rasped out his name. "You can't mean that."

"For the last six months, I've been a bear to work with. My team has noticed it, and they were gearing up to send someone to New York and beg for you to give me a second chance."

Jada snorted. "Like that would have worked."

Gideon cupped her cheek and traced her full bottom lip with his thumb. "I know it wouldn't have worked. I hurt you badly the last time I saw you in Kentucky."

Jada took in a deep breath, "you did," she agreed. "But I know you. At least I'm pretty sure I know you now. You push people away. Me, maybe your mother..." she let her voice fade away.

"Ma, no. I haven't pushed her away—that's beyond complicated. You, yes."

"But why, Gideon?" her lower lip trembled. "You said you're too old for me. You said you were damaged. I don't see it. It sounded like a line, a different way to say, 'it's me, not you.'."

She hated the fact that she felt tears coming on. She looked up at him, hoping against hope that he would tell her it wasn't true.

"Ah, Angel, it was me. It *is* me." She saw his pain, it mirrored her own. It was too much.

"Can you explain it to me so I understand?" she begged.

"It's a long story, but yeah, I can." He held out his hand. "Come with me."

She took his hand and followed him down the hall.

14

He needed the comfort of his bedroom to have this talk. When he got to his bed, he pulled her into his arms, then gently settled them against his pillows so that she was cuddled against his chest.

"So, this is a bedtime story?" she attempted to tease.

That was his Jada, always bringing humor to any situation, even when he was twisted up inside.

"Well, it's a story that haunts my dreams, that's for damn sure. I hurt the people I loved."

He saw her frown.

"No, it's more than that," Gideon continued. "I didn't hurt them, I walked away from them. I made decisions that destroyed everything important and good in my life. When you hear this, you'll know who I really am, and the thought of that kills me."

"Gideon, I know who you are, and I love—"

He put two fingers to her lips before she had a chance to finish her sentence. "You love an image I project, not the real me. Hear me out, okay?"

She nodded.

He took away his fingers, but she pulled them back and kissed them. "But you're wrong. I don't care what you've done in the past. You're the man I called when I was desperate, you're the man who I counted on to save me, and you did. I *know* you, Gideon Smith."

He blew out a deep breath. "Just hear me out, okay Angel?"

She nodded again.

"You asked about my Ma. Let's start there. My mother hates me. Literally hates me. I abandoned her and Pops when they needed me the most."

Jada frowned and shook her head. "That's not possible."

"Shhh, you promised to listen, Honey."

"Okay."

"When I was thirteen, Pops got injured when he failed to lock a car lift into place at the body shop where he worked. It fell down on him and damaged his spine. He had multiple surgeries and was going to need extensive rehab if he was going to walk again. There were neurological issues too."

"Oh, Gideon, that's awful," Jada said as she stroked her hand down the side of his neck.

"Because of this, our family was going to lose the house. But before that even happened, Mikey was being recruited by the Crips, and that was when I pulled a runner."

Her hand stilled. "What—"

"During the middle of that shitstorm, I said I was leaving. Pops told me to never darken their doorstep again. He died before I ever had a chance to heal that breach."

She looked up at him. "You would never do that," she whispered. "You would never abandon your family."

He gave her a grim smile. "Ask Ma, that's exactly what I did. To this day, she won't speak to me. After Pops died, and Mikey decided to move to Virginia Beach to be near me, I bought her a house in San Jose close to her sister, but we had to say that Mike did, otherwise she wouldn't move in."

"I don't get it, what happened?"

Gideon swallowed.

"When I was just a little older than my nephew Felix, I started messing around with different video games. They were first gen. Nothing like today."

"And this was when you were thirteen?"

"I started when I was twelve, but yeah, I took apart my first Atari when I was thirteen."

"Sounds about right." She gave a small grin.

"Then there was a new console that came out of San Francisco. My friend Darnell got his hands on it. It was a game changer, pardon the pun. It was X-Box before there was an X-Box."

"Didn't that come out in two-thousand?"

"Two-thousand-and-one. Streetgamezzz had developed something that was out of this world much earlier, and I was in love."

"I've never heard of Streetgamezzz."

"That's because the company imploded when you were in kindergarten. The CEO went to prison."

"What happened? How'd you get involved?"

"When I got my hands on their version of X-Box, called Streetcube, I started adapting some of the current PC games to it.

"That's impressive."

Gideon gave a small smile. "There's more. Before I was fourteen I knew that I could tweak it."

"How?"

"I was positive I could incorporate wi-fi with Streetcube. I saved up to get a Nokia phone. Nokia had already created a game on their phone called Snake, the very first game on a mobile phone, so it seemed like a slam dunk."

Jada nodded and said with a smile, "Let me guess, you nailed it."

"Damn right. Streetcube went wireless, and I was asking my friend Darnell for another Streetcube so I could modify it so we could play head-to-head. That's when everything went to shit."

"Tell me."

"I'd just turned fourteen."

Jada nodded.

"Darnell had originally gotten the cube from his uncle. Neither of us knew it at the time, but his uncle was high up in the company and using Darnell as a tester to find out if the product would work with our age group. When my friend went back to Streetgamezzz for a second cube, his uncle got suspicious. Darnell couldn't lie for shit, so his uncle came and gave me a visit. Of course, I confessed all."

"Of course, you did, you were a kid."

"Plus, I was pretty proud of what I'd accomplished."

"I'm surprised that your friend's uncle didn't try to take credit for your work."

"I'm pretty sure he did. He gave me another cube and made some suggestions about what I should work on next. He met with me weekly at Darnell's house to see what new modifications I'd made." Gideon grinned. "I was pretty cocky back then. There were a couple of times when I could tell he didn't get what I was telling him, and that sent me over the moon."

"Are you trying to tell me you're not cocky anymore?"

Gideon leaned over and brushed his finger across the side of her nose. She smiled up at him. "Cocky is for test pilots. I'm *confident*."

"Okay, so what happened when you schooled Darnell's uncle?"

"One day I went over to Darnell's house and I found out that his uncle had been fired."

Jada shrugged. "Yeah, like I didn't see that one coming. Someone caught on that he didn't know what he was talking about. Then what happened?"

"Darnell told me I was in big trouble, and I had to come to his house the next day because somebody would be waiting for me." Gideon stopped talking. He remembered just how scared he was. His friend had told him he couldn't tell anyone, or he'd be in even bigger trouble.

"When I got to Darnell's house, there was a shiny, black town car waiting outside, and I was told to get in. I was driven an hour and a half to downtown San Francisco. There I was in my ratty Sacramento Kings jersey, jeans, and my knock-off Air Jordans, walking into the Transamerica Pyramid building. I was in awe, but also scared shitless."

"I can imagine."

"The driver takes me high up in the elevator, and then past this hot, blonde receptionist until I'm sitting in a leather chair facing a man behind a chrome desk who is giving me an oily smile. At fourteen, I might not have known much in life, but I sure as hell knew when I saw some con man, and this guy was like a visiting preacher at church who's looking to sell salvation for a hundred dollars a pop.

"He starts out all nice and complimentary, tells me how impressed he is with my coding and hardware skills on his proprietary property."

He looked down at Jada who was hanging on his every word. "I have no idea what the word proprietary means, but I can tell the hammer is about to drop so I thank him, all polite-like."

"Then he asks me if I ever got written permission to work on Streetgamezzz prototypes. Again, with a word that I didn't understand, and I'm beginning to sweat. I didn't understand prototypes, but I sure as hell understood written permission, and I didn't have that."

"At this point, I'm all 'yes sir, no sir,' and saying anything I think will get me out of trouble, and he's still grinning at me, which just scares me even more."

"Shit, who was this guy?" Jada asked. "He sounds like a complete prick coming down on a fourteen-year-old."

"His name was Kendall Douglas." Gideon sat up on the bed and rearranged the pillows, then he pulled Jada into a sitting position against the headboard.

"You just can't help but be a Neanderthal, can you?" she said with a cheeky grin. "Here I am, mad at you, and you're just moving me about like some kind of doll."

"I told you the story was long, and I wanted to make you comfortable." He smiled in return.

She shook her head in exasperation. "Okay, I'm comfortable now, please proceed." Gideon took it as a good sign that her eyes were twinkling.

He thought back to that meeting that changed the trajectory of his life. To this day he still hated Kendall

Douglas with a passion. It didn't matter that the bastard had been stuck serving a seventeen-year sentence in prison; as far as he was concerned, it hadn't been nearly long enough. Occasionally, there were times he thought of the man and he could almost put it behind him, knowing that he had to be old and pitiful now. But only sometimes.

"I didn't get it at the time, Jada, but I was miles further along than anyone in his development team, I mean by years."

Jada laughed. "Go figure," she teased.

"What can I say, I liked to play video games." Gideon shrugged. "Anyway, after forty-five minutes this guy picks up his phone and he has two guys in uniform come into his office. Looking back on it, I know it's just his security flunkies, but at the time I'm damn near wetting my pants, but trying to act all tough."

"Jesus." Jada sat up even more until she was almost face-to-face with Gideon. "That was a total dick move. Then what happened?"

"He looks at me and says he has no choice but to press charges. I might have done some innovative things with his product, but it was entirely unauthorized, and if he let me get away with it, what's to stop someone else from doing the same thing?"

"But he comes up with some kind of solution, doesn't he?" Jada guesses grimly.

"You got that right. I'm begging by this point. I would have sold my soul not to go to jail. My mom was working as a secretary at the church, and she was the volunteer choir director for God's sake—she'd die if her son went to jail. Plus, I gotta take care of things at home. It was really bad back then."

Jada nodded.

"So, there I am, a skinny, sniveling mess, begging for my life, and this asshole has me just where he wants me."

Jada let out a low growl and Gideon couldn't help but grin.

"Then he tilts his head at me and says 'but maybe.' That's what he says. 'But maybe.' He throws me that lifeline like he'd just thought of it. I grabbed a hold of that like you wouldn't believe. I begged him to tell me what I needed to do, that I'd do anything. The asshole knew he had me."

"He had to have been licking his chops."

"For real," Gideon agreed. He got up from the bed. Even thinking about that conversation over twenty years later still got him edgy. He began to pace.

"So, Kendall Douglas tells me that if I come to work for him and sign an NDA and a non-compete, he can arrange for me not to go to jail. Again, the only thing I understand is that I have to sign papers that will make it so I won't go to prison. I'm all in. What's more, I get to actually work on stuff that I want to do. But I tell him I have to work around school and ask my parents."

Gideon rubbed the top of his head. "The bastard laughed. He said that wouldn't be necessary. He would help me get out of schoolwork, and he would arrange it so that I wouldn't be living with my parents. I would have to move to San Francisco and devote all of my time to Streetgamezzz."

Jada looked confused.

Gideon nodded. "I see how you're looking. That's how I was looking, too. My parents weren't going to let me give up school and go to work for some company in San Francisco. I was only fourteen. But he laid it out for me. The bastard already knew that my dad had been badly injured at the body shop, and we were barely holding onto our house. He knew that the Crips were trying to recruit my little brother Mikey. He knew we were going to end up homeless. He knew everything."

"How?"

"Again, in hindsight, I can see it perfectly. He'd spent a lot of time investigating me before he'd made any move to confront me." Gideon sat back down on the side of the bed, and Jada pushed over next to him. She wrapped her arm around his shoulder.

"Tell me what happened next." She whispered the question into the side of his neck.

"There's not a lot more to tell after that. I gave in. I did everything he wanted. He wanted me to come and work for him? I did. He wanted me to quit school? I did. He wanted me to abandon my family? I did."

"That's impossible; you were only fourteen."

Gideon gave a harsh laugh. "Oh, you have enough money and lawyers on your side, you can do anything. Plus, he wasn't just scaring me by that point, he threw out the carrot. He promised me that my family would be taken care of, that my parents would get the money they needed to move out of North Highland, which was Crips territory, and he could get Pops the physical therapy and hospital care he needed to get well."

"This doesn't make any sense. There isn't a chance in hell that my family would have let me go. I know you, I've heard you talk about Mike, I can't imagine that the parents who raised two men like you wouldn't have fought tooth and nail to keep you with them."

Gideon pulled away so he could stand up again, but Jada wasn't having any of it. "Jada, let me stand—"

"You just keep your ass planted on this bed and tell me what happened," she said fiercely.

"*I* happened. It was all me."

"What are you talking about, baby?" she asked gently.

"I did exactly what he said," Gideon whispered. "His lawyers were slick, but without all my help and my subterfuge, there is no way I would have been able to get away with getting emancipated from my parents at fourteen. But I managed it."

"That sounds impossible," Jada gasped.

"You woulda thought."

"Jesus, Gideon, how horrible for you. They made you do that?"

"What are you talking about? I'm the one that did that. I'm the one who lied and tricked my Pops into signing paperwork he didn't understand because he was so sick. I'm the one who turned my back on my family."

"Yeah, you did all that because you didn't have a choice," Jada protested.

"Didn't I? At any point, I could have just talked to my parents, told them what was going on. We could have figured it out together. They'd always been my foundation."

"Sure, you, the skinny little black kid from the hood, up against some powerful CEO with his security guards telling you that you were going to go to prison. You thought you were going to be able to fight this? Give me a break." She squeezed him harder. "Then that bastard says he can fix it so that your father will get well, and your family will have a place to live outside of gang territory. You didn't stand a chance."

Jada got up on her knees and pulled him to her chest.

"Please, God, don't tell me that you are still beating

yourself up for this."

"Of course, I am. I destroyed my family. My dad disowned me, and he died believing that I turned my back on my family when they needed me most. My mother still won't talk to me to this very day."

"I'm so sorry, baby."

Gideon closed his eyes and blew out a long breath. "God, I can't even remember the last time I thought about all that shit, let alone talked about it."

Jada cupped the side of his neck, and he turned to look into her beautiful brown eyes. "Gideon?"

"Yeah, Angel?"

"Who else knows?"

"Mike. Kostya."

"And your mother? Does she know?"

Ah, God, were those tears for him? "Jada, there's nothing to be sad about. I'm living a great life. After I was done with Streetgamezzz, and before I decided to join the service, I was recruited by a legit team in Silicon Valley and made ridiculous coin."

Her fingers dug deeper into his neck. "I don't give a shit about any of that. Answer the question, Gideon. Does your mother know what happened? Does she know what that monster did to you?"

Gideon pulled her hands away from him and then tangled them with his so that they were palm to palm.

"Angel, it's best to leave things as is. I've never seen two people so in love before like my mother and father; it was sacred. When I betrayed my father the way I did, according to Mikey, I broke him. My mother will never forgive me for that, no matter what my reasons."

"That's not fair," she whispered.

"Who said life was fair?"

15

Jada stared at the man who wasn't just one of her country's heroes like her father, but a man who had been tested in the hottest of fires while he was still just a child. How could she have ever believed that he would be so cavalier in his treatment of her? How could she have not realized that there was something deeper going on?

Looking at his beautiful face, and into his warm brown eyes, she slowly smiled.

"So that's it, huh? Those are your words of wisdom, Chief Petty Officer Smith? "'Life isn't always fair'?"

Gideon gave her a funny look, then shrugged.

"Yep, that's all I've got."

"What happens if I want more?"

Gideon pulled her into his arms so that she was almost sitting in his lap. "Do you mean it, Jada? Are you willing to listen to me?"

She giggled. "I'm pretty sure I've been listening to you for the last half hour, Honey."

His eyes rolled upwards and he gave her a little shake.

"Be serious, woman. I want to talk to you about what an utter ass I was in Kentucky, and why."

Jada swallowed. Deep. "Uh, you were—"

"More than an ass. I was an ass*hole*. Just let me explain."

"I'm not sure you need to," she said quietly.

Gideon shut down. It was like the light went out of his eyes. "No," she rushed to assure him, "that's not what I meant. I meant that I don't think you need to explain why you were acting the way you were. I kind of get it now, the baggage you've been hauling around all these years. I wondered how a man like you hasn't ever been married or lived with some woman in the past. It seemed really weird to me, you know?"

He slowly shook his head.

"Men," she rolled her eyes. "We women have questionnaires a mile long for men. You don't know it, but we do everything we can to make sure we're not going to end up with a horse's ass, we want somebody nice and stable."

"I thought it was all about the car and the size of his cock," Gideon teased.

"That's when you're a freshman in college. It changes after you graduate," Jada said primly. "One of the things on our questionnaire is whether the man has been able to sustain any kind of long and healthy relationships in the past. You got an A-plus when it came to guy friends, but you failed miserably when it came to romantic relationships. But I totally let it go, because...well because you're you."

Gideon frowned at her. "I thought the deal that I wasn't coming into the relationship with an ex-wife and a bunch of kids was a good thing."

"Honey, a man like you? I'd love to love on your kiddos."

His grip tightened. "You kill me, Angel. You know that? Every single minute that I think I can't love you any more than I already do, you go and prove me wrong."

Everything went quiet. Jada couldn't even breathe, let alone feel her heart beat. "You love me?"

"With all that I have, with all that I am." Gideon's voice was low, deep, and sure.

He wasn't kidding. She could see the emotion shining in his eyes.

"When? How?"

"Angel, I was scared as hell that I was falling for you when we danced at Sebastian and Gianna's wedding."

"My God," she breathed.

"But then I was even more scared that you were falling for me, and it was the worst thing in the world for you. I had to get you to understand that I was poison. Not only was I too damn old, I was just a bad bet. The only thing I was good for in this life, was being a SEAL."

"That's not true," she whispered.

"It is. Or at least I thought it was."

Jada let out a jagged laugh. "Who would have guessed that I'd have to work on Gideon Smith's self-esteem?" She slapped him on his chest. Hard. "I love you. I'm in love with you. You broke my heart, but now I understand that you were just being a man with your fucked up logic."

He choked out a laugh. "I don't know whether to be happy or mad at that comment."

"Happy, definitely happy."

"Do you know what I said to you on the yacht? What I said when I thought it was almost too late?"

She shook her head, her curls flying everywhere, but she didn't care.

"I told you that I was too old, too damaged, but that if anyone was strong enough to handle me, it was you. I said that you were right all along and that I needed someone exactly like you in my life."

She lifted her head so she could peek up at him. "You said that?"

"I did."

"Did you mean it?"

"I meant it with my whole heart."

It was like her soul took a breath. Jada sank into Gideon's arms. He held her close, and her world clicked into place. She soaked in the beauty of the moment.

HE'D BEEN FLUNG out of hell and thrust into heaven. It had happened in Oregon when he'd known Jada was going to live, and it was happening again here in his bedroom. Jada was a vision here in his arms. And she was finally his. Completely.

"Kiss me," she whispered. "Don't make me wait."

He cupped the back of her skull and brought her head up so that he could take her mouth in the type of kiss he'd been hungering for, for months.

His Jada's taste was sweet, bold, and lush and made him crazy, and then when she opened her lips and he thrust his tongue inside her, he thought his head would explode. Sensation after explosive sensation washed over him as he worked to meld them together. He wanted to take things slow, he really did, but Jada made it impossible. Her nails were scraping at the back of his neck, down the collar of his uniform, until she was scratching his upper back.

"Off," she moaned.

"What?"

"Take off your shirt, Honey."

Those were the only words she said before they both went back in for deeper, lusher kisses. Gideon shoved his right hand underneath the back of her thin sweater, luxuriating in the warmth of her soft skin. She squirmed, then broke off their kiss and backed away from him. She swept her sweater off, then went to work on her bra and flung that off the bed.

He looked down and winced when he still saw faint traces of bruising.

"It doesn't matter," she whispered.

Her nimble fingers started unbuttoning the front of his uniform and he couldn't help but laugh. Making love with Jada was joyous. This time he pulled back and stood up. He made quick work unbuttoning his khakis and then pulled his t-shirt over his head.

"Yes," Jada hissed. She was up on her knees, her fingers splayed against his chest, her short nails scraping over his nipples.

Gideon groaned. He gripped her wrists, then took them in one hand and took her down to the mattress. He had to kiss her, had to feel her breasts against his naked chest. Had to. It was an imperative.

Jada squirmed against him. He knew what she was doing—his woman was a tactile lover. He moved his chest up and down, giving her nipples the stimulation they needed, and she moaned in pleasure. He thrust his thigh between her legs and she bucked up against him, squeezing, trying to get as much pressure as she could. Being with Jada set him on fire.

He backed up again so that he could unbutton and unzip her jeans. He needed to see all of her. This time she winced when he tugged the denim off her hip.

"Fuck, baby, that has to hurt."

He pulled her jeans and panties off her legs and threw them on the floor, then he traced the bruise on her hip with tender care.

"It doesn't hurt," she assured him.

"Liar."

"Kiss it and make it better," she teased.

Gideon slid down her body, intent on doing just that.

"Wait!" she exclaimed.

He looked up. "What?"

Had he hurt her?

"Do it naked." Her grin was wicked.

"You naughty, naughty, girl."

"And you love that about me," she crooned.

He got up off the bed and shucked out of his boots, socks, pants, and skivvies. He didn't know how he managed it, but he got even harder as she stared at him. Jada reached out to touch him, but he brushed her hands away. She pouted.

"But, Gideon," she started.

"No way, Angel. This is my show."

"It's always your show."

"I don't remember you having any complaints."

Jada slowly laid back on the bed. "You're right, I didn't." She raised her arms above her head.

He about swallowed his tongue, but that would be a waste; he had so many other uses for it.

"That grin of yours has me worried," Jada whispered.

Gideon didn't bother to respond—it would be another waste, this time a waste of energy. He circled one delicate ankle and pulled her toward him, savoring her hum of approval. The idea of any part of Jada Harlow being delicate, when she was the strongest woman on Earth, confounded him. But that was her, a puzzle that he would gladly spend the rest of his life trying to solve.

When her ass was finally resting on the edge of the bed, he got down on his knees in front of her.

"No," she whined. "I want a turn."

"In a minute," he lied.

He looked down at her flushed sex and smiled.

So pretty, so wet...so mine.

Gideon didn't bother with a tentative taste; he claimed her with one long lick that had her bucking upward. He laid his arm over her stomach, making sure he didn't do anything to hurt her bruised hip. Jada wiggled and tried to bring up her thighs to get a better purchase, but he pushed her knee outward, intent on keeping her open to his ministrations.

He curled his tongue, slipping deep, feeling her tighten around him.

"My God," she wailed.

She stopped moving her torso, but her legs kept trying to grip him. Time for a new tactic. He moved his arm from her tummy and plunged two fingers into her tight channel, curling them up, hitting a spot deep inside.

"Gideon. Gideon." Her nails scraped against his scalp.

She was so close, and his dick felt ready to burst. He licked her again and again, then sucked her clit deep. He closed his teeth around the delicate nub, nibbling in time with the scrape of her nails.

She screamed out her pleasure.

Vaguely he heard Lucy barking. Thank God he'd had the presence of mind to close the door when he'd brought Jada into his room.

"You better have a condom," Jada panted. "Otherwise, I'm going to be pissed."

Gideon burst out laughing. How did she always make him laugh? "I think I'd be more pissed than you, Angel."

He scooped her lax body up and placed her in the middle of the bed. He pulled a condom out of his nightstand. He tore it open with his teeth and laughed again when Jada's greedy fingers circled his cock.

"I can help," she purred as she held out her hand for the condom.

Gideon closed his eyes as she stroked him up and down. "If you want me inside you, Ms. Harlow, I suggest you stop what you're doing."

"But I like how you feel," she protested.

"You'll like how I feel a lot better in just a minute if you let go."

Jada's brown eyes twinkled up at him, even as she pouted. "Okay, but remember, I get to taste you before the day is through."

Jesus, I'm going to die before the day is through.

Gideon rolled on the condom, then knelt on the bed, between her legs. Jada opened her arms, but there was no way he was going to put his weight on her, not when her hip was still so bruised. He reverently touched her breasts, taking the time to roll her nipples between his fingers, and she moaned her pleasure.

He couldn't help himself; Gideon bent and sucked one of her plump nipples into his mouth, toying it with his tongue. Again, Jada's short nails dug into his scalp. He gave a distant thought to how he would explain all the crescent-shaped indents on his head tomorrow, but then the thought disappeared as he positioned his cock against the tender entrance of her vagina.

Jada bucked up, trying to seize onto a connection, and now his heart wanted to explode. The fact that he was so wanted and needed, about killed him.

"Please, Honey." No pouting. No teasing. Just an honest ask.

He watched her expression as he gently pressed himself deep inside her. When a tear slid down her temple, he knew she wasn't sad, she just felt their connection as deeply as he did. She was no longer digging her nails into his scalp. Instead, she was petting him.

When he started the rhythm that would take them further, take them higher, she undulated with him, intent on giving as much as she received, because that was Jada.

He pulled her legs around his waist.

"I'm not fragile," she whispered.

"No, you're not. You're precious."

He drew out, then pressed in again, and kept on with that slow, languorous tempo, driving them both insane.

Her hands moved from his head and slid down to caress his chest, then trace his abdominal muscles, until she brushed the spot where they were connected. Jada scraped one fingernail—just one fingernail—against the root of his cock and he lost his mind.

Gideon plunged deep and she groaned his name. Passion swept through his body, like sparks from a fire. Jada's breasts heaved with each forceful thrust, and she laughed and moaned her pleasure.

"More. Give me more. Give me everything," she cried.

It was as if those words unlocked something buried deep inside him, and Gideon let loose all he had—every emotion, every pent-up desire, every want and need that he had been holding back—safe in the knowledge that Jada would always love him, no matter what.

With that last conscious thought, he drove one last time into her body, bringing them both to the pinnacle of ecstasy.

16

I'm glowing. I'm literally glowing. What in the hell?

At least she wasn't skipping as she went down the hall to Gideon's den, that would just be embarrassing.

"Yeah, yeah, I'm late. But I knew enough not to bring my Fritos and Coke into the Throne Room of Tech and Wizardry," she said to Gideon and the three men and one woman who were currently displayed on the monitors. Two of the men laughed and the woman giggled. One of the laughing men saluted her with his bottle of grape Fanta.

Gideon turned to her and whispered, "If you're not careful, I'll make you sit in my lap for this meeting."

"Bring it," she dared him.

"Young love," the woman crooned. "Reminds me of you and A.J., Kane."

"Shut it down," the non-laughing blond man said.

He must be Kane.

"We don't have time for this shit. I promised A.J. a night out tonight, and if I bail on her again, she's going to force me to watch another pilot of some reality show. I will hold *all* of you responsible for that, and you won't like how I retaliate."

"That sounds like fun," Jada piped up.

"Don't mess with Kane, Angel. He hates reality TV, and his wife produces it. She keeps threatening to do a series around the dating lives of special operatives. It keeps him in line."

"What you forget is that all of us are paired up," another blond man spoke up. "You're the one who should be scared, Gideon. Omega Sky would be the team on the chopping block."

Jada and the other woman giggled.

"Enough," Kane roared. "I want to get down to business. Dex got information for us on Bonham. It doesn't make sense how it relates to anything to any of us, but hopefully, it will make sense to Jada."

Jada sat down on the other rollie chair in Gideon's office and pulled it up next to the bank of monitors on Gideon's huge circular desk. "Okay, let's hear it," she said.

"Hi, Jada," the man who was drinking the grape Fanta said. "I'm Dex Evans. Let me do the gentlemanly thing and introduce you to everyone, since all Gideon seems to be able to do is look at you with puppy dog eyes."

"It's true," the woman said with a big grin.

Dex grinned big. "I handle computers and communications for the Black Dawn SEAL team out of Coronado. The beautiful woman who just agreed with me is Lydia Hildalgo-Archer. She is married to the man sitting next to her. He is Clint Archer and he has the same job as the rest of us, only for the Midnight Delta team, also out of Coronado, California. Lydia can run circles around the rest of us, and she props Clint up on a regular basis."

"Archer," Lydia said. "I'm not hyphenated."

Jada noted that she had a Hispanic accent. It sounded Mexican.

"Good to know." Dex smiled. "Now, the last guy is Kane McNamara, he is on the Night Storm team near you in Virginia Beach. He can be a bit of a pain in the ass, but you're used to temperamental geniuses like Gideon, so this shouldn't be a problem for you."

"Hey, don't be trying to dress me down. I just got back on her good side," Gideon protested.

"Find out her favorite video game and play it with her, then you'll be golden," Lydia said. "Clint and I fell in love over League of Legends."

Jada looked at Gideon and burst out laughing. "I think we'll find something else to do," she told Lydia.

"Okay, okay, let's get back to work," Kane said irritably. "I really don't want to watch a show about humans and dolphins falling in love or some such shit. Dex, tell them what you found out about Bonham."

"Bonham was working on ensuring that Risk Guard's clients' firmware wasn't compromised."

Jada shrugged. "Yeah. There's a whole department devoted to that, which only made sense. I mean, yeah, software is where most of these companies are most vulnerable, but if somebody can get into a company's firmware, they are really up shit creek."

Everybody nodded.

"Bonham was doing something a little bit different than the rest of the team members," Dex explained. "He came from Homeland Security, and he was actually devising tech that could be installed into companies' hard drives."

Both Jada and Gideon rolled their chairs closer to the desk.

"How?" Gideon asked.

"It was really interesting. He moved from the CIA to Homeland Security when that was created after 9/11. He retired with Homeland Security and then tried to start up his own business for a couple of years."

"Doing what?" Kane asked.

"Fixing computers. He tried to be his own little Geek Squad. It was a bust. That's when Risk Guard picked him up for a third of the salary he should be paid."

"Assholes," Jada muttered.

"Anyway, besides just creating tech that could be installed at the lowest levels, it was his job to figure out how to install it."

"Wi-fi, e-mail?" Lydia asked.

"When I went through his computer, what he was working on wasn't anything like that. It was pretty damn sweet. He was going back in time to some of the old Soviet cold war days of spying. He was figuring out how everybody was installing things on copy machines and typewriters so that they could download exactly what an embassy was up to. Real James Bond shit."

"So, this would be more like bugging an office," Jada clarified.

"Exactly."

Jada's mind started to whirl. If she were to get into some place like the Pentagon and get close to one of their servers, there was no end to what she could download. But getting in would take an act of Congress, literally.

"What are you thinking?" Gideon asked.

"Getting into one of those companies is one thing, then getting close to one of their computers or servers is another. Then there is having something sophisticated enough to download the information without being detected...? That's a hell of a lot of dots that would need to line up."

"Yep, that's what Bonham concluded," Dex said.

"So why torture and kill him?" Jada asked. "That doesn't make any sense either. Hell, by the sounds of it, everything they would have wanted to know was right there on his computer."

"Jada," Gideon tapped her on her shoulder. "This man worked for the CIA and Homeland Security. It's pretty damn likely that he had shadow set-ups at home, the same as you. He was probably a suspicious bastard."

"But suspicious of what?" She was beginning to get really frustrated.

"That's what we were hoping you could help us with," Dex said gently.

"Well, I can't. I just know what I was working on. And I'm pretty damn sure that work was bogus. Yeah, I'm good. But you all saw how easy it was to check out those potential clients' systems. Risk Guard could have had their in-house employees do it and for a shit-ton less money than what they were paying me. I've been trying to figure it out ever since I was in the hospital. There was no reason for them to hire me for that gig."

"I've checked you out, Jada. Nothing against you, Gideon, but you're not necessarily thinking logically, so I wanted to see if Jada was as good as you said she was," Kane explained. "Not only is she good, she's better than you told me." He turned his focus back to Jada. "But Jada, even with your skillset, I agree there is no reason for Risk Guard to be paying you the coin that they're paying to do those checks. There're other hackers out there who'd do it for a lot less."

"None with my clothes sense," Jada said flippantly.

"But I agree one hundred percent. Since I've been thinking on this, something just feels off."

"Jada?"

She turned her attention to Lydia. "Yes?"

"I'm sorry to say, but I dug a bit into your background too." Lydia looked apologetic.

"Don't be sorry," Jada rushed to assure her. "If I'd known your name ahead of time, I would have done a little snooping too."

Lydia gave her a blinding smile. She'd been pretty before, but when she smiled like that, she was gorgeous.

"Anyway," Lydia continued. "Your reputation precedes you. One thing that is very clear, you like to vet all potential employers."

Jada nodded.

"So, anyone from Risk Guard who hired you would expect you to do a thorough background check on their company."

Jada nodded again. "Tim Sloane hired me, he's the Chief Technology Officer. He introduced me to the CEO once I was hired, but just in passing. Tim's been my point of contact. I liked him, except for the pressure tactics."

"What pressure tactics?" Gideon asked.

"I told you," she reminded him as she turned to him. "Remember? I only had forty-eight hours to sign on the dotted line, otherwise, I wouldn't be hired."

"Oh yeah. But then you went back and checked out the company after they hired you. That's when you found out about the suspicious activity and how it related to Miles."

"Exactly," she nodded. "Still..."

"Still, it seemed too easy," Dex chimed in.

"Yes!" Jada said.

"Which brings us right back to Bonham," Kane said. "We know that Miles and his merry band of psychos were busy torturing him. Obviously, he had information they needed, and it had to do with the firmware he was working on."

Everyone on the call nodded.

"Somehow, this is the real issue, not how Risk Guard made it big three years ago. I just don't know how." Jada bit her lip.

"Neither do I," Clint said. "Anybody else have a guess?"

Everyone shook their heads.

"We need to come back to this when we're fresh."

"Hey, Gideon," Kane gave him an evil grin. "Is your team still talking to you?"

"What are you talking about? My team loves me."

"Even after the shit you pulled on them in Fort Knox? What with everything that went wrong during their Urban Warfare Training, I would have thought they would have put Ben-Gay in your jockstrap by now."

"Again, Kane, I don't know why you think my men would be upset with me. Now, are they holding a grudge against you and Commander Clark? Hell yeah. But me? Hell no; they know I was rescuing my woman across the country in Oregon."

Dex snorted out a laugh.

"Holy hell, he's got you on that one, Kane." Clint grinned. "What'd you do to the poor men of Omega Sky?"

Kane held up his hands. "It wasn't me. Gideon came up with the idea to fuck with their equipment, radios, and sat-nav while they were training at the Urban Combat Training Center at Fort Knox. I was just helping him out when he had to leave."

"What are you talking about?" Gideon asked innocently. "I'm confused."

"You're an asshole, Smith," Kane said pointing toward Gideon through his monitor. Jada chortled.

"You got Commander Clark to go along with this?" Dex asked. "That sounds like something that Liam McAllister would do, but I didn't know Simon Clark had it in him. That's cool."

"Yeah, it was," Gideon agreed.

"Sounds to me like you better be checking your jockstrap from now on," Clint told Kane.

"Sounds like," Kane agreed.

"Let's meet back here in a couple of days if we have anything to report," Dex suggested.

"I will as long as my balls are intact and I haven't buried myself in a bomb shelter after watching episodes of dolphins and humans falling in love," Kane moaned.

"You can handle it, Kane. I have faith in you," Jada smiled.

"WHY ARE YOU NERVOUS?" Gideon asked.

"You're kidding, right?"

He watched Jada as she adjusted her blue pinstripe corset-style top that went with her matching pinstripe flared slacks and red high heels. With her height, she looked like some kind of model. She raced out of Gideon's bedroom and he followed her into the guestroom and watched as she pulled a cropped, fitted, red leather jacket out of the closet and threw it over her arm.

"There. I'm done. We're not going to be late, are we? I

needed a jacket in case they seat us outdoors and there isn't a heat lamp."

"You're fine. According to Kostya, Lark isn't known for always being on time."

"But I want to make a good impression," she said as she tried to pass by him.

Gideon caught her around the waist. Jada looked up at him. "What?"

"You can never do anything but create a good impression," he assured her.

"But Kostya is so important to you," she breathed.

"So is my brother. He loves you. Felix, Kyle, and my dog all like you better than they do me. You're going to do fine tonight. I'm the one I'm worried about. Lark might be sick of me because of some of the shit I pulled before."

Jada frowned. "What are you talking about?"

"I might have pushed my way into her little adventure with Kostya down in Florida."

Jada pushed at his chest. "Wait just a damn minute, Mr. Smith. Are you feeding me a line to make me feel less nervous?"

Gideon's lips twitched. "Maybe."

"Dammit, man."

"Angel, I'm telling you, they're going to love you." He bent down and brushed his lips against hers. It took long moments before he came back up for air.

"Okay," she whispered.

"Okay, what?"

"I'll believe whatever you want to tell me."

"Your lipstick isn't smeared," Gideon said with a straight face.

"I'll believe anything but that."

JADA NOTICED that Lark was observing Kostya and Gideon just as much as she was. In some ways, Kostya and Gideon seemed more like brothers than Gideon did with his actual brother Mike. Lark looked over at her and gave her a quick wink.

Jada suppressed a grin.

"The waiter is being too slow with our drinks," Lark said. "I'm going up to the bar. Want to join me, Lark?" she asked as she stood up.

"Aw, hell, they're going to talk about us," Kostya moaned.

"That was going to happen sooner or later." Gideon shrugged. "I'm just happy they're doing it out of earshot. I don't think my ego could have handled them dissecting my traits while I was sitting in front of them."

"Good point."

"Do you want another glass of Jameson?" Lark asked Kostya.

"I'm driving, so I'll stick to one. Thanks, though."

Gideon shook his head before Jada had a chance to ask.

They walked into the restaurant from the patio and Jada admired how Lark sauntered up to the bar. When she planted her tushie up on a barstool, Jada did the same thing. A bartender came up and they placed their orders.

"Bourbon, huh?" Lark said.

"Got a taste for it while I was in Kentucky. Just glad to see they're serving my brand."

"So, which came first, your love for a bourbon called Angel's Envy, or Gideon calling you Angel?"

Jada chuckled. "They do bourbon flights in Kentucky,

and I might have over-indulged during brunch. I had intended to share, but..."

"But, they all tasted so good," Lark grinned. "I can't imagine being in Scotland and sharing a flight of whiskey with Kostya. So, Angel's Envy was the winner?"

"Hands down."

Lark held up her hand and caught the bartender's attention. She came back over to them. "Can I also have a small taste of the bourbon my friend is rhapsodizing about?"

"Sure thing." The bartender grinned.

She was soon back with three highball glasses of amber liquid, and a glass of water. Jada frowned, and Lark explained. "She wants me to be able to cleanse my palate after the bourbon so I can go back to the Jameson. The woman is definitely earning her tip." Lark put out her credit card.

"Let me get the bill," Jada protested.

"I'm writing this dinner off. I want to hear more about Risk Guard." Lark picked up the tumbler with the splash of bourbon, took a sip, and swished it around in her mouth, letting the burn settle, then swallowed. "Ooooh, that's nice." She finished off the rest. "No wonder you like this. There is just a little hint of candy to this, after it's knocked you on your ass," Lark grinned.

Jada laughed.

"It's nougat and vanilla, but just a little essence." She picked up her glass and took a sip, as Lark took a drink of water. "Are we going back to our table?" Jada asked.

"No, let's get to know one another a little bit. I want you to tell me where you got that beautiful vintage leather jacket, and what is going down with Risk Guard, and I'll let you know every one of Gideon's annoying habits."

"I've read most of your investigative articles and all of your op-eds. My mother is from Puerto Rico. Her whole family immigrated to the U.S. before she married my father. The work you did to spotlight what goes on in the favelas in Brazil was desperately needed. My mom is going to freak when I tell her I met you."

Lark blushed and took a long sip of her scotch.

"Okay, let's talk about how Gideon interfered with your investigation down in Florida. He said that he ticked you off."

"He said that? He's bullshitting you. He was a big help. We couldn't have found my sister without him."

"Really?"

"Really." Lark took another sip of her drink. "He talked about you, too."

"He did?" Jada found that hard to believe, but she wanted to.

"He was struggling with the age difference between the two of you."

"He's an ass." Jada ran her fingers through the ends of her hair. "And it was more than just the age difference."

"I figured as much," Lark said. "These men." She lifted her glass, and Jada touched hers against it.

"To our men and their twisted thinking," Jada toasted.

"And why we love them anyway."

17

"WE HAVE TO BAIL, BUT THIS IS GOOD STUFF," GIDEON SAID to the people on the screens.

"Yeah, well, I sure wouldn't have put it together if Jada hadn't mentioned that Risk Guard was also working with different correctional facilities to update their mechanized locking systems," Clint said.

Gideon looked over at Jada, once again amazed at how her brain worked. "I told you she was good at this."

"She should go to work for my old company," Kane said. "I already told Bruce all about her." He turned his attention toward Jada. "Seriously, Jada, you could work full-time from anywhere you want, and the pay and benefits would be outstanding."

"It's something to consider," Gideon prompted. "You could move out of that New York hovel that you call a home."

Jada glared at Gideon then turned her attention to Kane. "Thanks, Kane. It's definitely something to think about. But right now, my job will be consisting of doing diapers for the next twenty-four hours."

"Huh? I thought Gideon was potty-trained," Dex said.

"We're going to watch our Godson, you ass," Gideon explained. "Sebastian is going to be here any minute."

"Okay, then, we'll sign off," Clint said as Lydia waved at the screen.

Every screen went dark and Gideon turned his chair so he could study Jada. "That was really good work. It helped explain what Bonham was working on."

"The only thing is, somebody had to download the worm at the facility before they were able to get it to function." Jada shook her head as she got up from her chair and headed out to the great room. Lucy got up from her doggie bed and looked at the two of them expectantly.

"Are you ready to play guard-dog again?" Gideon asked his big Russian terrier.

Lucy perked up even more and headed to the front door.

"It's like she knows that Sebastian is bringing Neil."

"She was fascinated by him the last time we babysat," Gideon said. "Do you want anything from the kitchen?" he asked as he headed to the fridge.

"A glass of water." Neither she nor Gideon liked proliferating the world with additional water bottles when re-using glasses or filling up their own water bottles was just as easy.

"Got it," he replied.

The doorbell rang.

Woof. Woof. Woof.

"Settle," Jada said softly, and Lucy plopped down on her butt and stopped barking.

"Good girl," Jada patted her head as she went by her to open the door for Sebastian. She stuffed down the giggle when she again saw the khaki baby carrier strapped to the front of Sebastian, cuddling his son close to his chest. Neil had already managed to curl up next to Daddy in the few yards that it took Sebastian to walk from the car to the house. Besides carrying Neil and a diaper bag over his shoulder, he was holding a portable playpen in his right hand and a baby walker in his left.

"Shit, man, did you leave anything at home?" Gideon asked as he came to the door.

"Yeah, my wife," Sebastian said as he shoved the playpen at Gideon. "And I want to get back to her as soon as possible. If I timed everything right, I have eighteen minutes to pick up the food from Il Giardino's then get it home and plated."

"Plated? Did I hear you say plated? When did you ever work in a restaurant?" Gideon wanted to know.

"Gianna's been making me watch episodes of Iron Chef. She's convinced she can learn to cook."

"God no! Don't let her near the kitchen!" Jada rushed over to Sebastian and held out her hands for Neil.

"Don't I know it? Her idea of making nachos is pre-sliced cheddar cheese nuked on top of chips," Sebastian said as he started to unbuckle the baby carrier and Neil started to wake up. His beautiful green eyes began to focus on the world around him.

"So, what else did she put on the nachos?" Gideon asked.

"Nothing," Sebastian and Jada said in unison.

"My mom tried to teach her to cook, her granny tried to teach her to cook. She's missing the cooking gene. I never realized it was a genetic trait like blue eyes, but it is. She doesn't have it," Jada explained as she nuzzled Neil's neck.

"For real?" Gideon asked.

"Yeah, but I never said it. She's still making attempts. This seems to be important to her, and I don't want to hurt her feelings."

"Sebastian, be careful, she could end up killing you. That girl is one day going to try to feed you raw chicken," Jada warned.

Sebastian's eyes twinkled as he watched Jada with her Godson. "You know she's too OCD to do anything like that. Now, will it taste awful? Yes. Kill me? No. I want to make one of the bedrooms into a studio so she can focus on her art; that way she won't focus on the kitchen as much."

Jada wasn't paying attention now that she was holding Neil. She'd forgotten to put her hair in a ponytail, and he now clutched a tiny fistful of dark curls in his hand, trying to bring it to his mouth. She vaguely listened to Sebastian and Gideon talk as she went to her favorite spot on the sofa and sat down with one leg curled up under her butt.

"Did you miss me, kid? I haven't seen you for six whole days. Not since I was over visiting you and your mom."

Neil didn't make any noise. He just stared at her, watching her mouth move and her facial expressions. That's the kind of baby he was, solemn and transfixed by everything around him.

"Hey, Jada," Sebastian whispered. He was standing above her, out of Neil's line of sight. "Gianna and I really appreciate you and Gideon taking Neil for the night."

Neil's head bobbed as he heard his father's voice. Nothing got by this baby. He tried to turn around to look at his father.

"You're not fooling your boy, so you might as well stop with the whispering," Gideon teased.

Sebastian took a step to the right then crouched down

and looked at his son. "Is Gideon right? Do you see right through me?"

Neil bobbed his head again and all the adults laughed.

"Hey, young man, how about we don't snatch Auntie Jada bald-headed, huh?" Sebastian asked as he gently pried open his son's fist to release her hair.

"As for you thanking us, we love taking care of our Godson," Gideon said as he stood next to Lucy. "We'll take care of him anytime, just bring him on over."

Jada sat up straighter. "Well, until Miles is caught and I go home, then Gideon won't be as available."

"We'll cross that bridge when we come to it," Gideon growled.

"Gideon, I don't want to mooch off you forever," Jada frowned at him.

Sebastian stood up and looked speculatively between the two of them. "So if I were to tell you that you could move into our house tomorrow...?" he asked Jada.

She bit her lip and glanced up at Gideon.

"Not happening, man. She's staying here."

Sebastian laughed. "Thought so."

He looked down at his watch. "Shit. I'm going to be late." He bent down and kissed Neil's forehead. "Have fun, kid. Make sure to vomit your peas on your Uncle Gideon."

Jada shook her head and rolled her eyes.

"Bye, you two."

She sat there snuggling Neil to her chest as Gideon walked Sebastian out to his car. Lucy padded over and placed her head on the arm of the sofa and let out a low whine.

"You've missed your friend, haven't you girl?"

Neil reached out toward Lucy. Jada had been concerned the first time Lucy and Neil had interacted.

Especially since Neil liked pulling Jada's dark hair and she knew that the baby would probably want to pull Lucy's long, shaggy dark hair too.

It hadn't been a problem.

Gideon had explained about Lucy and her sister being raised together with the Ellis family, and how they had grown up as pups around a toddler, so Lucy was used to being very gentle and protective with babies. Still, Jada discouraged Neil from pulling on the big dog's hair.

"Come on you two, let's get down on the floor and see if your crawling has improved, big boy."

Gideon had already moved the coffee table in preparation for Neil, so there was lots of rug space to put down his baby blanket. Jada set him in his playpen while she laid out the baby blanket.

"Caught you," Gideon said as he came back in from outside carrying a portable crib. "Are you already planning on getting down and dirty?"

"Darn right I am. I want as much playtime as I can get with the kid."

Lucy's nose was up against the playpen and Neil was batting at it. "I think my dog wants to play as much as you do," Gideon said.

Jada stopped herself before saying, 'our dog'.

God, what am I thinking?

She lifted Neil out of the crib and got down on her hands and knees and proceeded to play with Lucy and Neil, delighting in how far and fast Neil could now crawl.

"You're a champ, kid. You take after your Godfather."

"I don't know Jada, all that energy and speed reminds me of you," Gideon grinned.

GIDEON HUNG UP HIS PHONE. He hadn't been surprised by Sebastian's midnight call; it was the first time that he and Gianna had been separated from their son overnight and they were jumpy. Jada had shared with him her friend's concerns about her marriage, but his teammate was doing a great job getting everything back on track.

It seemed that Gideon and Sebastian had a lot more in common than he would have thought. Guilt was a pernicious emotion, and so often you didn't even realize how deeply it had its hooks in you and how it was souring every aspect of your life until you were drowning in it. When Sebastian told Gianna just how culpable he felt for getting her pregnant so soon after Neil's birth, she had laughed. She went on to explain that she was ecstatic at the idea of having children close in age so they could have strong connections like Jada's older brothers. Sebastian had started feeling better immediately.

"Did you calm him down?" Jada asked as she walked into the bedroom.

"Yep. He tried to say he was calling on behalf of Gianna."

"Did you call bullshit?"

"No, because I figure he was calling for both of them."

Jada nodded as she put the baby monitor on her nightstand, turned off the light, and got under the covers.

"You know, the way that thing works is, Neil has to make noise before you need to check on him. You do realize that, don't you?"

"I thought I heard something," Jada defended herself. "Anyway, it's hard to hear anything over Lucy's snuffles."

Gideon laughed. "That's true. But she would let us know if something were wrong."

"Maybe," Jada said doubtfully.

"For real. Shasta, Lucy's sister, would always let Felix and Pam know when little Isaac was attempting to climb out of his crib. One time, the kid got into Pam's purse, and Shasta pulled the purse away from the kid. She's quite the babysitter."

Jada laughed. "I wonder if Lucy could be taught to do that."

"She spent a fair amount of time over there when I was on missions, and according to Pam and Felix she was just as good with Isaac as Shasta was."

"I'm loving this."

Gideon put his arm around Jada's shoulders and pulled her close to his side. "Loving what, Angel?"

"This. You. Here. Everything."

"Well, that clears it up, thanks," he teased. He switched off the light on his nightstand, then pulled Jada in and caught her mouth with his—needing her mouth, needing a kiss, which Jada readily reciprocated. He drew them deeper under the covers, and Jada rolled on top of him.

CHIRP. Chirp. Chirp.

It was his home alarm system ringtone on his cell phone. He snagged Jada around the waist and rolled so that they fell onto the floor beside his side of the bed, her small body landing on top of his.

"What? Gid—"

"Shhh," he hissed, while reaching up to his nightstand and pulling out his pistol. "Get under the bed."

"Neil—"

"Now, Jada." He shoved her and as she started to

squirm under the bed. He pounced into a crouch and turned toward the French door that led to his patio.

Woof. Woof. Woof.

Someone was coming in through the front of the house.

Glass pelted the floor as someone reached in one of the French doors to open it from the inside.

This isn't a quiet intrusion, this was a blitzkrieg!

Gideon shot at the figure who was trying to break in. It was a headshot, and he went down. This time he heard a loud noise from the great room and turned his head when the French doors crashed open.

Another intruder!

Woof. Woof. Woof.

Lucy was going crazy. Gideon could hear the snarls, punctuated by Neil's cries through the baby monitor.

"Neil!" Jada shouted.

Gideon got off another two shots. One was a kill shot.

Woof. Woof. Woof.

"Stay put!" Gideon shouted when he saw Jada squirming out from underneath the bed. He leapt over the bed, intent on getting down the hall to Neil.

"Fucking dog!" somebody yelled.

More snarls.

Woof. Woof.

Neil was past the point of crying—he was screaming.

Woof.

Lucy howled, then whined, then nothing.

"I've got the brat, drop the gun."

Gideon stood at the mouth of his bedroom door and stared at two men dressed all in black. One had tiny Neil crushed to his chest with one arm. He held a cattle prod against the baby.

"Drop the gun, or it dies."

Even with Neil's screams, he could hear Jada's gasp and knew she was coming out from under the bed.

Lucy must have been stunned, that's why she wasn't barking. He saw blood dripping from the guy on the left. His thigh looked torn to shit where his pants were ripped. If Gideon took the shots, there was too much of a chance that Neil would be stunned, and there was no way an eighteen-pound baby would survive a jolt of electricity.

Gideon slowly crouched down, then lowered his Sig Sauer onto the floor, but stayed with his knees bent so he could still get to it quickly.

"Let go of me," Jada cried.

Shit. Another man must have come in through the French doors and gotten ahold of Jada. Just how many were there?

Gideon didn't take his eyes off the tableau in front of him, even as he heard the crackle of electricity and a thud.

"I've got her. The bastard killed Ronnie and Jim," the man called from Gideon's bedroom.

Gideon never felt so helpless in his life.

"When the boss gets ahold of him, he'll regret that and every other moment of his life."

No wonder they were using tasers, they wanted him alive. Neil's cries sounded wretched.

"You're holding him too tight," Gideon said to the man holding Neil.

"Shut up," he replied.

"You want to live, and you want to take me alive, but that won't be possible unless I know the baby won't come to any harm," Gideon threatened.

The man holding Neil darted his eyes to the man beside him.

Jesus, Gideon saw yet another shadow at the mouth of the hallway in the great room. That meant at least four, and probably one in a van outside. He needed to stall. The alarm went to the local sheriff's and to Kostya and to Nolan since he lived the closest.

Gideon took a step to the side, still in a bit of a crouch, so that his back was against the wall. He was still within reach of his gun. He had eyes on little Neil, but could see the behemoth behind him with Jada over his shoulder.

"Quit moving," the injured man snarled.

"We're at an impasse," Gideon said.

The man holding Neil chortled. "How do you figure that?"

"My neighbor is armed to the teeth. He'll have heard the shots. My silent alarm didn't go to just the sheriff, it went to my SEAL teammates and they'll be here in minutes."

"Fuck," the man behind him muttered.

"I'll go quietly if you put Neil back in his crib and we all walk out of here together."

"Do it quick, Ketterman," the man behind him said. "He's already killed two of our guys."

"Kick your gun to me," the injured man said.

Gideon didn't have a choice. He did it.

The man holding Neil lowered the stunner and went into the spare bedroom with a whimpering Neil.

When he rushed back out, Gideon could still hear his Godson's mewls over the baby monitor, and his knees sagged with relief.

"Get moving," the man from behind shouted. "To the front door. Fast."

Gideon started down the hallway. The man who had held Neil had backed into the room so that he could follow Gideon as he passed by. Now Gideon had two men at his back and two men in front of him as they marched him out his front door. Jada was helpless.

The only.

Only.

Saving grace out of anything, was that she had put on his tee and panties after sex, and he'd put on a pair of workout pants because they might have to check on the baby during the night.

Outside in his drive, he was surprised to see a Mercedes Sprinter instead of the expected white windowless van. That was his last thought as he was stunned into unconsciousness.

18

"Ahhhhhh!" Jada screamed and shuddered, then her mouth filled with salt water and her eyes stung as she snapped them shut. Her body automatically stopped sucking down water, and she began holding her breath as she realized she might drown. Her instinct was to swim to the surface, but her arms and legs wouldn't work.

She was tied up!

She opened her eyes again in panic and started to flail around. Anything to get to the surface. But she couldn't.

Someone was holding her shoulders, forcing her underwater. She flung her body back and forth, her hair tangling in front of her eyes. She was losing consciousness. Her elbow banged against something hard, and she clamped her mouth shut even tighter, fighting back a scream of pain.

More pain.

More pain.

Someone grabbed her hair and pulled her up out of the water.

Air.

"Pretty tits."

"He's right. You've chosen well, Gideon."

Jada looked for Gideon but couldn't see past her hair plastered across her face. She was waist deep in water; at least her bound feet were touching the bottom.

"Get her out of there!" she heard Gideon yell.

"You look really upset, Gideon. I'll leave her where she is. I like to see you suffer."

Was that Miles Albright?

Why is he doing this to me? To us?

Jada's lungs seized. The cough that crackled through her lungs shook her entire body. As huge ugly sounds came out of her mouth, she thrashed around in the small space of water. Her ribs hit the side of the oil barrel she was in, cutting into her skin.

"Unnhhhh." A howl of pain interspersed with her coughs as the saltwater hit her broken skin. It felt like someone had taken a red-hot knife and stuck it between her ribs.

Jada couldn't stop coughing. She flopped against the side of the barrel again, this time scraping her upper arm, then cutting into it.

"Owwwww," she started to cry as she coughed. She couldn't make out what Gideon was saying. He sounded like *he* was in pain.

Someone yanked her hair again, then grabbed her under her armpit and wrenched her shoulder as they pulled her out of the barrel. Her thighs to the tops of her feet were scraped raw as she was hauled over the side.

"Ahhhhh."

Is that me screaming?

Her body turned to lava with the pain, then mercifully she passed out.

GIDEON COULDN'T AFFORD to feel anything. Jada was alive. Neil was alive. That was what mattered. No emotion.

I need to assess the situation.

"Aw, your pretty little girlfriend has a boo-boo. Aren't you upset?"

A well-dressed man in a suit, who looked like the pictures of Miles Albright, pushed himself off the back of the SUV near the closed bay door of the warehouse. He walked over to Jada where she was lying on the rough wood floor. He pushed at her with the toe of his expensive loafer.

"Weak."

He looked up at Gideon. "But you're not. Not like you were. The army made you strong."

Gideon didn't correct him. He'd been trying to undo the heavy-duty zip-ties that bound his wrists and ankles. He'd woken up on the floor with Jada's first cries.

"Oh, aren't you going to tell me your allegiance belongs to the Navy, Gideon Henry Smith?"

Miles seemed pretty proud that he knew his middle name. It was as if the man really wanted to get under Gideon's skin.

"Henry, that was your father's name, right?"

Gideon's skin began to crawl.

He stared hard at the man.

"Aren't you going to hurt him too?" The woman who had been leaning next to Miles against the SUV marched her way over to the old man and slid her arms around his shoulders. "You promised you'd let me play, Miles. She's almost dead, so she's no fun. When can I start in on him? I brought my knives."

Gideon could care less about the blonde; she meant nothing, and her threats were meaningless. On the other hand, there was something about the man's eyes.

"Are you catching on? I should hope so." Miles whispered. "You were such a wunderkind. You were supposed to blaze new trails. But now it seems you're nothing. Just a grunt answering to Uncle Sam, led around by his dick. You're pathetic."

He turned his attention to the woman. "Jenny, you're going to get to play, but this time you're going to have to be patient. If you're not, I'll let Timmy play with your knives on you. Do you understand?"

God, the blonde almost licked her lips. She was a psycho, just like Jada had said. But to Gideon, she was a subplot. He turned his attention back to the man who was watching him like he was a bug under a magnifying glass.

What was his damage?

"Still nothing?" Miles taunted Gideon.

He scraped Jenny off him and walked closer to Gideon until he was standing over him. His face looked odd. The skin around his jaw was too tight, the same around his eyes.

His eyes.

I remember those eyes!

"Are you catching on now?" Miles grinned. "How about if I offer my condolences for your dad's passing? Such a shame that he died hating you."

"Douglas," Gideon hissed as he twisted his wrists, working at getting his bindings loose, using his blood as a lubricant.

"Oh, don't stand on ceremony. You can call me by my first name, after all, we've known each other over twenty-five years, Gideon. Call me Kendall." The man cackled.

"What is this?" Gideon cringed that he'd asked the question. He needed to keep silent, he couldn't afford to play into this madman's game. He needed to work on getting free.

"I am so glad you asked. Do you know I always saw you as my greatest protégé?" Gideon said nothing, and Kendall Douglas shrugged. "Well, I did. I taught you. I groomed you. Then you betrayed me."

Gideon turned his head away from him. He couldn't roll over, then Kendall would see he was trying to break free.

"Wake her up!" Kendall yelled.

Gideon heard movement, then there was a large splash, and Jada moaned.

"Jenny, feel free to start having some fun with our dear girl. Somebody needs to be getting some satisfaction, and since Gideon isn't conversing with me, then let's make Jada sing."

Panic flared. "What do you want me to say? Call off your sicko bitch, and I'll talk." Gideon turned his head back immediately, catching Kendall's glance.

"I want you to admit you manufactured evidence against me."

"Call off Jenny."

"Fine. Jenny, hold off for a minute. Gideon and I are going to talk about old times."

"But, Miles," the blonde whined.

"Do as I say," Miles ordered sharply. Gideon could tell that Jenny would regret not obeying him. She must have sensed it too.

"All right," she acquiesced.

"So, tell me how you phonied up the evidence," Miles prompted again.

Gideon gave a harsh laugh. "You're kidding, right? By the time I went to the F.B.I., you had managed to do everything but rob a kid's lemonade stand and the March of Dimes."

"I was on my way to an initial public offering. Streetgamezzz was valued at fifty million dollars, you little fuck!"

"Only because you'd managed to embezzle five times the amount that every one of your investors was willing to invest with you. You even tapped into the Special Olympics, you idiot."

"There was absolutely no way the fumbling imbeciles at the F.B.I. could have found anything. There was nothing to find. I did the coding myself!" The toes of his shoes were brushing Gideon's forehead. His eyes were wild with anger. "My plan was bulletproof. You had to have manufactured something to give to them."

"I didn't have to do shit. You were careless. You were always careless. Because of hubris, you were just sure you were smarter than everyone else. Just like now. But we were on to you. We know about Sid Bonham and what he was working on. You're going down...Again." Gideon forced a laugh.

"You know nothing." Kendall's laugh sounded genuine. "I'm going to rule the world. I'll be bigger than Elon Musk or Jeff Bezos, just watch and see."

"You're psychotic."

Kendall kicked him in the chest. "I don't like that word. I'm a genius. How else would I have been able to take over the real Miles Albright's identity and life as easily as I did? That was the work of a creative genius. I've been willing to play the long game."

"How did you do that?" Gideon asked, forcing himself to sound impressed.

"I'd hatched my plan in prison. I knew I had to find some civil servant with a strong technical background. Someone who had a fantastic bio, but absolutely no life, no nothing. He had to be a ghost, with no friends or family." Kendall laughed. "It was really surprising how many poor slobs I had to choose from."

Gideon imagined that was true. He worked to keep Kendall talking. "Well, that didn't take a genius," he taunted.

"But the next part took fortitude. Not many men have it in them to follow through when it's really necessary, but I can. I *can*," he mumbled the last bit to himself.

"What did you do?" Gideon asked in a bored voice.

"Why I killed him, of course. But only after he retired and went to that wretched fishing cabin that he'd bought by the lake. By that time, I'd already had some surgery done, and I'd shaved my head so I looked like him. It was perfect. Nobody from his old life would ever run into me when I went to Reynolds as the CTO, but even if they ran into me, they'd walk by me, because nobody at DoD realized that Miles Albright existed there." Kendall laughed. It wasn't nice.

"Why didn't you just apply for a job with Risk Guard, if that's where you needed to be? Didn't they want you?" Again, Gideon worked overtime to ridicule his old tormentor.

"I couldn't be that obvious," Kendall told him like he was explaining things to an elementary school child. "You wouldn't be any good at this, my boy. It's all about keeping things at arm's length. Being a member of the Board of Directors for Risk Guard was perfect. It kept me in the know and able to affect change, without being directly responsible."

Fuck, Kendall Douglas is still as intelligent, devious, and sleazy as he ever was.

Kendall crouched close, looking Gideon dead in the eye. "And now you're going to pay for what you did to me," he whispered. "Make her scream," he yelled over his shoulder.

Gideon did an ab curl and powered up, He butted his forehead up into the bridge of Kendall's nose, doing what he could to push the cartilage up into his brain. Blood spurted all over Gideon, but he was prepared and had his eyes closed.

Kendall screamed out with pain. His screams mixed with Jada's cries of pain.

"What the fuck?" It sounded like the behemoth who had carried Jada out of Gideon's house. He heard running feet heading toward him, then he was kicked in the ribs hard enough to send him sliding across the rough floor. He squinted through the blood obscuring his vision and saw the big man picking up Kendall and slinging him over his shoulder.

"Miles!" the blonde psycho cried out. "Somebody help Miles!" she ordered. Gideon heard even more feet come running toward him.

Jada wasn't making any noise.

From far across the warehouse, Gideon heard breaking glass.

"Shit! Someone's breaking in," a man yelled.

"Get in the SUV," someone else shouted.

"Kill them!" the blonde yelled.

Now, Gideon couldn't see anything past the blood in

his eyes, but he knew it had to be his team breaking the glass.

"We're alive!" he yelled.

"Shut up!" he heard a man yell at him. Gideon squinted again just in time to see the man pull back his foot. Gideon tried to roll away from the kick, but he felt it hit the back of his head.

Pain.

Not again!

Black.

19

Gideon recognized the smell; he was in a hospital. His eyes snapped open. His head pounded, his hand stung. Nobody was with him.

Thank fuck.

He yanked out the IV from his hand and swung his legs out of the bed. He stumbled as he tried to walk.

Gotta get to Jada. To Neil.

His ass was hanging out, like that mattered. He made it as far as the door to his room, then fell against the wall, his shoulder taking the hit.

"Goddammit, Gideon," Kostya growled as he came into the room. He pulled him upright. "What in the hell are you thinking? Let's get you back to your bed."

Kostya looked fuzzy.

"Where are they?"

"Who?"

"Ja—"

"Right." Kostya was steering him toward the bed. "Jada and the baby are fine. So's your dog." He pushed him down so Gideon was sitting on the side of the bed.

"Kendall?"

"Who?" Kostya asked again. He tried to press Gideon into a prone position, but he wasn't having it.

"Kendall Douglas, you remember him." Gideon shook his head and pain sliced through it, but that managed to cut through the fog. "Miles Albright. Where is he?"

"Was he at the warehouse?" Kostya asked. He'd finally managed to shove Gideon down, despite his best efforts to stay sitting up.

"Dammit, he must have gotten away," Gideon muttered. "Where's Jada? Tell me about Jada. I've got to get to her." He did an ab curl and tried to shove his Lieutenant so that he could get up, but there was no way he could match Kostya's strength in the shape he was in.

"I told you Jada's fine. Lots of superficial wounds, but they've got her here, and they're treating her."

"I need to see her." Gideon took another swipe at Kostya, but his friend easily blocked it. "Neil? What happened to Neil?"

"Lucy was waking up when Nolan got to your house. She tried to attack him when he was searching the house and heard Neil's whimpers and tried to get into Neil's room."

Gideon almost smiled. First good news he'd heard since he'd woken up.

"I can then assume my Godson and dog are doing fine?"

"Absolutely," Kostya grinned. "It took Nolan more than a minute, but he managed to get to Neil and get him to Sebastian and Gianna. He wasn't part of the op."

"He was doing the important thing."

"That's how he saw it," Kostya agreed.

"How'd you find us?"

"We didn't, it was either Kane, Dex, or Clint. Something about a real estate subsidiary of Risk Guard. I didn't get into it, but they were able to pinpoint you."

"I owe them."

Kostya shook his head.

"I need to see Jada. Where is she?"

"She's with Lark, at my place."

"For fuck sake's, how long have I been here?"

"Since yesterday."

"And they let her out of the hospital already?" Gideon was pissed.

"She wouldn't stay. She was sick of hospitals."

"You're telling me that Lark is the only one who is with her?"

Kostya raised his eyebrow.

Gideon laid back on the pillow. "Sorry. I wasn't thinking. Of course you wouldn't have left them alone. Who's with them?"

"Nolan, Jase, Ryker, Jonas and Lincoln. Lincoln and Jonas are up in the trees with their rifles. Jase is patrolling outside, Nolan is inside watching her condition and Ryker is inside for comic relief."

Gideon nodded. It's how he would have deployed the men. *But...*

"Isn't Commander Clark crawling up your assh having so many of our menz babysitting Jada?"

Did I just slur my words?

"Gideon, you've got to take a rest. The docs want you to stay at least one more night."

"Fuck that noise. I'm leaving now." He pushed against Kostya.

"You're in the same shape Jada was in, in Oregon. You have a bad concussion and—"

"And nothing. Don't make me slug you. Simon isn't going to be impressed when you show up to the base with a black eye, and you have to explain you were fighting with me while I was in the hospital." He stared at Kostya and his friend could see he was serious.

Kostya tried one last ditch effort.

"Gideon, think about it, you're slurring your words, you're having trouble walking and you're getting Miles Albright confused with Kendall Douglas. Stay in bed."

"I'll give you the first two, but the third is true; it's a mindfuck, but it's true."

Kostya gave him an incredulous look. "Explain."

"Kendall's aged twenty-five years. He shaved his head, and he's had some plastic surgery. But his eyes and voice are the same."

"Are you sure you're not imagining things?" Kostya asked carefully.

"Damn sure. He called me his protégé, then he said he was sorry my dad died. It was him all right."

"Holy hell! But why would he be pretending to be Albright? Why would he kidnap Jada and you? It doesn't make any sense."

"He's a madman, and trying to understand what goes on in his twisted mind is impossible for someone sane."

"Should we ask Jase his opinion?" Kostya suggested.

Gideon laughed for the first time since he woke up, thinking about their less than sane teammate. "We'll keep that option open."

Then Gideon sighed. "Kendall was intent on making me suffer. That's why he took Jada. I think that's why he took her before. We never could figure out a good reason for the first time they abducted her; I think it was to get to me."

"You think he would really become Miles Albright, just to set you up?"

"No, I think that's something else, but I think he always planned to come after me, and when he found out about Jada and saw he had an opportunity, he took it. So, I think Kendall/Miles has something else going on, something bigger planned."

"Shit, and we let him get away," Kostya said with disgust.

"How did the op go down?" Gideon finally asked.

"Uh."

This time it was Gideon who raised an eyebrow. Then he winced. Raising an eyebrow hurt.

"Tell me."

"As soon as your alarm came in, I busted ass over to your place. Nolan and I beat the sheriff by seven minutes, tops. Your neighbor was there, and he helped to get Lucy back to his house, and that's where Nolan took Neil. They had a car seat, so Nolan was able to take Neil straight over to Sebastian and Gianna's house. He didn't tell them ahead of time what went down."

Gideon agreed with that play.

"And you?" Gideon asked.

"Jesus, I was standing there with my dick in my hand, needing to do something, but not knowing what to do. There I was, with two dead men near your bedroom, blood in the hallway, you and Jada gone, and knowing the sheriff will be there any minute. Both yours and Jada's phones are on your nightstands, there was no way to track you, so I drive Nolan's Jeep, then my Bronco over to the neighbor's driveway and call Kane, who forwards me to Dex."

"And that's when Dex tracks a warehouse at the Colonna's Shipyards back to Risk Guard."

Kostya nodded. "Half the team is out of commission, you know that. Night Storm and a bunch of ours are back at Fort Knox playing reindeer games at the Urban Combat Training Center. So, I had Ryker and Linc. I gave coordinates to Jase and Jonas but they were camping."

Gideon nodded, and Kostya continued.

"By the time we got the info, the three of us were loaded for bear. The problem was the docks were really busy by the time we got there. There were two container ships. They were unloading at the same time, and there was a shift change. One of the ships had come in from China and must have had high-end product, because security was tight."

"Shit."

"Yeah, your warehouse was basically surrounded, and the last thing we wanted was civilians injured. Ryker was the one who came up with the idea of coming through windows on the second story."

"Good man, it got us out alive."

"Yeah, but fucking Miles, Kendall, or whatever the hell his name was, got away. We did capture one of his guys alive."

Gideon was getting impatient with the replay of events. "Okay, thanks for the blow-by-blow. Now that we know I only have trouble walking and talking, and nothing's wrong with my thinking, get me out of here."

Kostya sighed. "Gideon, I really—"

The door flew open and a pissed-off Ryker came into

the room. "Thank all that is holy, you're finally awake. Let's get you back to Kostya's. Jada is a royal pain in the ass without you there."

Gideon shot Kostya a 'told ya' look.

"Fine. I'll talk to your doctor," Kostya said with an air of resignation. As he started out the door, he turned to Ryker. "Keep his happy ass in bed until I'm back," he ordered.

"Aye, aye."

Kostya left.

Ryker looked around the room, then zeroed in on a little cupboard in the corner and opened it. "Shit, man, all that's in here are some grungy sweatpants. Can't smuggle you out in these. I'll be right back." Ryker left as fast as he came in.

Now Gideon's head was swimming again. He needed out of here. He needed to make sure Jada was okay. Flashes of her being tortured in that barrel of water, then scraped raw against the rusted sides would remain with him the rest of his life.

Besides that, there was Kendall Douglas. Bile rose in his mouth just thinking about the fact that because of him, Jada had been put through hell. Not just two days ago, but also the sexual trauma back in Oregon.

Set it aside. It's time to focus.

The door slammed open again. Ryker stood there holding a pair of scrubs. "I couldn't find shoes. This will have to do." He turned, then backed in a wheelchair. When the door closed behind him, he threw the scrubs at Gideon. "Dress."

Gideon had to take it slow, getting out of bed.

I hate this.

"Need help, grandpa?"

"Fuck you, Ryker." Gideon chuckled and finished dressing. "How's Jada?"

"Antsy. Hurting. Once again she's against the pain meds, but I think Lark has her turned around on that. She actually got Amy on speaker phone. The two of them wore Jada down. It was funnier than fuck." Ryker grimaced, instead of smiling.

Gideon wondered at his expression, then remembered that Ryker was still hung up on Amy. Gideon felt like a shitty friend for not finding out how things had been going between the two of them, but in all honesty, he'd had a lot on his plate.

"Got your cell phone with you? I need to talk to Kane and the others."

"Your geek squad?" Ryker asked.

"Yeah," Gideon reluctantly agreed to the crap name.

"Wait 'til I've got you in my Riviera."

"Are you telling me I don't get to ride bitch on your Harley? I'm hurt."

"If I had the Harley, I would have had you continue to wear your hospital gown so your ass would be showing," Ryker smirked. "Now enough with the chitter-chatter and plant your ass into the wheelchair."

Gideon sat down in the chair, and Ryker had them down the hall and at the banks of elevators in no time.

"Give me your cell phone," Gideon demanded again.

This time Ryker handed it over. Gideon dialed Kane's number from memory.

"Ryker? How's Gideon?" Kane asked. Ryker shoved the chair into the elevator.

"It's Gideon. In elevator. Going to lose you. Stay put." Gideon hung up and waited for them to get into the hospital lobby, then called Kane again.

"Thought you needed another day in the hospital," Kane commented.

"Yeah, well, you thought wrong. I'm headed to Jada. Need you to gather the team. Here's what's going on. Miles Albright is really a man named Kendall Douglas. Douglas used to head a gaming company in San Fran, called Streetgamezzz. He went to prison. When he got out, he had plastic surgery, killed Miles, and took over his identity a few years back."

"Jesus, is this for real?" Kane asked.

"Yep."

"Sounds like a James Bond movie."

"Yep. Especially when I tell you he considers me his arch nemesis and he went after Jada so he could hurt me. I was the one who sent him to prison."

"Motherfucker."

"He's out there, and he's plotting something. He said it would make him on par with Bezos and Musk. We've got a hell of a problem on our hands. I'm woozy, and I can't figure it out. We need everyone working on this." He glanced up at Ryker who was looking at him wide-eyed. "I should be with Jada in?" Ryker didn't respond.

"Ryker," Gideon said sharply. "How long to get to Jada?"

"Forty minutes, but I can make it in half that time."

"I'll call back in twenty minutes," Gideon told Kane.

"I'm bringing Rylie into this," Kane muttered.

"Huh?" Gideon asked. He didn't know anyone named Rylie. "I'm not willing to trust some guy named Rylie."

"Rylie is a woman, and she's married to Dare Stanton on the Midnight Delta team. Trust me, we want her."

"Okay. Get them all together in twenty." He hung up

the phone as Ryker parked the wheelchair at the lobby door.

"Are you good enough to walk to my car?" Ryker asked.

"Damn right I am."

"Good enough."

20

When Gideon walked through the door, it took everything Jada had not to burst into tears. She'd called her mother yesterday just so she could have that feeling of being hugged. She hated being so needy.

She wanted to get up off the couch and rush to Gideon, but her legs were becoming one big scab, so Gideon did the rushing.

"Jesus, Angel, look at you," he said as he knelt down beside her. He pulled her gently into his arms. He acted like she was spun glass, and God help her, this time she needed that.

Don't cry.

Don't cry.

She started crying.

"Sweetheart, I have you. I have you. Let it out."

Jada tucked her face into Gideon's neck, needing to smell him and feel the comfort that she could only get from him. His big hand gripped her nape and pressed her even closer.

"That's right, Angel, you cry as much as you need to.

I've got you, I'll always have you. Just remember one thing. We know who he is, and that bastard won't get you again."

"I don't care about that," Jada sobbed. "I thought he would kill you. You can't ever be dead. I love you too much. You're my everything."

"I love you too. I'm not going anywhere. Just hold on to me, I've got you."

Finally, Jada could take a free breath and she kissed Gideon's neck. Licked him. Proving to herself that he was here. Alive.

Gideon chuckled. "I guess they did get you to take the pain meds."

She pulled away so she could look him in the eye. He had such a warm and loving look on his face that she thought she would melt all over him.

"Yep, I took some pain meds. Lark's friend Amy threatened to come down from D.C. and whup my ass if I didn't. But what was worse was when Lark said she'd tell my mother what had happened."

"Brought out the big guns, did she?"

Jada nodded.

A phone rang. Jada turned around and looked at the coffee table to see if it was hers.

The front door opened.

"Goddammit, Chief Petty Officer Smith. When I tell you to stay in bed, I mean stay in bed!" Kostya's voice boomed across his living room and Jada winced.

Gideon pulled out a cell phone from the front chest pocket of the scrubs he was wearing.

"Yeah?" Gideon said into the phone. He looked up at the angry Kostya. "I'm going to need your laptop. Kane and the others have set up a Zoom call, and we need to log into it."

Kostya shook his head in disgust, then stomped over to a room off the side of the living room. Gideon stood up from his crouch and went to follow him.

"Now wait a damned minute. I might be injured, but you're not excluding me from this." Jada heard the whine in her voice and flinched.

"You're right, I'll bring the laptop out there," Gideon called from the other room.

"It's okay, I can come to you," Jada said as she started to move her legs.

"Get real," Gideon said as he came back into the front room holding the laptop. He set it down on the coffee table which he then pulled closer to Jada.

Gideon brushed his finger down her nose. "Stay put, I don't want you hurting any more than you already do. Of course you were going to be on the call, Angel," he assured her.

"And me," Kostya said.

"And me," Ryker called out.

"Don't forget about me," Lark said as she came in from the kitchen with a tray of snacks.

"Lark, you're definitely invited to be on the call; you brought food. Kostya's invited because it's his computer. Ryker, you're shit out of luck."

Ryker laughed. "That's the story of my life, but I will be listening in. Your story is too unbelievable, and since it's not a government mission, just a tiny little dust-up concerning your girlfriend, I can write the script for Hollywood and make my millions."

"Make him stop," Gideon groaned to Kostya.

"What is he talking about?" Kostya asked Gideon.

"You'll see," Ryker smirked.

Gideon pressed the button on the laptop to start up the Zoom call.

"What the hell, are we having a party?" Kane bitched. "We don't have time for this, Gideon. You said this guy is going to do something big, so we need to figure it out."

"Shut it, McNamara," a pretty blonde pixie said. "We need all hands on deck. In the twenty minutes since you gave me the info on Kendall Douglas, I can see we have a sociopath on our hands with a genius level I.Q. who doesn't mind killing people. I've accessed his prison records, and there is no way in hell he should have been let out on parole. It might have shown that he was a model prisoner, but according to the infirmary records at the Solano State Prison, he shanked three guys and one died."

"So why was he let go?" Dex asked.

"Because he got to those records and added a different middle initial to his name, and they never matched up to his permanent record."

"Good job, Rylie," Kane grinned. "How did you—"

"I'm good, it's what I do."

Jada loved it; this girl didn't bother with false modesty, and Jada suspected that the big, adoring man beside her might have something to do with it.

"Real fast, introduction time." Dex cut in. "Y'all just met Rylie Stanton; she's married to the big SEAL sitting next to her. He's on the Midnight Delta team, and his name is Dare Stanton."

Dare nodded.

"The grumpy guy is Kane McNamara, second-in-command and computer geek for Night Storm out of Little Creek, Virginia. Wave like a good boy, Kane," Dex commanded.

Kane raised his middle finger.

"We then have Clint and Lydia Archer. Clint is the computer and communications genius from Midnight Delta out of Coronado California, his wife runs circles around him. Wave." They both waved.

"I'm Dex Evans, the computer nerd from Black Dawn, also out of Coronado. Now it's your turn to do the introductions, Gideon. See if you can match my level of entertainment."

"Jesus, Dex, did someone put drugs in your Cheerios this morning?" Kane asked.

"Bet you Kenna was extra nice to him this morning," Clint grinned knowingly.

Jada stifled a giggle.

"I'm Gideon Smith," Gideon started. "I'm second-in-command of Omega Sky here at Little Creek, Virginia. The beauty beside me is Jada Harlow, and I'd put her skills up against all of yours."

"You go, girl," Rylie cried.

"Then we've got my Lieutenant, Kostya Barona standing behind the couch. He probably has his arms crossed and is looking grim." Gideon pointed his thumb behind him without even looking. "The goofy-looking guy next to him is Ryker McQueen. He's our breacher, which is probably how he made it into this meeting. The gorgeous woman seated to the right of Jada is Lark Sorensen. She is a top-notch investigative reporter and engaged to Kostya. Are we caught up now? Can we start the meeting, Dex?"

"You have my permission to begin," Dex said magnanimously.

GIDEON HATED THIS.

Hated this.

He'd never had a mission be so personal.

As he opened his mouth to speak, Jada slid her hand into his and tangled their fingers together so that they were palm to palm. Gideon felt himself calm down.

"That was outstanding work, Rylie, figuring out what Kendall had been up to in prison." Gideon praised. "I hope to God we can figure out the rest. I'm going to start from the beginning to get everybody up to speed who hasn't heard the situation. This will also make sure nothing was missed as the story was repeated to others."

Every person on the screen nodded.

"Jada was kidnapped twenty days ago after being hired six months and one week before that by a company called Risk Guard. Risk Guard's business model is to determine if potential clients are vulnerable to cyber threats. If they are, they come up with ways to stop those threats in their tracks and come up with ways to ensure that their security is bulletproof going forward."

"Let me guess, it's like a gym membership; they get you on the hook and you have to pay monthly dues forever," Ryker griped.

"You got it in one," Gideon nodded. "These clients can be cash cows on into perpetuity. Now, there are more than two-hundred-and-fifty employees at Risk Guard, but the CTO hired Jada for an obscene amount of money to work as a 1099 contractor and start trying to penetrate the security and firewalls of all new potential clients."

Rylie put her fist up in the air. "Righteous! I'm liking the obscene amount of money part. You rock!" Gideon looked over and he could see Jada blushing. He was liking Rylie more and more each minute.

"I agree with you Rylie, Jada is worth every penny, but Risk Guard had an ulterior motive. They have a guy on their Board of Directors, his name is Miles Albright. He's actually employed by Reynolds Inc., but he's very involved with Risk Guard. He became a board member three years ago."

"He's our bad guy? Not Kendall Douglas?" Rylie looked perplexed.

"Patience, Honey," Dare said to his wife.

Gideon continued. "Three years ago Risk Guard landed some huge clients. They really turned things around for their business. I'm not going to explain how, but it was Miles who arranged it by doing shady shit."

"Betchya I know how," Dex mumbled. All the other people on the Zoom call nodded.

"Anyway, now Risk Guard is the hot ticket for companies to come to, to check out their firewalls and security. That's where Jada comes in. The CTO sources her and hires her. Now Jada has a reputation for checking into the companies she works for, and it isn't long before she discovers the shady shit and is kidnapped. But she reaches out to me right before she's taken."

"Lucky for her." Kane frowned.

"This isn't a coincidence, is what you're telling us, right?" Clint asked.

"Nope, I'm the one they want on the hook. Turns out Kendall Douglas has killed the real Miles Albright. Twenty-five years ago I was the one who provided the evidence that sent him to prison. He has a vendetta against me. This last abduction was his big reveal. He explained everything to me, including the plastic surgery he'd had to look like Miles before he killed him."

"Holy shit," Jada breathed. "That is crazy."

Gideon gave her a tender hug, bringing her even closer, but ever mindful that he didn't hurt her. "I'm so sorry, Jada. I can't believe I brought this down on you," he whispered.

He was met by silence for a long moment, then he watched a fierce look overtake his woman's face. "I will whoop your ass if you take on guilt for this. We're dealing with a psychotic bastard who sees himself as some kind of super-villain straight out of a comic book."

She turned to the people on the screen. "Could any of you guess that something like this would be done in real life?"

Rylie tentatively raised her hand.

"Figures," Clint said, shaking his head. "Rylie's already lived a double life. She's not psychotic, but she's definitely walked a tightrope between reality and Hollywood shit."

Dare looked like he was in pain.

"That's great!" Jada exclaimed.

"Rylie, you're our secret weapon," Lydia grinned.

"What are you talking about?" Kostya demanded to know.

"I don't get it," Ryker complained.

"This could work," Kane smiled.

"Just hold on. Before we figure that Rylie can work magic, let me finish my story," Gideon interrupted everyone.

The team nodded their heads. Gideon continued. "As he's bragging about what an evil genius he is, we talk about Sid Bonham and what he was working on, and then the bastard says he's going to rule the world. He says that he's going to be bigger than Jeff Bezos and Elon Musk."

"Come again?" Ryker said.

"Yeah, it's not making sense to me, either. But I think

fucking with me was just an opportunity that presented itself, and it was too good to pass up. He's always been planning something else. Something big. It has to do with the tech that Bonham was working on."

"Okay, what was Bonham working on?" Dex asked.

"He was working on ways to physically introduce things that could be directly installed onto a company's firmware. This would make it virtually impossible to detect."

"How about to kill?" Kostya asked.

"We could stop it, once we know what it is. We just have to write and install the correct virus. Installing the virus is going to be the problem. If Kendall somehow figured out a way to get into the firmware, that means he was physically onsite. Meanwhile, we have to either get onsite or find a zero-day to get into their systems remotely."

"What's a zero-day?" Lark asked.

"It's a vulnerability that the target doesn't realize they have. That's where Kendall or any other bad actor would install malware."

"Got it," Lark responded.

"So all we have to figure out what he's planning and stop it. That's not going to be hard at all," Ryker added sarcastically.

"We need to come at this a few different ways. Dex, start taking notes," Gideon ordered. "First, we need to try to track down where Kendall is. Next, we need to figure out what his over-the-top master plan is and stop it. Third, we have Naomi Sims in custody in Oregon. She's the sister of Kendall's girlfriend, so maybe she has some ideas on how to track her. Fourth, we need to create some kind of malware that will counteract the firmware that would be corrupting the target, whatever it is. Let's parse out the jobs."

"I'm on for Naomi," Lark said. "I can get a flight today. I have a knack for getting in to see people, and then getting them talking."

"Boy does she," Kostya grinned.

"Okay, next?" Gideon asked.

"I want the over-the-top master plan," Rylie said.

"Sounds like you'd be our girl for that," Gideon agreed.

"Rylie, let's team up since we have so often in the past," Lydia said. Rylie gave a thumbs up.

"I'll watch the police interview on the guy at the warehouse and check out his past. My gut says he's going to be worthless, but we need to tie up that loose end," Dex said.

"Jada, how about you and I check out Bonham's work, then build some malware that would counteract his firmware?" Kane asked.

Jada nodded.

"That leaves me with finding Kendall." Gideon rubbed his hands together with a satisfied smile on his face.

21

"This is so frustrating, it's been four days and we hardly have anything," Jada complained.

Gideon cared, but he was so relieved to see Jada's body beginning to heal he was having a tough time focusing on their operation. Despite what she said about 'whooping his ass' he felt guilty for the pain, danger, and suffering she'd gone through. When she let slip the little nugget of information that the water in the oil barrel had been seawater, he wanted to kill someone.

"Are you done with dinner?" Gideon asked. They were now staying at a beach house rental overlooking Grove's Beach, five minutes from base. This allowed Lark to come check in on Jada when Gideon went to work.

"You know, Honey, you don't have to keep waiting on me. I'm really feeling pretty good. The salves they've given me have really worked on most of the scrapes, and I'm not feeling stiff at all. What's more, the doc said that even the cut on my arm isn't going to scar, so it's all good."

Gideon cupped her jaw, his thumb brushing her bottom lip. "I can see you healing right before my eyes. As for scars, you've seen mine. I wouldn't care how many you acquire—just not because of me, okay?"

She grabbed his hand away from her face. "Okay, Gideon," she said right before placing a kiss in the middle of his palm.

She heard him hiss.

"I was planning on taking the dirty dishes into the kitchen," he said huskily. "Maybe rinse them off and put them in the dishwasher."

Still holding his hand, she trailed her tongue down to the base of his thumb and then gently—or not so gently— bit down.

Gideon groaned. "To hell with the dishes."

His free hand sank into her hair until he was gripping the back of her head, he angled her and then swooped in for a deep kiss. Boy, did that man know how to kiss.

Jada let go of his hand and slid both of her palms up his chest until they finally wound around his neck. His lips tasted hers and coaxed her mouth open. He thrust his tongue inside, invading and overwhelming her senses. Jada's head would have fallen backward if it weren't for his steady hold.

Jada tried to match his onslaught, but she couldn't, she just couldn't. Gideon was fully in charge, and she loved every moment of it. The kiss was unlike any they had shared before; it was as if Gideon was claiming her on a cellular level, and Jada's soul felt and welcomed the claiming. Gideon was relentless in the way that he gave her pleasure. His tongue stroked against hers, then when she needed air, he took the opportunity to bite her bottom lip. The sting morphed into pleasure as he licked it better.

His kiss makes me feel like I'm flying.

She let out a giggle when she figured out he was

carrying her out of the dining room and she hadn't even realized it. He was holding her gently against his chest.

"Please say you're heading to our bedroom," Jada whispered.

"You're such a smart woman." He grinned. "It's one of the many things I love about you."

She cuddled closer to him and let herself bask in his tender treatment. When they got to the bedroom, he laid her softly on the light blue comforter and crouched beside the bed. She saw him eyeing her legs.

"You better be admiring my legs in these short-shorts, not obsessing about a few scrapes," Jada warned.

Gideon chuckled. "Thank God I'd already swallowed my sip of OJ when you came into the kitchen this morning, otherwise I would have choked on it. If you ever decide to stop wearing those shorts, we need to have them bronzed."

Jada smirked. "Then my evil plan worked."

"What evil plan?"

"We haven't made love since we got here, even after I threw myself at you last night."

"Angel, I was worried about your injuries." Gideon's brown eyes still showed concern as he glanced back at her legs.

"So, we take things slow. I know you know how to do that, Gideon, and don't tell me you don't want this. I checked your nightstand, you stashed condoms in there."

She saw him flush.

Gotcha!

"I'd be an idiot not to bring condoms when I knew I was going to be sharing a bed with you."

Jada felt herself relax, knowing they were going to

make love. She gripped the bottom of her crop top, but he stopped her.

"Let me. You're my present, and I want to unwrap you."

"Is that a pun?"

"Yep, not only are you a gift, you're my present, my future, and my forever."

Jada's eyes stung as Gideon got up and sat on the side of the bed. He pulled her shirt over her head, winding the thin cloth around her wrists. Jada's legs began to get restless as she felt her nipples tighten and her panties dampen.

"No fair," she whispered. "I want to touch you."

"So fair," Gideon disagreed. "We agreed on slow, and when you touch me, I can't go slow." He unclipped the front fastening of her bra and hissed with pleasure as her breasts fell into his hands. "You are the perfect size for me to caress." He rolled both nipples between his thumbs and forefingers for long moments until Jada whimpered, moaned, then called out his name. Then he got serious and sucked one of her sensitive buds into his mouth, driving her insane.

"I've got to touch you," Jada panted.

He let go of her left breast so that it could wander down her stomach, then tickle her navel, before unbuttoning and unzipping her shorts. He looked up at her, his pupils blown.

"Angel," he groaned. He got up and knelt in front of her, then took off her shorts and panties, being careful not to hurt her scrapes. When he was done, his finger skimmed the seam of her sex, finding her wet and wanting. Jada spread her legs, inviting more of his touch. When he started to lower his head, she quickly closed her legs again.

"Oh no, I want your cock. I've been dreaming of being filled by you."

He gave her a long look. Then nodded. "Well, it's Wednesday, and that *is* traditionally Ladies' Night." Gideon waggled his eyebrows.

Jada giggled, but her laughter soon stopped as she watched the man she loved and lusted after strip out of his clothes.

And he's all mine.

Jada worked a little harder on untangling her hands and succeeded. Then with a defiant look, she sat up and slid the fingers of both hands around his cock and looked up at him.

"Ladies' choice." She took the head of his shaft into her mouth, savoring his warmth, loving the clean and spicy taste of him. She sucked him deeper, circling his thick penis the best she could with her hand, and started stroking him up and down as she licked and sucked... licked and sucked.

Is that me humming?

She was lost in the daze of pleasuring Gideon, of the sensuality of the moment, and she whimpered when he backed up and caressed her jaw. "Just a moment, Angel. Lie back."

She wanted.

She needed.

Gideon rounded the bed and took a condom out of the nightstand and was back to her in a moment. He knelt beside her, tenderly moving her to the center of the bed, giving her a kiss, then touching the side of her nose, making her smile.

"I love you so much, Jada Harlow."

She didn't know how it had happened. It was as if all

of her dreams had coalesced into one and here, she was, with this man who was her everything.

He brushed the one lonely tear that slid down the side of her face, almost making it to her smile.

"Being loved by you is a gift beyond measure."

His big hand drifted down her sternum toward her sex. Jada's legs relaxed, welcoming his touch. He caressed the unblemished skin of her inner thighs. He smiled when she opened further so that he could touch her intimately. When he was sure she was ready for him, he carefully positioned both of her thighs around his hips and watched her face for any signs of discomfort.

Jada cupped the side of his neck and looked him in the eye. "Honey, I'm fine."

Silly man.

When he finally filled her, it was sublime, but even better was watching the look on Gideon's face. Relief and joy. She kept her hand on his neck as he bent and sucked her nipple into his mouth. Electricity jolted throughout her entire body. Soon she couldn't feel or think of anything else but Gideon's strong thrusts and the way he caressed and sucked her breasts.

"Look at me," Gideon demanded as he nipped her chin.

Jada lifted her lids as far as she was able, seeing the power in his eyes.

"Yes," he smiled. "I want to get lost in your eyes."

Those few words shot her over into ecstasy.

JADA GIGGLED when they heard the distinctive tones of texts coming into both of their phones simultaneously.

They were just meandering back into the beach house's office where they'd set up their computers.

"Group text," she said needlessly. "Your timing is impeccable, Mr. Smith."

He bent down and captured her lips for a kiss.

Their phones beeped again but they took their time ending the kiss. When they were done, it was back to business. The office setup was sweet—there was a large, curved desk that overlooked the ocean and could seat two. Gideon had brought in his whole setup from his house, so once again it looked like tech geek central. He logged into the Zoom invite and everyone but Ryker and Kostya popped up.

"Who's moderator?" Gideon asked.

"Last one to join is stuck moderating," Dex said as he took a sip of his grape Fanta.

"Dammit," Gideon muttered.

Before he could say anything else, Jada started.

"Okay, Lark, we all got your encrypted e-mail with the info you got from Jenny's sister." Jada didn't want to say her name, so she didn't. "There wasn't a lot of meat on the bone; did you get any nuances or hunches that didn't make it into the factual report?"

Lark nodded. "I did. Now let me preface this by saying I'm not a psychologist, just took a few classes in college, but I'd classify her as a sexually deviant narcissist. That made it really difficult to get her to talk about her sister, unless it somehow included her."

Jada shuddered at Lark's description of Naomi. Gideon pushed his chair closer to hers and put his arm around her. She let out what she hoped was an unnoticeable deep sigh.

Lark continued. "She's proud of her big sister, and

she's proud of herself. Made a big deal of her social media accounts, both individual and those she shared with her sister. I've checked them out, and some of them connect to dark places. I'm hunting those down. This could totally be a dead-end, but I'm hoping there is some possibility that Jenny might have posted something about Miles/Kendall."

"Great work," Jada complimented her. "I think you're really onto something."

"How dark is dark?" Dex asked.

"Stuff that just shouldn't exist," Lark said with a grimace.

"Unfortunately, I've worked on ops that have required me to check that kind of shit out, so I've got you covered. I can work with you," Dex promised.

Lark smiled and nodded.

"Also, you got my encrypted e-mail that told you your guy from the warehouse was nothing more than hired muscle, former military hired out of Texas. He's got nothing, he just came into town a week ago," Dex reported.

"Yeah, we got that," Jada acknowledged. "I'm sorry you and Lark have the ick duty, but I think it has possibilities." Jada turned her eyes to Kane. "Kane, why don't you update them on what we figured out since our e-mail."

Kane squinted into the screen. "I took a little trip to New York City. By the way, Lark and Jada, hate your hometown, just saying."

Lark laughed.

"Quit putting down the greatest city on earth and give them the good stuff, Kane," Jada prompted.

"Anyway, hypothetically, I might have remembered to look up my old buddy Sid Bonham, and when he didn't answer his door, I let myself in. I knew he wouldn't mind. What's more, my backup external hard drive might have fallen into his computer and accidentally copied his shadow computer's hard drive."

"You always were kind of clumsy," Gideon chuckled. "Even when I knew you back in the day in Silicon Valley."

"Yep, it hasn't changed," Kane said with a hint of a grin.

Jada gave Gideon a hard look. She hadn't known that Kane and Gideon had a connection outside of the SEALs. How did she not know this? Jada gave herself a mental shake and got back to business. "Yeah, yeah, you're clumsy, but when you got home after visiting Times Square and the M&M store, tell them what we found on Bonham's computer," she ordered Kane.

"You tell them, you're the one that figured it out," Kane said with a smile.

"Okay." Jada cleared her throat. "Bonham was definitely old school. He was thinking just like a spy back in the cold war days, so you have to put yourself into his mindset. They had some pretty sweet operations back in the day, even with the limited tech they had. So, Bonham was trying to figure out different ways that you could get the firmware installed into different companies' systems. His best effort, which he didn't share with Risk Guard, was installing the virus into people's phone's connection cords, and then if they charged or paired them with their company laptop, they would then drop the malicious firmware into the laptop port via the connection cord."

"If he's doing firmware, wouldn't that have only captured the stuff on that laptop? Isn't that how firmware works? I'm confused," Lark admitted.

"I'm sorry, I should be saying firmware malware. As

opposed to a software virus that works on your applications, firmware malware can and will, depending on the bad-guy, corrupt high-privilege layers. Compromised firmware will then screw with *all* of your software and allow remote access to your machine, and to answer your question, Lark, because the firmware is also malware, it spreads like the virus it is."

Lark shuddered.

"We've got you covered, Lark," Gideon assured her. "Remember when you left your laptop behind that day you went up and visited Amy in D.C.? I put in some serious, and I'm talking serious, security. You're safe now."

"Gonna have to talk to Kostya about being less sneaky but let me thank you, Gideon, for covering my ass," she smiled.

"Well, we get the idea of what he was thinking to install the firmware. It's not bad, but it's not great. Did he have something developed that he could attach to the phone cords?" Clint asked.

"Yep," Jada answered.

"Now that's interesting. Can you replicate it?" Dex asked.

"Kane can," Jada immediately answered.

"This *is* good stuff. Great job, you two," Gideon gave her a blinding smile. Having him so impressed was almost as good as sex with him...almost.

Jada turned back to the computer screens. "Okay, Rylie, you and your team are up. You didn't send up an update, so I figured you'd hit a wall."

"We had," she said. The problem with this project is, there aren't really any strings to follow. It's more trying to think like he does and figure out what he might be doing,"

Rylie admitted. "But in the last day, the three of us began to have some ideas."

"Lay them out," Jada requested.

"Obviously, Kendall likes playing different roles," Lydia began. "Kendall played Miles, but even while he was Miles he was playing at being the CTO at Reynolds and also the mover and shaker board member at Risk Guard."

Everybody nodded in agreement.

"So, it makes sense that he might have another persona he's ready to slip into when the Miles one was uncovered."

Again, everybody nodded, but Jada moved closer to the monitors, and Gideon, God bless him, moved with her, his arm remaining around her shoulder.

"Kane, you should have told me you were going to Manhattan," Rylie said with a big grin. "You could have met up with a good friend of mine, Melvin Powers. He ended up taking a trip to Miles Albright's penthouse apartment with another friend of ours, Aretha Heyer."

"Aretha Heyer, the model?" Lark asked.

"Yeah, that Aretha Heyer," Rylie replied. "Thanks to her, they were let up to the top floor. Anyway, Melvin scoured Miles/Kendall's home and found something hinky. He had an extensive library, but a lot of it was not on tech, it was on History, specifically on medieval law. I mean a lot, a lot of books. He took pictures."

"And his computer?" Jada asked.

"Everything was wiped clean. He found nothing." Rylie sighed, but then grinned. "But Aretha noticed something else."

"What else? Don't keep us in suspense." Dex was clearly exasperated.

"There were four books throughout the library all about Loyola University. When Melvin did a quick check, he found a class taught at Loyola called Medieval Crime and Community. It's been taught online by a new professor for the last six months, by the name of Gideon Rydell. The picture of the guy is blurry, but I would say it's him!"

"Hell, when does he have time to juggle all of this?" Kane wanted to know.

"I don't know who this Melvin guy is, but tell him I love him," Jada grinned.

Gideon gave her hair a firm tug, and Jada smiled even bigger. "Okay, so we know who his next persona is, but he could be located anywhere."

"And he still is planning something big, and my gut is telling me it's going to be soon," Gideon reminded the team. "Let's share all the compiled information that we have and see what we can come up with in the next twenty-four hours."

Jada's fingers ached to start in on her keyboard. "Agreed," Kane said, then his Zoom window went blank. Four more windows went blank almost simultaneously, which left Jada and Gideon staring at one another.

"Ready to get to it?" Gideon asked.

"Absolutely."

22

JADA YAWNED FOR THE SECOND TIME IN TWENTY MINUTES. "Do you want me to brew another pot of coffee?" she asked Gideon.

"Angel it's after one in the morning."

She smiled. "I can tell time, thank you very much, I just wanted to know if you wanted to join me as I have another cup of that delicious blend of Kona coffee that our hosts left for us."

Gideon shook his head in defeat. "Yeah. That sounds good."

She went over and kissed the top of his head, then left the office. Gideon picked up his phone and called Kane.

"I take it Jada's not with you," Kane said as he answered the phone.

"Affirmative."

"Dex and Lark are going down a dead end, but that keeps Lark out of anything heavy," Kane said.

"Agreed. I already explained that to Kostya. He was relieved," Gideon replied.

"I don't think it matters one little bit that your enemy is

some history professor, we're not going to find him that way. That was his backup-backup plan if he had to totally drop out. He's not dropping out. He's going to go for the gusto."

"Not only that," Gideon said. "Like this little side history thing he had going with Loyola, he's had his big event planned for months or even a year. As you go through Bonham's computer, check for any sign of a security breach. My guess is that Kendall has known about Bonham's shadow computer since the beginning, and he's already modified his firmware malware."

"Okay, if that's your supposition," Kane mused, "then why kidnap and torture him?"

"My gut tells me they wanted to know if he'd shown any of the tech to anyone at Risk Guard. Remember, they said something about him leaking information."

"I like it. You're firing on all cylinders tonight, Chief. So how do we make sure that the women stay safe?"

"I want them all working with Rylie," Gideon said. "Somehow we need to arrange it so they are all working on tracing Kendall via Loyola, while you, Dex, and me work on the firmware and how he might have improved it, then who he would target."

"Why not Clint?" Kane asked.

"I'm thinking he wouldn't be able to get this past Lydia."

Kane chuckled. "I think you're right. I also think you're skating on thin ice, my friend."

"I hope not. I want Jada safe. She's been through enough."

"You'll get no objection from me."

"Got to go, I hear her coming back."

"Good luck, Gideon."

Two days later the email came in a half hour before their Zoom call. It came to Gideon's personal e-mail account that he only shared with his very close friends, and he didn't recognize the sender.

He had a bad feeling.

"What's up?" Jada asked as she continued to work on code beside him. She must have felt him tense up.

"We'll see," Gideon said as he clicked to open the e-mail.

YOUR FRIENDS ARE IMPRESSIVE. I LIKED ARETHA HEYER TOUCHING MY PERSONAL THINGS. SO GLAD WE GOT A CHANCE TO CATCH UP. FINDING OUT THE PATHETIC LIFE YOU ARE LIVING GIVES ME PLEASURE. AND YOUR MOTHER? SO SAD THAT YOU DON'T TALK. IF YOU DID, MAYBE YOU'D LEARN SOMETHING.

BEST WISHES,
KENDALL DOUGLAS

"What the fuck?! He's dragged Ma into his psychotic games?"

For a moment he looked to Jada to disagree, to tell him he was reading the message wrong, but she didn't.

"He's left a clue for you with her. It's part of his over-the-top master plan," she whispered.

"My mother?!" He slammed his fist so hard on the desk that the wood cracked.

Jada stood up and placed her hands on his shoulders. "Gideon, Honey, you need to calm down. You're giving him the exact reaction that he wants."

"But, Angel, it might not be a clue, she could be the target. He could be out there planning on killing her right now. Or worse, planning on kidnapping her, like he did with you."

She curled her hands around the sides of his neck and forced him to look her dead in the eye. "Listen to me. You do two things. You call your brother Mike and have him check in with your mother. If she doesn't answer, have him pull some strings with the nearby precinct to do an immediate welfare check. Got that?"

Gideon closed his eyes and blew out a deep breath. "And the other thing?"

"Trace that motherfucking e-mail, find out where he is."

His eyes squinted, his mouth grim. "On it."

Jada was handling the Zoom call as Gideon was on a three-way conversation with his mother and brother. Jada had heard the start of it and she wanted to start crying. It hurt to hear her man's voice damn near tremble as he talked to his mother for the first time in almost twenty years. But she couldn't think about that now, she had a job to do.

"Since Gideon could get ahold of his mother and she's

all right, we've got to assume she has some kind of message from Kendall."

"What happens if she doesn't realize what it is and can't tell Gideon about it."

"He'll get it out of her," Jada assured Lydia.

"Anybody have anything new to report since yesterday?"

"We do," Lark and Dex said at the same time.

"You go," Dex said, deferring to Lark.

"There's this dating site for sadists, but you can only be invited in if somebody has met you in person and can vouch for you."

"Lovely," Lydia grimaced.

"It gets worse. When I dug down deeper, I found that there was a spot that showed where people were putting themselves up for auction as sex slaves, and men, women, and couples were buying them. I told you, sick. That's where I found Naomi and Jenny; they were auctioneers."

Jada trembled and forced back her nausea.

"Are you fucking kidding me?" Dare Stanton damn near shouted. "We work our asses off to stamp this shit out, and people are selling themselves into that kind of life?"

"Honey, calm down." Riley grabbed his arm and laid her head against it. "It's not our place to judge. It's really not."

"It is when you see some of these kids who look like they just graduated high school, if that," Dex said grimly. "This is definitely something we're going to be sending to the F.B.I."

"But, let's get back to the sicko sisters. They actually have a page where they offer their auctioneering services. Lots of pictures, including just candid shots. That's when I spotted our guy. And we were in luck. Naomi tagged this to every damned account she could think of, which included a social media account owned by one K.D. Smith."

"How long and how far has his grudge gone for Gideon? He even has an alias using his name?" Clint asked incredulously.

"Seems like," Dex answered. "We're pulling that string as we speak."

"Anything else?" Jada looked at all of the tired faces. Everybody else shook their heads. "Okay, let's just wait until Gideon joins us."

"How are you doing, Jada?" Lydia asked. "I've been in your shoes, having someone hurt me."

"Fuck, baby, call it what it was," Clint said as he put his arm around his wife. "They tortured you."

Lydia nodded. "So how are you doing, Jada?" she asked again.

She could actually see on the woman's face that Lydia had been through the same kind of thing that she had. "I'm getting there," Jada said. "I'm almost all healed."

"Your body is healed, but what about the psychological scars?"

Jada snuck a peak at the other faces on the screen. All she saw were men and women looking at her with compassion.

"Yeah, and the bad dreams," Jada admitted. "It helps that I'm not sleeping alone."

Lydia grinned. "Yes, that helped me a lot during my recovery, too."

Jada could hear Gideon coming back into the room. She turned to catch a glimpse of him before he sat down. His face showed nothing. No emotion.

Her heart sank.

"Kendall sent something to my mother at her church. It was an offer of funds from a new donor who wanted to remain anonymous. The donor had one caveat—they wanted a portion of the funds to be used to purchase computers and start a youth class to learn basic coding skills."

"So how do you know this is from Kendall? Did it say his name?" Jada asked.

"No, like I said it was anonymous, but he suggested the classes teach the kids the basics of social media and how to limit their exposure in order to have a balanced life. She and the Pastor really liked everything they were reading, until they got to the end of the letter. He had provided them with a link for more information, and to register for the donation."

Gideon shook his head.

"What, baby?" Jada prompted.

"I went to it. It seemed innocuous enough until you scrolled further down the registration page and saw where Kendall had candid shots of Mikey, his two boys, and me. It was at a barbeque last year. There was a sentence underneath that said, *Look to the children, they predict our future.*"

"When did this letter come in?" Clint asked.

"Two days ago."

"Your mother didn't immediately talk to Mike?" Kane asked incredulously.

"That was Mike's response. He lost it," Gideon said. He was still unemotional. "Mike left to pull his boys out of school. He didn't know what all had been going on with me, or what I'd been working on, but as soon as there was a hint that his kids could be part of this mess, he wanted them safe."

"Where is he taking them?" Kane asked.

"He's trying to figure that out," Gideon admitted.

"He can stay at my house at the lake. There's plenty of space for him and the boys until this blows over."

"Appreciated," Gideon nodded. "I just wanted to take a minute to update all of you, before heading over to their house. There has to be something there that will lead me to Kendall's next fucking clue. He's trying to lead me around like a fish on a hook."

"I'm going with you," Jada said.

Gideon glanced over at her and nodded.

FELIX, the genius in the family, was able to pinpoint the clue as soon as Gideon explained they were looking for a message that might have been relayed to either him or Kyle.

"I didn't think it was anything but a bug, Uncle Gideon," Felix explained as he took him to the family room and turned on the large flatscreen television set.

"What?" his father asked him.

"I can't remember it exactly. I figured some programmer was just fooling around and forgot that they wrote a message to another programmer and left it in the code, and their QC team sucked. It's in my Lego Star Wars Skywalker video game."

"Call it up," Mike ordered.

Felix grimaced. Gideon immediately guessed the problem.

"What level was it on?" Gideon asked.

"Twenty-three or twenty-four, I think, and I'm way past that." Felix looked at his uncle in consternation. "I'm sorry, I didn't really read the message, I just blew past it. I'm not sure how to go backwards." By that time Felix had the game pulled up and Mike, his young son Kyle, Felix, Jada, and Gideon were all looking at the television screen.

"Can I take control?" Gideon asked.

"Yeah, sure." Felix was obviously relieved.

Gideon immediately saw that both Kyle and Felix were listed as players. He looked down at his four-year-old nephew. "Hey, champ, do you like playing the Lego game?" he asked.

Kyle nodded. "But I'm not good like Felix. I watch him, and I learned. But I like Mario."

Gideon grinned. "Good choice. I like Mario too."

"Wanna play?" Kyle asked.

"Maybe later."

Gideon handed the controller back to Felix. "Play as Kyle, he's only at level two. Get it up to twenty-three, and then we'll see the message."

"You bet," Felix said eagerly. I can do it real fast, I'm good at this now."

"I know you are, kid."

"How long, Felix?" Mike asked his son.

"Maybe a half hour."

Gideon raised his eyebrows, he was impressed.

"Let's go to the kitchen and I'll get you some coffee," Mike suggested. Gideon and Jada followed him as he left the room. While they were in the kitchen, Gideon explained to his brother where Kane's lake house was.

"I thought it went good with Ma," Mike said tentatively.

"Let's not go there right now, 'kay?" Gideon asked.

"We're going to need to discuss this. She talked to you, Gideon, that was huge. I've been telling you that things have changed. This proved it. I know you think you did wrong, but you didn't. If you talk to her, Ma would see that. She'd understand. She'd realize there's nothing to forgive."

"That's not true, Mikey. That's just not true."

"Uncle Gideon," Felix cried from the other room. "I have it!"

The three of them rushed to the family room. Gideon immediately spotted what Felix had been talking about. He could see why his nephew thought it was a coding error. He read the message.

A SMART MAN WOULD KNOW THE END ALWAYS STARTS AT THE BEGINNING.

It took him seconds to think it through, and when he did, he was furious with himself. He pulled out his phone and pulled up streetgamer.com. It was what Streetgamezzz.com had eventually morphed into after the bankruptcy and restructuring. He found the list of board members, and there was the new guy—a history professor by the name of Gideon Rydell. It gave his personal website address. Gideon clicked on it.

Kendall Douglas' smiling face appeared.

"You found me! I'm so proud of you, Gideon. Maybe I did teach you something after all. I finally figured out why you joined the Navy and had to become a SEAL. You just had to punish yourself after your father died. So much guilt." Kendall looked at him sadly and shook his head.

"So, there you were, going on mission after mission, trying to save the world to make up for your sins. Well, I'll give you the chance to really make a difference. Not that you'll be able to."

Kendall laughed, and Gideon's flesh crawled. He felt Mike and Jada watching on either side of him.

"Listen to this web address carefully, then you'll see what I have planned. You may have minutes to stop me, hours, or maybe even a day. Depends how quick you were on the uptake. I'd wish you luck, but I wouldn't mean it." The screen went blank.

Gideon was vaguely aware of Jada texting. He assumed it was to the tech group, but he was too busy typing in the address.

23

"Boys, go to your rooms."

"But, Dad," Felix whined.

"Now," Mike said.

Jada watched as both of Gideon's nephews trudged out of the room. Mike had already set her up at the home computer in the corner of the family room. It was an older Dell, but it would get the job done. She could hear something coming from Gideon's phone, but she didn't have time to care. Everybody needed to be hearing everything at the same time.

Rylie had set up a Zoom call in a joint e-mail. She clicked on it and immediately saw everybody but Dex Evans. Kostya was on the same screen as Lark.

"I'm doing a screen share now, so we can all watch whatever message Kendall has for Gideon. I think this is his final big play."

"This is it, huh?" she heard Ryker whisper behind her.

Kostya must have called him to come over to Mike's house she thought.

She turned around and besides having Gideon on one

side of her and Mike on the other, Ryker and Nolan were behind her. She moved the monitor so everyone could see.

"Everybody ready?" she asked.

After everybody either nodded or said yes, she changed the view on Zoom so everyone could see her internet window on her screen, then clicked on the web address. They could all still hear one another.

"Check it out, this is set up as a pre-post," Jada pointed out.

"Wait a sec," Lydia said. "Am I seeing what I think I'm seeing? Has he configured this so that it can go up on social media and potentially all news media and streaming channels?"

"That'd be pretty tough to do," Clint said.

"But doable," Gideon said over Jada's shoulder. "We all could do it with enough time, and this bastard has been planning this for God knows how long."

"Yeah," Kane sighed.

"Look at the clock on the post. It's set to eastern standard time. We've got ten-and-a-half hours before it is set to go live." Gideon gritted out the words.

"Let me play the video," Jada said quietly, aching for Gideon, but knowing that she needed to focus on the task at hand.

Kendall Douglas came on screen. It was the best he'd looked since Jada has been introduced to the man. She was positive he was wearing make-up. Beside him was Jenny Sims, and Jada was almost blinded by her white teeth and cleavage.

"Check out that green screen backdrop," Rylie noted. "It looks like someplace you'd find in Dubai."

"Hello, my fellow Americans," he started to talk. "I'm

so glad we get to have this time together. Allow me to introduce myself. My name is Kendall Douglas."

Jenny scooted even closer to him and whispered into his ear.

"Oh yes, and this is the lovely Jenny Sims." He glanced down at her and shook his head. "She has her uses, but this is my show. Now, I'm sorry to interrupt your regularly scheduled bit of mind-numbing mush, but this is important—at least it is if you, or someone you know and like, lives near water and wants to continue living." He gave a fond smile to the camera.

"Did you know the United States has over ninety thousand dams? I didn't think so. What do they teach in our schools these days? Anyway, I have the capability to unleash four hundred and eight of them at my fingertips. Again, let me dumb that down. By unleash, I mean, open them up and make the water come out. That would be bad, right?"

He chuckled and held up his phone. "I created my own application called 'I don't give a dam.' Clever, huh? Anyway, this app is only available to me. And there are a couple of different settings. The one I like the best is where I will give you an example of what I can do. After all, why would I want to destroy all four hundred and seven when I could just destroy one, give you an example of my power, and get rich?"

He sighed. "Jenny, hold my phone for a moment, and for the love of God, don't press any buttons. I need to make something clear to everyone, especially all those one-percenters."

He handed off the phone to Jenny, who immediately giggled and slipped it into her cleavage.

"Now I'm not blackmailing the government. That's so

tedious and usually takes an act of Congress to get anything done, and I hate waiting... So, I'm coming directly to you, the people who care."

His grin stretched from ear to ear. "I'm thinking that many of you little fellows might want to donate five or ten bucks to save your ass. And then there are the one percenters; you know, the poor little rich boys who like to send rockets to the moon. Maybe they should donate a little more, don't you think? After all, they've made so much off your backs, shouldn't they pony up some to save their fellow Americans?"

"Now boys and girls, I'm not made like most people. I can't be reasoned with, and it will just make me giggle when I use my fun little app, so I suggest y'all start digging in your couch cushions because in the next forty-eight hours I will destroy four hundred and seven of the ninety thousand dams here in America. Who knows, maybe it will be a dam near you. Now, wouldn't that be fun?"

He smiled big into the camera.

"Friends, I want you to think of this as the world's biggest GoFundMe, and to make it really interesting, your names will be shown next to the amount you donate. This will be displayed in real-time as you donate. Nothing like a little bit of peer pressure."

Jenny giggled.

"Since there are four hundred and seven dams, I'm looking to raise twenty million a dam. That's a tad bit over eight billion dollars. That's not a bad investment. Oh, and for those of you who worry about little 'ole me, you don't have to. I have a way to get the funds converted to an actual safe, untraceable crypto-currency so I can enjoy my well-earned money."

He trailed his fingers over the top of Jenny's breasts and pulled out his phone.

"Now remember when I said I had the ability to unleash four hundred and eight, and then changed the number to four hundred and seven? I do hope that at least a minuscule number of you noticed," he said with a sigh. "Anyway, that's because I'm going to let the waters loose right now on the lucky residents of....drumroll please."

He handed Jenny the type of envelope that you would see at the Academy Awards. She opened it.

"Now tell our lucky guests who today's winner is."

She smiled up into the camera, then looked down at the card and read, "Warren County and Alle...Alleg..." Jenny looked up at Kendall helplessly.

"Oh for fuck's sake. I told you she was only good for one thing. Anyway, the fortunate people near Allegheny National Forest in Warren County, Pennsylvania will be getting a tad wet in just a few hours as I...oops, I can't tell you how I'm going to unleash the water from the Kinzua Dam, just know that I will. It's always so much more horrifying to leave it to your imaginations. I wish you all the luck in the world getting out of the way of the floodwaters..."

He gave a jaunty wave, then looked at Jenny.

"For God's sake, woman, wave goodbye to our viewers."

"Oh, sorry, Miles." She started to wave.

"Women. Useless, I say. Useless." Kendall gave a disgusted sigh.

He held up his phone and waggled it, then grinned right before the video ended.

THE SILENCE WAS DEAFENING EVEN when Jada flipped the Zoom screen so everyone was looking at one another.

"Who called him a comic book villain?" Dare Stanton asked.

"That'd be my woman," Gideon answered, referring to Jada.

"Ten and a half hours?" Clint said.

"Ten hours and fifteen minutes, now," was Gideon's answer. He was still in shock. It was like he was looking at everything from a forty-thousand-foot level. Normally he would be working out the problem and coming up with plans A, B, C, and D.

He heard a noise behind him, but he didn't turn around. He couldn't. He was still watching himself and Jada as they looked at Mike's computer.

Jada stood up and turned to him. "This is not because of you," she said fiercely.

"Fuck no, it isn't," Kostya said from his place on the screen where he was sitting beside Lark.

Gideon didn't respond.

"Chief, you listen to me. You are dealing with a psychopath who is blackmailing the entire United States of America!" Kostya roared. "He was a psychopath before you met him, he turned into a murderer in prison and now he's intent on turning life into a Hollywood movie at the expense of millions of lives." Kostya paused. "Look at me, Gideon," he said softly. Gideon came back to himself and his entire focus turned to his best friend's face.

"Do you know why he's been baiting you? Torturing you?"

Gideon shook his head. He didn't. He really didn't.

"It's because you were a snot-nosed kid, and you took him

down. You beat his ass and sent him to prison. You fucking *beat* him. You had the guts to do what you needed to do for your family, and then you had the smarts and the bravery *to take that fucker down*. That's why he's been gunning for you. And Gideon, because of you, we have an advantage."

Gideon's body went solid. Kostya was right. He was absolutely right. Because Kendall was so intent on proving how much smarter he was than Gideon, he'd tipped his hand early, and they had a chance to stop not just the four-hundred-and-seven dams from unleashing a billion gallons of water, but they had a ten-hour head start on saving those people in Pennsylvania!

His eyes took in everybody on the screen, then he turned to Jada. "Kane, Jada, how are you two doing on coming up with a virus to counteract Bonham's firmware malware?"

"We have something," Jada answered. "Our problem is if Kendall modified the malware—which you know he has—our virus won't work."

"You know Clint discovered a record of thousands of boxes of power strips, extension cords, and batteries being sent from Reynolds, Inc. to dams across the country. Will it matter if the methodology changed from Bonham's telephone charging cords to power surge protectors?" Gideon asked.

"Nope, that won't make a difference," Kane assured him.

"So, you'll be able to modify your virus on the fly to counteract his virus. It's not going to be a problem for you two."

He watched his lover look at him with her big brown eyes. She hesitated, then her eyes fired up, and the powerful woman he loved shone through. "You're right, it won't be."

"Once they have that, we'll have to get that virus physically patched into each site," Clint noted.

"It would be great if we could find out which dams he targeted, but if we can't we'll go to all of them," Gideon said.

"A lot of these were built by the Army Corps of Engineers, I think we could use them and the National Guard to get the patch onsite and installed," Ryker said.

Everybody nodded.

"We're going to need—" Gideon started to say.

"I'm already on it," Kostya interrupted as he looked up from his phone. "Commander Clark is authorizing a chopper to get us to Pennsylvania as soon as we can all make it to base."

24

"GOOD TO FINALLY MEET YOU IN PERSON," KANE SAID TO Jada as the big man gave her a hug.

"Same," she said as she hugged him back.

Gideon had found out that the reason why Dex Evans hadn't been on the last call was that Black Dawn had been called out on a mission somewhere in Eastern Europe. Right now, Clint, Lydia, and Rylie were working on tracing back multiple feeds. The one from Kendall's manifesto, his website from the Streetgamer.com board of directors' biography, his address to 'donate' money, and tracking down all of the places that Jenny Sims had tagged 'Miles' on her post. They had a lot of slogging to do, but currently, it was their best chance to track Kendall down.

Lark meanwhile was taking one last crack at Naomi Sims via teleconference. Her thought was that Jenny was going to be feeling humiliated after the video and she would be reaching out to her sister who was currently out on bail.

Gideon looked around the Coast Guard Jayhawk that Commander Clark had been able to procure—once again the Commander had decided to come with them. Kostya took it in stride. It was three hundred and sixty-five miles to the dam, and it would take them a little over two hours to get there. Kane and Jada were sitting together huddled around Kane's tablet, still working on various virus scenarios. One of the things that had Gideon twisted was how in the hell did four hundred and eight dams get infected? All of them would have required an onsite visit to get the malware installed, but how?

Kostya nudged him then made the hand signal for Gideon to change the radio frequency so it was just the two of them.

"How are you doing and give it to me straight."

"Better," Gideon admitted. "What you said, and how you said it... it unlocked something for me. You're right, I've been holding onto a lot of guilt that just isn't mine. But to tell you the truth, I didn't even know I was carrying that much of a load until that asshole tried to do a number on me. I mean, talk about gaslighting a person."

"Exactly. You've been feeling like shit for almost thirty years for making the best decision a kid could make, and this bastard knew how to press your buttons, but he overplayed his hand. The net result is you pulled your head out of your ass. I'm happy for you."

"So am I." Gideon nodded his head toward Jada. "I also got it together about Jada too. I was just hiding behind the age thing. My damage was guilt, and I couldn't see it, so I threw her away. Biggest mistake of my life. Thank God I've got her back."

"Having a woman... a partner. There's just no way to describe that feeling and how great it is," Kostya agreed.

"How much do you know about Amy Linden?" Gideon asked.

"Some," Kostya said.

They both looked over at Ryker who was talking to Nolan O'Rourke. "Now that's another man who's twisted up about a woman. Does he even have a shot, 'cause if he doesn't, the kind thing would be for a brother to put him out of his misery," Gideon said.

"That's the thing," Kostya said. "Lark can't get a lock on her, and Amy's her best friend. I've only met her a couple of times, and the only time I spent a significant amount of time with her was the night those two met. Sparks were going off like the fourth of July."

"So? That's a good thing, right?"

"I can't get into any details with you. I won't share anything Lark has asked me to keep to myself, you know?"

Gideon nodded.

"And what she has shared, doesn't give me a real good clue as to which way she's going to go with Ryker *or* the best way for Ryker to approach. My gut is, it's because she doesn't have any idea how she wants Ryker to approach."

"Lieutenant, I hate to tell you this, but you're not making a whole hell of a lot of sense."

"Do you see why I don't talk about it?"

"Yeah," Gideon sighed.

"Look, Amy comes off like a sex goddess on stilettos. She had every man in that bar drooling over her, and that was even when Lark was beside her."

"Shit, that's saying something," Gideon said in surprise.

"Exactly. But Amy wasn't aware of it. What's more, if she had a clue, I think she would have been uncomfortable as hell. If you want my real opinion, I think she's pretty inexperienced."

"Come again?"

"This isn't anything that Lark's shared, just my observation."

"And our boy didn't pick up on that?" Gideon asked.

Kostya rolled his eyes. "As oblivious as Amy was to men falling all over her, I don't believe the word virgin is in Ryker's vocabulary."

"Holy hell."

"Exactly," Kostya agreed. Then he gave Gideon a patient smile. "Have we taken your mind off things enough, yet?"

"It worked for ten minutes, so that was nice," Gideon chuckled.

"Glad to be of service."

IT TURNED out to be Tanner Robb, their sniper and backup medic, who was their go-to when it came to having an in with the United States Army Corps of Engineers. His aunt retired from the USACE as one of the staff principals for civil works.

"Aunt Alice knows where all of the bodies are buried." Tanner laughed when Gideon got ahold of him after they landed.

"This is important. We're twenty minutes away from the Kinzua Dam here in Pennsylvania, and we need full access to their systems. This is going to take total trust, and what's more, we can't tell them why. We haven't figured out a cover story yet that will work with these people."

"Let me have Aunt Alice call you. I'll give her the details of who you are, first. Will that work?" Tanner asked.

"Absolutely."

"I'll make it fast, Chief."

"I appreciate it."

Gideon hung up and looked at Jada who was sitting with him in the backseat of the SUV. Kostya and Ryker were up front. Kane, Nolan, and Commander Clark were driving in another SUV ahead of them.

"Needed a break from Kane, huh?" Gideon teased.

"More like, I needed a little bit of time with you," Jada whispered back as she held out her hand to him. Gideon grabbed it and held it tight to his thigh. "You know this is going to work out, don't you?"

Gideon looked out the window. "I can't help but see this entire valley flooded, and it kills me, Jada. The man doesn't have a soul. Not only will people lose their livelihoods and homes, but some of them will also lose their lives."

"We're going to stop him."

He let go of her hand and put his arm around her shoulders. Even with the seatbelts, they found a way for her to rest her head on his chest for a long moment before his phone rang. Jada pulled away so that he could put it up to his ear. He didn't want the car noise to disturb this conversation and it would if he were to put it on speaker.

"Hello, this is Chief Petty Officer Gideon Smith, United States Navy."

"It's nice to meet you, Gideon, I'm retired Lt. Colonel Alice Tanner, United States Army Corp of Engineers. My nephew vouched for you but didn't have details for me, just that I could trust you implicitly. On a personal level that gets you one hundred percent of my trust, but my nephew is saying that this has to do with one of our dams, and I'm going to have to have a hell of a lot more information to get up to a hundred percent trust on that. What's going on in Pennsylvania, Chief?"

He liked her, he liked her a lot.

"Colonel, as you know a SEAL team does not work operations here in the United States."

"I'm aware," she agreed crisply.

"My girlfriend was kidnapped almost four weeks ago. I was able to find and rescue her with some help, but I knew she was still in danger. I am my team's communications and computer expert, and I pulled in some other experts to assist me in uncovering who was behind her abduction, and subsequently found out she was kidnapped by a man that I had sent to prison over twenty years ago." Gideon took a deep breath.

"Go on."

"When I worked for him, it was in Silicon Valley. He's a technical genius, but he's also a madman. He's held a grudge against me for years, and while I've been tracking him to make sure my girlfriend stayed safe, myself and the other experts found out about another plot that he has planned that involves over four-hundred dams across the nation."

"Are you saying that someone plans to sabotage four hundred of our nation's dams?" For the first time, Gideon heard a hint of panic in her voice.

"That's what I'm saying. What's more, this man intends to cause nationwide hysteria in about five and a half hours if we don't stop him. We must keep this between the fewest number of people possible, otherwise, we will not be able to stop it."

"I understand your reasoning at this point, but I need to hear more."

"Instead of trying to explain further, can I text you a

web address, and you just watch the video and call me back?"

They were minutes away from the dam, and Gideon needed her on his side as quickly as possible.

"Send me the address," she ordered. "I'll watch it and call you back."

After she hung up, Gideon texted the address. He looked down at his watch and grimaced. He knew the video took a minute and forty-three seconds to watch.

"Hey," Jada whispered to him. She hugged his bicep. "We're going to beat him. I know it."

Gideon gritted his teeth and nodded, watching the second hand round the face of his watch. It was two minutes and five seconds after she'd hung up that the colonel called him back.

"This is real, isn't it?" she said without preamble.

"Yes, it's real," Gideon answered.

"How do we stop him?" Her voice was pure steel.

"As I explained, my team and I have been working on this for a while now. We understand that he is implanting malware into these dam's firmware. When that happens, he will be able to take control of the dam. We have had a head start on replicating the type of malware he has probably created so that we can counteract it by implanting a virus directly into each of the infected dam's systems."

"Let's do it."

"Here are the obstacles we need to overcome first. One, now that we know Kinzua has been infected, we finally have an opportunity to interact with the malware he has created. We've needed to do this in order—"

"To create the antidote. I get it. What are your other obstacles?"

"We don't know the other dams that have been infected."

"Yep, that's an obstacle all right," the colonel agreed. "I don't mean to piss in your Cheerios, Chief, but what happens if you can't come up with the antidote? That's possible, right?"

"Yes, ma'am."

"So the other way you stop them is turn off all of the computers. Just unplug them, right?"

"What happens to the dams?" Gideon asked.

"I don't know the answer to that," the colonel admitted. "You're going to need a top-notch engineer with degrees in both electrical and mechanical engineering. That's your best shot at knowing the best way to disconnect all of the computer systems. I have to tell you, these babies are set up with backup systems galore and many redundancies. This will be tricky. Now, are any of you qualified for this?"

"No, ma'am."

"You have five hours and forty-eight minutes on the clock. I can get you one who's good from Pittsburgh. They'll be there in less than two hours."

"Ma'am, it's important—"

"That they know how to follow orders. I'll make it clear. I'm not going to tell anyone what you've shared with me. If this gets out, the shitshow starts, and we don't need that. I'm sending someone who used to work for me. She's smart, she'll be helpful, she'll take orders and push back for the good of the cause."

Gideon breathed a sigh of relief. Now that sounded like someone he could work with.

"Thank you, colonel."

"Call me Alice. Now go save the world."

25

Tanner's aunt definitely had some pull. She'd already gotten in touch with the Deputy District Engineer of the Pittsburgh District, who had tapped Allen Adams, the man currently running things at the dam since his supervisor was on vacation. When Jada and Kane introduced themselves, they stuck close to the truth and told him they were currently evaluating the public works projects' systems' firewalls and security for the entire Pittsburgh District.

Allen had been told to give Jada and Kane complete access to the Kinzua Dam's system and answer any and all questions that they may have. As for the other people who came with them, they were there to oversee the project, as well as tour the dam. Jada and Kane had been logged into Kinzua's system for less than twenty minutes when they discovered the malware, and as they suspected it was a botnet. Their system had already been taken over and no one, not even their computer support analyst, realized it.

"There, do you see it?" Jada pointed to a section of code on her screen.

Kane nodded. "Shit, let me get to it on my screen. This looks like a thing of beauty, but it's going to take more than a minute to figure out what he's done besides the obvious."

"Yeah, I can see where the malware has been installed, but what it is and what it does is something else, and we're going to need to know that to write alternate code to stop it."

"Hey, chin up," Kane smiled. "Who knows, maybe he embedded a kill-switch, and we can just use that."

"Yeah, like that would have happened," Jada said sarcastically.

"But we can dream, right?" Kane said.

Jada nodded.

"You ready to dive in?" he asked.

"Try and stop me."

She looked at the clock on the computer screen. They had five hours and ten minutes before this dam was due to fail.

ALLEN ADAMS TUCKED Jada and Kane away in the software analyst's office. He left Gideon, Commander Clark, Kostya, Nolan, and Ryker in his office, which barely fit them all. Still, they all appreciated the privacy.

"Jada told me that Kendall has remote access to the dam and could be anywhere. She would have given Clint and the team remote access to the server so that they could try to track it back to where Kendall might be like they're doing on all the other sites, but she and Kane agreed that would be a bad idea. I agree with them."

"Why?" Kostya asked Gideon.

"Because Kendall has access to the whole set-up here, so he might notice if someone else was granted permission to the system," Gideon answered.

"If that's the case, aren't they going to notice Kane and Jada creeping around?" Nolan asked.

"No, they're too good to be caught," Gideon assured Nolan and the rest of the men.

"So, what are we going to be doing?" the typically restless Ryker asked. "Stand around with our—?"

"Don't say it," Kostya interrupted Ryker before he could say the colorful phrase in front of their Commander.

Simon just laughed. "You know I've used that saying myself, right, Kostya? I also have to agree with Ryker at the moment—how can we be of use?"

"I'm not sure." Gideon was frustrated as all hell. "Part of me says that Kendall will still be somewhere in Manhattan because that's what he knows, and he'll want to be in the United States to watch the mayhem. Another part of me says he'll be here in Pennsylvania because he'll want to see the destruction that will follow after this dam's failure."

"Do we know how the dam is going to fail?" Kostya asked.

"That's something that Kane and Jada are going to tell us when they find the script. There are two types of turbines, and it depends on what kind they have here, and how they have it set up. The engineer that Tanner's aunt knows will be here and she can school us."

"But it could be that he just set explosives, right?" Nolan asked.

"There is always that possibility," Gideon agreed.

"Righteous! That means we could be looking for C-4," Ryker said with a grin. "I brought my full backpack with me—I have my scuba gear."

"Of course, you did," Kostya muttered.

Gideon eyed his friend. "Are you telling me that you didn't pack your full pack?"

"Nope, I'm not saying that. I've got scuba too. But we're going to need tanks," Kostya responded.

"I brought mine too," Nolan admitted.

"Me too," Simon said.

Everybody tried not to look surprised, but they were. It must be years since the Commander did fieldwork. But good for him.

"So, I'm the odd man out." Gideon chuckled.

"Looks like." Kostya's eyes twinkled. "I'll arrange tanks and get them here ASAP. Gideon, are you going to help Jada and Kane?"

"No, they've got it well in hand. I'm going to see if I can backtrack Kendall's remote access to the dam."

Everybody nodded.

"I'll get the dam specs so we know where to dive," Commander Clark said.

"You mean I'm still stuck standing here with my dick in my hand with nothing to do?" Ryker bitched.

Everybody laughed.

"Go over everybody's equipment with Nolan and make sure it's in order," Kostya commanded.

"At last, something to do." Ryker smiled.

JADA LOOKED over at Gideon where he was typing furiously on his laptop, parsing through lines and lines of code. All three of them had done their best to create mini-firewalls around what they were doing so their work wouldn't be obvious if Kendall were to do a sweep of the system. She could feel Kane's frustration beside her. They were now down to three hours and fifteen minutes and they still hadn't found the specific code within the malware that programmed out what the actual sabotage was.

Dammit, they needed to fucking find it!

"Hello?"

Jada and Kane both turned around when Allen Adams spoke. He was standing next to a middle-aged woman who held herself with a great deal of authority.

"This is Darla Creek," Allen introduced. "She works out of Pittsburgh for the USACE. The colonel said you'd be expecting her?"

Gideon turned around and stood up. "Hello, Darla, my name is Gideon Smith. You made good time, thank you so much for coming."

"You're welcome. Alice said it was urgent."

"It is. If you'll come with me, I have a group of men I'd like you to talk to." He smiled as he ushered her out of the room.

Jada turned back to her computer screen. Suddenly, she felt like she was looking at it from a brand new perspective.

"Holy shit, Batman. Look at this." She grinned and pointed at a large section of code.

Kane wheeled his chair over and his eyes lit up. "You know, I went over that about forty-five minutes ago, but blew past it. Oh, no wonder—it's tucked under this subroutine, there." He pointed. "That's slick, the bastard."

"Okay. We've got it. Let's isolate it and zap it." Jada rubbed her hands together.

"DARLA," Kostya spoke up. "So, what kind of turbine does this dam run on?"

All eyes were on the woman who was standing up in front of the conference room at the whiteboard.

"It's an impulse turbine." She uncapped a dry erase marker and began drawing a diagram on the board so everyone could see. "The water head is converted to high-speed flow by two nozzles to the turbine, right here, see?" She turned back to see everyone nodding. Then she turned back to the board and drew some more. "The turbine consists of these blades or buckets that are attached to the runner. They spin around as fast as the water is released to create energy."

"How is the water regulated to the turbine? Does it always flow to it at the same rate of speed?" Nolan asked.

"No, here's the intake from the reservoir. It goes into what we call a penstock, that narrows down into a nozzle. This spear, here," she pointed to what was basically a plunger on her diagram. "This spear regulates the flow of water. It can be pressed in to stop the flow or totally opened, which is very rare, and is done for limited amounts of time."

"When a lot of water flows from the nozzle to the buckets, the buckets just spin faster, right?" Kostya asked.

Darla nodded.

"Do they ever spin out of control?" Simon asked.

"No, that hasn't happened, thank goodness. That's why we control that spear as heavily as we do. We don't want the turbine overwhelmed. Plus, it would be bad if an unregulated amount of water would just be let loose out of the reservoir."

Kostya turned to Gideon and raised an eyebrow. Gideon nodded. This sounded like how Kendall could be sabotaging the dam if he wasn't using explosives.

"Is there any way to make sure that the spear stays in a certain spot?" Gideon asked.

"What do you mean?" Darla asked.

"Can you arrange it so that you manually override the spear, so that it can't stay open?"

"Actually, we just totally automated it two years ago. We're very proud of what we've done. There are three system redundancies to ensure that we will always be able to turn off the flow of water if we need to."

Fuck!

Gideon looked around at the rest of the men. He could see each of them thinking the same thing. They were screwed if they didn't find the code and stop this. At least Ryker wasn't making any smartass remarks this time.

GIDEON RUSHED into the computer room and immediately felt the buzz coming from Jada and Kane. They were on to something.

"Is it good?" he asked in a low voice.

Please say it's good.

Please say it's good.

"Yep, Jada found the script. We're both writing something to shut this down. Wanna join us?"

"Yes," Gideon said emphatically.

"Thought you might." Jada grinned. "Already sent it to your e-mail."

Gideon plopped his ass down in his chair and pulled up his e-mail.

This has to work.

They were now down to one hour and thirty-three minutes.

26

FASTER.

Faster.

Gideon knew they were going to stop the dam from unleashing water. It should take another forty minutes to get the alternate code written and disarm Kendall's big plan. But he desperately wanted to be working on backtracking the malware so that he had a shot of finding Kendall's whereabouts.

I want that man.

I want my hands on that man.

I want to make him pay.

"Gideon, we've got this," Jada shouted at him from across the room. "Work on finding Kendall."

Gideon looked at his watch. One hour and seven minutes.

"She's right. We're almost done," Kane said. "When the dam doesn't spill too much water, Kendall's going to know we've got him and he'll run. You've got to track him now!"

Gideon toggled over to another screen on his laptop

and focused on the backtracking script he had started. As his fingers flew across the keys, his head whirled in the best sort of way—he was in the zone!

You're not getting away this time.

He was deep into the code when his phone buzzed. For the last three hours, he'd had it set to buzz in ten-minute increments so he'd know where he was on Kendall's countdown. He looked up and found Kostya staring over him.

"What?" he snarled.

"Simon's got two Jayhawks waiting just in case Kendall ends up fucking with you on his whereabouts. Or Rylie, Clint, and Lydia come up with one thing and you come up with something else, then we have two different means of transportation."

"Good." Gideon turned back to his computer. They had fifty minutes.

"Fuck yeah!" Jada shouted.

"Great job, Honey," Kane's voice was equally loud.

Gideon took half a second to grin at Jada's success, but he was on a mission. He was getting pretty close himself. He would have asked for Jada and Kane's help, but he was now to the point where he was following different methods and routes that Kendall had taken to hide his location. Currently, Gideon's search had him routed through Lisbon when he'd just been in Minsk, but he knew he was getting closer.

"Gideon," Kostya whispered over his shoulder. "Lark called me a little over an hour ago. I didn't want to get anyone's hopes up, but Naomi Sims got a call from her sister Jenny. Naomi gave Lark her phone number."

Stunned, Gideon looked at his lieutenant. He knew that Lark was an amazing investigative reporter, but how in the hell had she developed such a rapport with that sexual deviant?

Jada and Kane had come over to listen in to the conversation.

"Anyway, Lark gave the number to Clint and he was able to trace it. You're not going to believe this, but the call came from Miles Albright's penthouse in Manhattan."

"When was this?" Gideon wanted to know.

"Jenny made the call to her sister last night."

"What's your gut telling you?" he asked Kostya.

"I don't know the guy like you do, Gideon." Then Kostya turned to Jada, "Or you. What do you two think?"

Gideon locked eyes with Jada. She nodded her head, and he agreed.

"He might have played that over-the-top game show host on the video, but there isn't a chance in hell that he would be back at his penthouse like a sitting duck," Gideon said. "He's past the point of trying to set traps. This thing here at the dam is his big gotcha." Gideon looked up at where Jada was standing.

"I agree. What's more, if he and Jenny were together right now, he wouldn't allow her to make a phone call on a phone that could be tracked. Nope, this is Jenny acting on her own."

"I'll call the authorities then, to go get her," Kostya said. "And Kendall?"

"He's here. He's going to want to watch his handiwork. I'm sure of it," Jada said confidently.

"I wholeheartedly agree. Now it's up to me to just pinpoint his ass. So, all of you, get the hell away from me."

Kostya chuckled as he started toward the hallway.

"Hey wait a minute—" Gideon started.

"Yeah, yeah, yeah. Of course we have this covered,"

Jada said. "Kane and I have already developed a patch so that it can be installed at every single hydroelectric dam with an impulse turbine. And before you ask, we checked to make sure that he hadn't written anything against reaction turbines."

Gideon sighed in relief. "But—"

"Jesus, Gideon, get to work," Kane growled. "Tanner's aunt is already working on a way for the Army Corp of Engineers and National Guard to physically get the patches to each dam in the next twelve hours. Are you satisfied?"

Gideon turned back to his laptop and heard Jada asking where the vending machines were as she started down the hallway.

HE TURNED off the alarm right before it was going to buzz again.

"I've got you, you motherfucker," Gideon said under his breath.

That word didn't come close to describing just how evil Kendall Douglas was, but he really didn't have time to come up with more adjectives. Gideon picked up his phone with a smile and got up from his chair.

He turned and saw Kane and Jada both sitting in their chairs, looking at him. Jada was sipping her Coke, one leg swinging over another wearing sky-high red heels. Why had he not noticed that before? Meanwhile, Kane was snagging chips out of the bag of Fritos they shared. Simon had also found a chair and a bottle of water. At a desk to Kane's right, Ryker munched on a packet of Oreos. It took

Gideon a second to spot Nolan and Kostya. They were holding up the wall near the door. Kostya was grinning.

"Aw, shit, did you people actually bet on me?" Gideon asked.

"Hell yes," Ryker exclaimed. "But I didn't win. Jada, who did?"

Jada looked down at her phone then over to her left. "Simon, you're the winner. You were off by thirty seconds. Everybody owes him fifty dollars."

"I don't take personal checks," Commander Clark said with a straight face. Then he turned his attention back to Gideon. "So where is Kendall Douglas, is he in Pennsylvania?"

"Did you all bet on that too?" Gideon asked.

Jada shook her head. "Nah, we were all pretty sure your gut was right, so all of us figured he was here. What did you find out?"

"He's here, and he's cocky, and I'm ninety-nine percent sure he's staying at the Manor House bed and breakfast in Warren. It does after all have suites available and an overall five-star rating."

Kane sat up straight in his chair. "Now wait just a damn minute. You were checking out IP addresses; there isn't a chance in hell you could have triangulated him to an actual address."

"Oh, ye of little faith." Jada smirked at Kane. She turned to Gideon. "I want to hear how you did it, Baby," she purred.

"After being routed around the world and back, I finally landed right back here in Warren County."

"That's a little bit less precise than a bed and breakfast," Kostya said. "And let's start walking and talking." He opened the door and they all started down the hall to exit the structure and get back to their SUVs.

"He said talking," Kane reminded Gideon as soon as they hit the outside. "How did you figure out the Manor House?"

"Once I gained access to his network, there were a couple of named devices. One was Manor House Guest Printer. I've already sent that info over to Clint, Rylie, and Lydia. They should have what guest room he's staying in by the time we get there."

"That was slick," Kane congratulated him.

Jada grabbed him around his waist and squeezed tight.

"I checked it. Manor House is sixteen miles from here," Ryker said. "I'm driving one of these."

"Agreed," Kostya said. Gideon knew that Ryker was one of their trained tactical driving specialists; here in the backwoods of Pennsylvania it shouldn't matter, but after all the shit that had gone down with Kendall Douglas, none of them were taking any chances.

"I'm driving the other," Kane said. "I'm certified."

Kostya, Kane, and Gideon looked at one another, then Gideon turned to Jada and pulled her a little to the side.

"Uh-uh," she said as she shook her head. "You're not leaving me behind at this point. He's arranged to have me kidnapped twice, he's used me as bait to get to you and I'm the one who figured out how to stop his evil plan. Nope, no way, no how, no sir."

"She's got a point," Ryker said as he sauntered up to the couple before Gideon had a chance to open his mouth.

Gideon scowled at Ryker, then turned to Jada. "Angel,

we don't know what we could be walking into," Gideon explained patiently.

"All that matters is that we're walking into it together," Jada said firmly.

"Well, I wouldn't go that far," Ryker drawled. "You should definitely stay in the car."

"Butt out!" Gideon and Jada yelled simultaneously.

Ryker laughed and went to stand next to Kostya and Kane.

"It's too dangerous," Gideon said softly.

"You're going to a freaking bed and breakfast!" she cried out.

Gideon could tell that Jada was at her wit's end, and who could blame her? This had been a major roller coaster.

"Do you promise to stay in the SUV?" he asked.

"Fine. Whatever. Let's just get a move on before he gets away. A-fucking-gain!"

Gideon heard both SUVs' engines start up. He grabbed her hand and headed to the one with Ryker behind the wheel.

MOST OF THE men had brought their packs and they had comm systems available as well as their weapons. Clint had gotten back to Gideon and given him the rundown on the current occupants of the B&B, as well as the staff. It wasn't good. There were four other guests besides Kendall. Kendall had registered under the name Henry Smythe.

What a prick!

Gideon continued to look at his phone to read the

incoming information from Clint. As for staff, there were also at least three, maybe four, depending if one of the maids had left yet.

The good news was that Kendall's room was in the back of the Manor and looked out over the valley, so he shouldn't see them approaching. They stopped their vehicles a half mile before they got to the Manor House to regroup.

"We've got seven, maybe eight people we need to get out of the Manor House," Gideon said as they huddled up around the hood of the first SUV. "If we send in the police, it could be a bloodbath, it could be a hostage situation, or somehow that sneaky bastard could get away again."

"He's going to get away if we don't do something fast," Jada said. "If I were him, I'd have a drone flying over the dam, watching things."

Gideon's eyes shot up to her face. "Shit, you're right. We've got to move fast. You should have mentioned that before, Jada."

"And if I had thought of it even thirty seconds earlier, I would have." She glared at Gideon and everyone laughed.

Gideon rubbed the top of his head and blew out a long sigh. "Sorry, Angel, that's a brilliant thought. We've got to get moving fast. Jada and I would be instantly recognized, so we need to stay outside. The rest of you might be able to pull off being guests or visitors if anyone trips over you."

"That could work," Kostya nodded.

"Two of you need to be in charge of vacating the civilians, and the other two need to target Kendall." Gideon looked up to see how Kostya and Simon would want people deployed.

Simon looked at Kostya and shrugged, then Kostya nodded.

"Nolan, you're with me," Kostya said. "We'll focus on Kendall. Commander, you and Ryker will work on getting the civilians out of harm's way."

Gideon put his phone on the hood of the SUV. "Clint's sent me a blueprint of the house."

Everybody bent low to see what he was showing, except for Simon, who first had to pull out a pair of reading glasses.

"There's two sets of stairs," Gideon pointed out. "This one will get you real close to Kendall's suite, as opposed to the grand staircase."

Kostya nodded. "Nolan, we'll both take the back staircase. We'll leave the front staircase for Simon and Ryker to clear out the guests if they're in their rooms."

Nolan nodded.

"Commander, here's a side door that goes straight to the kitchen, which is where you and Ryker will probably find two of the staff.

"Ryker, I'll take that side door, you go up the front staircase and hit the other two bedrooms on the front side of the mansion and try to clear out those guests if they're in their rooms," Simon ordered.

Ryker nodded.

"Commander, off the kitchen and down the hall is a room marked storeroom, but Clint points out that there are a lot of electronics that have been connected in there. I'm thinking that could be the office, and you might find more hotel staff there."

"Got it."

"You ready?" Gideon asked.

Everyone nodded and then put on their small comm

devices and hid their guns under their jackets or they untucked their shirts so they could cover them as they tucked their pistols into their jeans or slacks.

Gideon looked at all the calm men and watched as they got back into the vehicles. This time he drove one and Jada sat in the passenger seat so they wouldn't have to get out when they arrived at the B&B.

"You good, Angel?" he asked quietly as he started up the lead SUV.

"I want this over, Gideon," she whispered back.

"It will be Jada. It will be."

27

GIDEON PUT THE COMM UNIT DOWN ON THE CENTER console and Jada was surprised at how clearly she could hear everybody. Two minutes after listening to Simon talk to a woman in the kitchen, she and Gideon saw her scampering out the side door and heading straight to a little sky-blue Honda in the parking lot.

Ryker talked to them quietly as he made his way up the front stairs and tried the handle on the first of the three front bedrooms.

"The knob's turning," he whispered. "Must not be anyone—"

His whispering stopped.

"Hello."

There was the distinct sound of the door closing and Ryker continued to talk. "We have a bit of a situation here. We did some digging on the septic three days ago, and apparently, we stirred up a nest of timber rattlesnakes. We've already found one in the parlor, and there's one blocked off in the master suite, so I was just check—"

"We've got to get out of here," a woman's voice shrilled. "Howard, come on, let's go."

"Susan, hold on a minute and let me get my shoes on." The man sounded like a long-suffering husband.

Jada was doing everything she had not to bust a gut. "Can they hear us?" she mouthed to Gideon.

"No," he said.

"Where in the hell does Ryker come up with his bullshit?"

"From a dark well deep inside a twisted psyche."

"He's hysterical," Jada said, still trying to smother her laughter.

As Susan and Howard were vacating the room, they listened as Simon used the same story on the two people in the office. It worked like a charm.

Gideon and Jada saw four more people vacate the bed and breakfast and hit the parking lot at a run.

"Knob's not turning," Ryker whispered.

The distinctive sound of knocking came through.

Jada looked over at Gideon when she heard some muffled talking. "Could you understand that?"

Gideon shook his head.

Ryker knocked again.

"I'm sorry, but I really need to speak to you. We have a bit of an emergency on our hands," Ryker said.

Muffled voices again.

"They're having an intimate moment," Ryker said into his mic.

"Was he just diplomatic?" Jada asked Gideon.

Gideon nodded, then put his finger to his lips. He pressed a button on the comm device. "I don't care if it's an orgy, get them out of there."

"Aye, aye."

"I'm coming upstairs to help," Simon said.

"Nolan and I are going to cover Kendall's door in case he hears something and peeks his head out. We'll just nab him at that point," Kostya said.

"Good idea," Gideon agreed.

Jada and Gideon waited for three-and-a-half minutes as another disgruntled couple was forced to leave the bed and breakfast. It took another minute to watch them get in their BMW and drive away. At least these people took their luggage.

"We're clear," Simon said.

The parking lot was almost empty, except for the little Honda with the young woman sitting in it.

And a garish yellow Ferrari, which Jada would bet belonged to Kendall Douglas.

"I think we may have a problem," Jada said as she tipped her chin toward the Honda. "Why is she still here?"

She watched as Gideon rubbed the top of his head. "It's going to go over better if a woman goes up to her car than a man. Can you go and find out?" he asked.

"You got it."

As she exited the SUV, Jada heard Gideon telling the men to hold on before they made their move on Kendall. When she got up to the car, the girl was already rolling down her window.

"Who are you?" she asked. She seemed shaky, and who wouldn't be after seeing everybody scurry out of the hotel? "Are you with that guy who told me that there was going to be a raid and I needed to leave?"

"Yeah," Jada said. But how the girl could have thought that was true as Jada was prancing around in high heels was beyond her. "Why didn't you leave?"

"I'm waiting for my friend. I work in the kitchen. She

does the cleaning, but she's been cleaning the upstairs a long time. She should have come out by now, don't you think? Shouldn't your people have told her about the raid?"

"What's your name?" Jada smiled.

"Heidi."

"Heidi, what's your friend's name?"

"Rhoda."

"What time does Rhoda usually finish the upstairs?"

"She usually finishes almost two hours ago. Somebody must have really made a mess. That happens sometimes. But still, I woulda thought that big guy woulda sent her outside already."

"Heidi, do you see those two SUVs parked over there?" Jada pointed.

Heidi nodded.

"We're going to drive Rhoda home when the raid is over with."

Heidi gave a relieved grin. "That'd be great." She rolled up her window and started her car. Jada stared at her in amazement. Was she really going to just abandon her friend so easily? But then she rolled down her window again.

"Hey." Heidi waved at her, even though Jada hadn't moved.

"Yeah?"

"Is this about the old creepy guy in the manor suite?"

"Why do you ask?" Jada asked.

"I don't know. He's just creepy is all."

"Yeah, it's about him."

Heidi's brow furrowed, then her face cleared and she smiled. "Okay. Thanks for taking Rhoda home." She rolled up her window and backed out of her space and sped out of the parking lot.

Jada raced over to Gideon.

We have a problem.

"Handle this like a hostage situation," Gideon said into the mic as soon as Jada reported back to him.

"Aw, fuck, who does he have?" Nolan whispered his question.

"A young maid. Her name is Rhoda," Gideon answered.

"I can see and hear you. There's no need to whisper."

Gideon about dropped the comm when he heard Kendall's voice booming through the device.

What the fuck?

"Really, people, do you think I would check into a place like this and not plant some cameras and listening devices out and about to see what's going on around me? Now wasn't that dear Gideon's voice on the comm link who said treat it like a hostage situation? He's right. I have Rhoda here with me."

Jada's hand shot out and gripped his. He looked up at her. How could he not have been expecting yet another twist?

How?

"Now, I realize that you have crushed my hopes, dreams, and GoFundMe, which really, really, hurts."

"This fucker is nuts," Ryker said.

"You. The blond who just called me nuts. This is for you."

A woman's scream came through the door.

"Now don't make me hit Rhoda again. She's a tiny little thing, not like that Amazon Jada. This girl will break too fast. So, blond man with the big mouth who lies about snakes, get the fuck out of here."

"Go," Simon said.

"Now, where was I? Oh, my throat is sore, my knuckles are bruised, and so is my ego. It's time to end this. Gideon? I assume you're listening. This is simple. You want Rhoda here to live? Trade yourself. That's it. A life for a life. I don't intend to come out of this alive, but someone is going to die with me. Is it going to be little Rhoda here, or is it going to be you?"

Gideon unbuckled his seatbelt.

"What are you doing?" Jada squawked as Ryker opened up her passenger side door. He handed a gun over the top of her to Gideon.

"Here you go, never hurts to have an extra gun. Now go get that crazy fuck."

"How are you going to do that?" Jada screeched. "You can't do this. He just said he's going to kill you and himself. This is a no-win situation."

"There's no such thing, Sweetheart," Ryker grinned at her.

"Is that true?" Jada stared at Gideon. "Do you have a plan?"

Gideon couldn't lie to her. "No, Angel, I don't have a plan, per se. My plan is to save Rhoda and stay alive."

"Let me be more specific—how do you intend to accomplish this?" she snarled.

"It's a fluid situation, so I'll just go with the flow." He gave her his best reassuring smile, but it didn't seem to be working.

"Gideon." She reached out and gripped the side of his

neck. "I want you in my life until I'm old and gray." Her bottom lip trembled.

"I want to grow old and gray with you too, Angel," Gideon said fiercely.

Please don't ask me not to go.

Jada cleared her throat. "Just don't piss him off like Ryker, okay? There's no reason to add more fuel to the fire."

He laughed with relief. "That's not my style, Angel. I'm totally chill."

She snorted.

He ran his index finger along her nose, then gave her a swift kiss.

"I love you, Angel."

Then he got out of the SUV and headed for the house.

***

WHEN HE GOT to the top of the stairs, he wasn't surprised to see Kostya gone. He'd be trying to get into the room from one of the back windows. Ryker would be getting one of the rifles they had stashed in the SUV and seeing if he could line up a shot. There were options, there were always options.

Simon nodded at him.

Nolan thumped his back.

Gideon stood by the side of the door and then knocked on it so he could avoid any gunshot blasts.

"Oh, for God's sake, Gideon. I told you, we're going to die together. I'm not shooting you through the door. Now come on in, it's unlocked," Kendall said loudly enough for them all to hear.

He screwed up; he should have taken the comm

system out of the SUV so Jada couldn't hear what they'd say.

Enough of that, Smith, it's game time.

Gideon opened the door and let himself in.

The girl was lying in a heap on the floor in front of the bed. Kendall was sitting above her, his gun trained on Gideon.

"Honey, can you stand up?" Gideon asked.

She raised her head and looked at him through glassy eyes.

"Rhoda, can you get up and walk out of the room?"

"He has a gun," she whimpered.

"So do I." Gideon motioned with his. "See? Now get up and leave."

She pushed herself up slowly off the rug and looked back at Kendall. He grabbed her arm and put the gun to her temple. "Hold up, Rhoda. Gideon, throw your gun out into the hall, then close the door. I'm sick of seeing your little army friends."

Gideon did as he was told.

"Now, Rhoda, walk toward the door, and Gideon, you walk toward me. Rhoda, you can't open the door until Gideon is kneeling in front of me, do you understand?"

"Yes, Sir."

Kendall looked like shit and his hand was trembling holding the Glock. *The idiot should be using two hands.* He was wearing a short-sleeved shirt and the man had no muscle tone. If it weren't for the fact that this guy had outmaneuvered him fourteen ways from Sunday, this should be an easy takedown.

Gideon took his time walking over to Kendall, wanting as much time as possible to scrutinize his opponent. He gave Rhoda a reassuring smile as she came close to him and was beginning to pass him.

"Oh, God," was all she said before she fell on him. Gideon still had all of his focus on Kendall, even as Kendall's strayed to the maid. Gideon pulled Ryker's gun from behind his back and pointed it at Kendall.

"Drop your weapon," Gideon yelled at the man.

Kendall's gun was about ready to fall out of his fingertips as it was.

"Drop it!" Gideon repeated himself.

"My nemesis," Kendall said as he worked to raise the gun.

Dammit, he *wanted* Gideon to kill him.

In the second before he had to pull the trigger, so many thoughts floated through Gideon's head. Gideon had his gun pointed at Kendall's hand, then lifted the barrel and took the headshot.

EPILOGUE

Jada looked around her small apartment. It looked so empty with all the pictures off the walls, and the rugs gone. Then there were all her plants that she'd given away. Her friends damn well better take care of them!

God, the pictures, the rugs, the plants, they'd really covered up a lot of cracks, water stains and...

"Oh. My. God. Is that mold?" She shouted as she ran up to look at the corner of her kitchen where she'd always had plants sitting. She relaxed when she saw it was just ants.

Okay, maybe her place had been a bit of a dump.

Her door opened and her brother Ricky and her mother walked in. Both of them were grinning ear to ear.

"Hey, what's the deal? You're supposed to be all sad and stuff that I'm moving out of state."

Ricky came over and picked her up and spun her around in the empty space. "No way, Baby Sister. The fact that somebody actually found a way to get you to move out of this dump, I don't care if you're moving back to

California, I am just that damned happy that he's getting you somewhere safe."

"Put me down, you big oaf," Jada slapped at her brother's shoulder.

She was laughing when he put her down on the ground.

"Mom, how do you put up with him living so close to you?" Jada griped.

The door opened again and her oldest brother walked in. Jada couldn't believe her eyes. She whirled around to look at her mother. "Did you know about this?" she squealed.

Her mother's smile was incandescent. Jada hadn't seen Arturo for three years. He was currently stationed at Camp Pendleton in California. She threw herself at her big brother and he caught her in a bear hug. Arturo gave great hugs. Behind her, she heard the door opening again, but she ignored it.

"Hey, do we get hugs?"

Jada recognized her brother Ben's voice. Wasn't he supposed to be on vacation with his wife? She turned around and saw that it wasn't just Ben, it was Luis and Raymundo too.

"What in the hell is going on?" she demanded to know. Again, she turned to look at her mother. "We haven't had the whole family together for two years, and now these idiots show up too late to pack a box? What gives?" She was really ready to burst into tears, so pretending to be mad was the best way to cover it up.

"Same little brat," Arturo said as he enveloped her in a huge hug again.

Jada hated it, but she couldn't stop the tears. She loved getting a hug from Arturo. He was eighteen years older than her, and when he had come home on his leaves, he'd always seemed bigger than life.

She took a step back and looked around in wonder at her five older brothers. Could anything be better than this?

Yes

Having Gideon here.

It was too bad that Gideon was out on a training mission right now. That was the reason he hadn't been here when she had filled only fourteen paltry boxes into a moving van and donated the rest of the furniture to St. Vincent de Paul. Last night when she'd been without furniture, she'd intended to stay at her mother's place, but she'd ended up staying at Darlene's apartment instead because her mother said she was having plumbing issues. So it was nice that everybody was here today.

"You guys should have told me you were all going to be here, then I wouldn't have booked my ticket to fly to Virginia this afternoon."

The door opened again.

Now who?

"You should cancel your flight to Virginia, stay another night, little sister," Raymundo, the retired Marine said.

"I can't," Jada said.

"Yes, you can," Gideon said.

She peaked around Ben and Luiz and saw that Gideon was the last person who had entered the apartment.

"In the name of all that is holy, can somebody please tell me what is going on?" Jada demanded. It had been great when all of her brothers had gotten together to see her off, but now Gideon was here, and not out training? What the hell was going on?

Somehow, in her now empty apartment, Jada found her standing in the middle with Ben, Luiz, and Raymundo standing to her left and her mother, Ricky and Arturo standing to her right.

She stared at Gideon as he walked toward her. He stood there looking down at her for a moment, then dropped down on one knee.

He is not really on one knee, was he?

He looked up at her, his eyes twinkling.

"Now that I have successfully survived a night with your five brothers, I have a question to ask you."

Holy shit. This is happening!

Jada raised one eyebrow. "And that would be?"

He pulled a light blue ring box out of his jacket and opened it up. It took everything she had not to squeal. For the fourth or fifth time that morning, her head whipped around to look at her mom. Then she pulled herself together and again gave Gideon the best bored-face she could under the circumstances, which were *not* boring at all. She was excited as hell.

Gideon pulled the luscious, gorgeous, fantastic ring out of the box, and tugged her left hand toward him. "Will you marry me?" he asked solemnly.

"Oh yes," she breathed out. "I love you, Gideon Henry Smith. I want to be with you until forever ends."

Gideon slid the ring on her finger and it fit perfectly. He stood up and pulled her into his arms. "That sounds like it might just be long enough."

Two Months Later

. . .

GIDEON LOVED COMING HOME NOW that Jada was living with him. He'd liked it before, but now he loved it. He'd really been looking forward to this weekend. He'd been out with his team at the Zussman Urban Combat Training Center at Fort Knox in Kentucky for three days, and after the hell Kane and Simon had put them through six months ago, they were in top-notch shape.

When he parked his Land Rover in the garage beside Jada's Mini-Cooper, he was surprised he didn't hear Lucy barking. His gut clenched. Ever since that night when the intruders had shocked her, he always watched out for her to make sure that there were no long-lasting effects.

After closing the garage door, he went into the house.

"Jada, is everything all right?" he called out.

"Everything is perfect," Jada replied. "I'll be right there, Honey."

"Where's Lucy?" he asked as he walked through the mudroom into the kitchen. He spotted Jada winding around the kitchen island to greet him. Then his head shot up when he saw Lucy sitting next to the couch with her big head in his mother's lap.

"Jada?" he asked, his voice hoarse. "What's going on?"

"Your mother wanted to come for a visit."

He lowered his voice. "Do you mean to tell me my mother called you up out of the blue and said, 'Hi, Jada, I want to reconcile with my son, can you arrange it?'"

"Well, uhm."

"It's not polite to whisper, Gideon." His mother's reprimand was said in the same old soft and loving way that she'd always had. Never belittling, just a way to remind and teach.

Gideon's heart clenched.

"Ma." He didn't know what to say. He had too much to

say. Jada wrapped one arm around his waist and the other around his bicep.

"Your Mom and I were just thinking about what to cook for dinner," she said as she began to usher him toward the couch.

"Ma, you're here in my home," Gideon breathed. "Why? Why after all this time?"

She stood up and held out her hands and he grasped them, clutched at them. "I was so torn apart after your father died, that I couldn't get out of my own way. You tried to get ahold of me. You wrote me letters telling me what happened, but I didn't want to read them. Mikey told me, but it seemed like I would be betraying your father if I forgave you."

He tried to let go of her hands, but she held tight. "No, Son, listen to me. I was wrong. I was so wrong."

"Ma, I understood why you were mad and disappointed with me. I got it. I deserved it."

Her small little body pulled up straight. "You most certainly did not deserve it. You were put in a terrible position and no adult could have handled it better than you did. I'm proud of you, Son."

Again, Gideon felt his heart clench. "But what about Pops?"

"I knew that man to the bottom of his soul. If he had known what I know now, he would be just as proud of you as I am."

Gideon shook his head in denial. "I'm not sure, Ma."

"You listen to me, Gideon. I hope it's not going to be my time to go for a good long time. But when I'm let into the pearly gates and welcomed into my father's arms and see my beloved Henry again, his first words to me are going to be how proud he is of his first-born son."

"You can't know that, Ma." Gideon could barely get the words out.

"I can. I do." She stood up on her tiptoes and brushed away his tears.

"Now give me a hug, Son."

LATER THAT NIGHT

"I AM NOT GOING to make love with you with your mother in the house," Jada hissed.

Gideon chuckled as he tugged at her little cotton tank top again. It was so much fun to tease Jada Harlow.

"Stop that!" She slapped his hand.

"Okay, Honey, not full-blown intercourse, but maybe something else?" he wheedled.

"Yeah, you want something blown all right," Jada giggled.

Gideon let out a laugh. "I hadn't meant it that way, but now that you mention it..."

Jada wrestled him to his back and propped her elbows up on his chest. "How do you feel?" she asked.

"About Ma?"

"Partly."

"About Pops?"

"Partly."

"Then what?"

"You didn't talk much for a couple of days after you killed Kendall, and then when you did start talking again, you never mentioned how it felt having him dead. Or having him dead by your hand. So, I guess my question is, my little snuggle bunny, how are you feeling about all of it?"

Gideon sighed. "Snuggle bunny, huh?"

"I'm going to keep coming up with terms like that until you spill your guts," she warned.

He saw she was serious, God help him.

"Kendall wanted me to kill him. It was a death-by-cop kind of thing."

"Okay." She continued to look at him.

"I could have easily incapacitated him, shot him in the hand, sent him off to prison again. In a way that would have been the real revenge." Jada nodded. "But Kendall Douglas has no place on this earth. I made that judgment. I would make it again. So I killed him." Gideon paused and looked closely at Jada. "I'm okay with what I did, are you?" he asked softly.

"Yes, Honey, I am." She placed a kiss over his heart.

"Now, you want to know about Ma and Pops, besides being fucking thrilled?"

Jada's smile could have powered a city.

"Or are you asking about my fiancée being a sneaky little thing and how I feel about that?"

He saw her look of concern and realized that *was* what was really worrying her.

"Aw, Jada, don't you realize, I know you. I know your sneaky ways. I know so many things about you, and I love them all. And as I come to learn so many other things over the next hundred years, I'll love those things even more."

"Well, okay then," she smiled.

"Okay what?"

"Okay, we can have full-blown intercourse tonight."

Gideon shook with laughter and delighted in knowing

that he had this woman to look forward to for the rest of his life.

Don't miss reading about Ryker and Amy in Her Wild Warrior (Book #3). Coming out this fall.

If you want to know about Nolan O'Rourke, read about him in Defending Home, part of the Long Road Home Series.

ABOUT THE AUTHOR

Caitlyn O'Leary is a USA Bestselling Author, #1 Amazon Bestselling Author and a Golden Quill Recipient from Book Viral in 2015. Hampered with a mild form of dyslexia she began memorizing books at an early age until her grandmother, the English teacher, took the time to teach her to read -- then she never stopped. She began re-writing alternate endings for her Trixie Belden books into happily-ever-afters with Trixie's platonic friend Jim. When she was home with pneumonia at twelve, she read the entire set of World Book Encyclopedias -- a little more challenging to end those happily.

Caitlyn loves writing about Alpha males with strong heroines who keep the men on their toes. There is plenty of action, suspense and humor in her books. She is never shy about tackling some of today's tough and relevant issues.

In addition to being an award-winning author of romantic suspense novels, she is a devoted aunt, an avid reader, a former corporate executive for a Fortune 100 company, and totally in love with her husband of soon-to-be twenty years.

She recently moved back home to the Pacific Northwest from Southern California. She is so happy to see the seasons again; rain, rain and more rain. She has a large fan group on Facebook and through her e-mail list. Caitlyn is known for telling her "Caitlyn Factors", where she relates her little and big life's screw-ups. The list is long. She loves hearing and connecting with her fans on a daily basis.

Keep up with Caitlyn O'Leary:

Website: www.caitlynoleary.com
FB Reader Group: http://bit.ly/2NUZVjF
Email: caitlyn@caitlynoleary.com
Newsletter: http://bit.ly/1WIhRup

facebook.com/Caitlyn-OLeary-Author-638771522866740

twitter.com/CaitlynOLearyNA

instagram.com/caitlynoleary_author

amazon.com/author/caitlynoleary

bookbub.com/authors/caitlyn-o-leary

goodreads.com/CaitlynOLeary

pinterest.com/caitlynoleary35

ALSO BY CAITLYN O'LEARY

Her Daring Seal (Book #5)

Her Fierce Seal (Book #6)

A Seals Vigilant Heart (Book #7)

Her Dominant Seal (Book #8)

Her Relentless Seal (Book #9)

Her Treasured Seal (Book #10)

Her Unbroken Seal (Book #11)

BLACK DAWN SERIES

Her Steadfast Hero (Book #1)

Her Devoted Hero (Book #2)

Her Passionate Hero (Book #3)

Her Wicked Hero (Book #4)

Her Guarded Hero (Book #5)

Her Captivated Hero (Book #6)

Her Honorable Hero (Book #7)

Her Loving Hero (Book #8)

THE FOUND SERIES

Revealed (Book #1)

Forsaken (Book #2)

Healed (Book #3)

SHADOWS ALLIANCE SERIES

Declan

Made in United States
Troutdale, OR
07/02/2023